I0596543

SEDUCTION SERIES REVIEWS

"Good read!!! …I didn't want it to end. Nor did I want to put it down." L.V.

"A good thriller. Story progresses well; plot line clear. Author weaves modern technology into the lives of the characters along with slowly revealing the past. Well done." B.T.

"…great read that incorporates positive ideas on some modern issues." F.A.

"Wild story. Great ending!

"Very enjoyable. Imaginative story line and characters. The ending was great. Couldn't put it down." Gracieon

"A great, fun read. Excellent story line with enough twists to hold your interest, but not so many as to feel contrived." Mozartnyon

"Excellent read! I am an avid fan of Coben, Crais, Parker, Silva, Child, Eisler and now I can add Bluestein to the mix." A.B.

"Loved the series. Can't wait to see it as a TV series or a movie." L.S.

"An intriguing mix of fact and fiction with story lines woven into a surprising conclusion. Couldn't put it down." C.M.

"This book's a page-turner. Couldn't put it down." M.B.

"Politically savvy thriller threads its way through covert politics, those leveraging wealth and power by manipulating the most vulnerable within the dark, chaotic reality of betrayal and greed. DECEPTION, 4th in the Seduction Series, holds your attention. Big screen ready." B.T.

"The series would make the coolest TV miniseries... wonder if any TV writers are looking for brilliant new projects." C.L.

BOOKS BY C.L. BLUESTEIN

Political Thriller
SEDUCTION SERIES

#1 <u>SEDUCTION</u> – Love, Loss, Leverage, Murder
#2 <u>PERCEPTION</u> – Love, Loss, Leverage, Murder
#3 <u>ISOLATION</u> – Love, Loss, Leverage, Murder
#4 <u>DECEPTION</u> – Love, Loss, Leverage, Murder

You Want Me To Do What? is available now. Walk in the sandals of our ancestors through this engaging interactive contemporary scripted Story of the Exodus/Passover for Jewish and Interfaith Families. Targeted but not limited to tweens.

REVIEW: "You Want Me To Do What" is the most innovative addition to the Passover literature I've seen. This is not just another pretty Haggadah....these interactive mini-dramas will make ANY Seder using any Haggadah come alive for all ages." Cantor Charles Bergman, Los Angeles, CA

Free download at <u>http://carolbluestein.com/</u>

PERCEPTION

LOVE. LOSS. LEVERAGE. MURDER.

A Novel by

C.L. BLUESTEIN

SEDUCTION Series • Book 2

Perception: Love, Loss, Leverage, Murder

Copyright © 2016 by Carol L. Bluestein,
C.L. Bluestein Books
A Division of Bluestein Publishing
Slingerlands, NY

ISBN Print October 2016 ISBN: 978-0-9966210-3-8
ISBN ePrint October 2016 ISBN: 978-0-9966210-4-5
ISBN audio October 2016 ISBN: 978-0-9966210-5-2

2021 Edition V.2
This is a work of fiction. The characters, incidents and dialogue are
drawn from the author's imagination and are not to be construed as real.
Any resemblance to actual events or persons, living or dead, is entirely
coincidental.

All rights reserved under International and Pan-American Copyright
Conventions
US Copyright Office registration #TXu 2-009-643

No part of this book may be reproduced, reverse engineered upload-
ed, or transmitted in any form or by any means, electronic or mechanical,
including photocopying, recording, or by any information storage and
retrieval system without the express written permission of the author and
copyright owner.

Editor: Anne Frazier Walradt

DEDICATION

With my love and gratitude to and for
my late husband, Michael R. Bluestein,
our children Sandra, Mark, and Lisa,
and their families

They are my inspiration.

ACKNOWLEDGEMENTS

First and foremost, I'd like to thank my family for their unwavering support.

Also, I want to note those who have passed but, in their own way, made my journey possible: Michael Bluestein, Roslyn and Noah Levine, Alynne Levine Sharp, Jack D. Main, Abraham and Selma Bluestein, Daniel Bluestein, and Ilse Bluestein Vanderpot.

As I worked on each chapter and phase of the book, I shared my words with my monthly writing group, Women Who Write. They listened and critiqued chapters with open hearts, frank critiques, and generous suggestions that contributed to the overall process and book.

In particular, my appreciations goes out to the following people.

My professional editors: Paula Chaffee Scardamalia for story, and Anne Frazier Walradt for genre and overall final edits.

My beta readers: Carol Marchewka, who keyed into the emotional connection; Barbara Traynor, who caught the non-essential passages and pacing; and William Petell, who identified the logic breaks and pacing; and Kathleen Pooler, who helped smooth out difficult sections.

My working editors, family and friends, read the story in various phases and helped me hone the language and grammar as well as replace telling with showing. Kal Van Avery, Sandra Bluestein Carrk, and Barbara Traynor.

Thank you to my teachers and friends at The International Women's Writing Guild (IWWG) who continue to replenish my soul and offer insights into to the wonderful world of expression. It takes a village to support an author and the IWWG is all about encouraging writers and sharing stories.

Finally, the patience award goes to Cooper and Kelly, my rescued schnoodles. They fill the exalted positions of snugglers, walkers, jesters, kissers, listeners, and protectors.

Table of Contents

PERCEPTION

Chapter 01▶Paris, France

Vanderhagen slapped his hand-carved desk and jumped to his feet, sending his chair crashing into the bookcase. Jaw clenched, he jerked the thumb drive out of the computer and threw it into the fire. Handfuls of micro-taped conversations followed, sending sparks onto the hearth and up the chimney. He stirred the fire, turning the evidence over and over until the heat melted the plastic and destroyed the data on the magnetic tape.

A downdraft sent noxious fumes into the room, and he gagged. Whipping his handkerchief out of his pocket, he covered his nose and mouth. It didn't help. The trim eighty-five-year-old financier staggered to the window and threw it open to purify his lungs and the library, with the fresh, cool Parisian February air.

Cleansed, he returned to his desk, housed in a den lined with a large collection of bound books and framed photographs that documented his long and prosperous career. Beside his computer, next to his father's gold pen and pencil holder, sat a golf-ball-sized paperweight made from Tawandian raw diamonds—a tangible reminder of his newest financial venture.

At the double knock on the door, Vanderhagen looked up and said, "Come in," as his son burst through the door.

"Dad, is everything all right?" James wrinkled his nose and said, "What's that smell?"

"I burned all the Donovan tapes." Vanderhagen shook his head. "After spending years befriending our boy Ted, welcoming him into our family, and financing his projects, the bastard left everything to PRAISE and one Rachel Allen."

"How do you know?"

"Lawyer. But that's not our biggest problem." Vanderhagen leaned back in his chair. "Shut the door and sit down."

Vanderhagen watched James, a younger visual version of himself, ease into the visitor's chair. The old man waited a few seconds before speaking. "We are losing control of Franklin. My explicit orders were to assassinate the Tawandian President, and, when Franklin had the chance, he took it upon himself to abort the mission."

"Dad, Franklin is President of the U.S. He had to act in what he thought were the best interests of the country."

"I didn't fund his election for the good of the country. He's bought and paid for, and he better damn well do what I ask."

"Dad, I think…."

"I don't care what you think." Vanderhagen turned, pulled a file from the shelf, and extracted a sheet of paper. "Here."

James scanned it and said, "This is a two-year-old newspaper article about Governor Sandford giving a senior girl-scout contingent a tour of the state offices. What am I supposed to do with this?"

"Why do I always have to spell it out for you, James. You've got to toughen up or you'll never be ready to take over when the time comes." Vanderhagen put the file away and sat, hands linked and resting on his abdomen.

James leaped out of his chair, leaned on the desk, his face contorted with anger. A microsecond later, his brows lifted, and his jaw dropped. "No. Don't say it. Don't ask." He fell back into his seat.

"He must be taught the lesson of obedience."

"I can't," James said. "Besides I thought you already had evidence that, as a councilman, he ordered the seduction of a local hood in his ward."

"I do, but only Donovan could prove it. Now that he's dead, I need another carrot. Therefore, you'll suck it up. Get me the story of Sandford's fondness for teenage girls with one or more witnesses. Have it ready to go on my say so."

"It won't stick."

"Who knows?" Vanderhagen raised his hands and shrugged his shoulders. "In any case, it doesn't matter. The internet media gossipmongers will jump on it in less time than it takes to tie your shoes. The damage will be done before anyone thinks to check the facts."

James's body sagged. "I'll take care of it. Anything else?"

"The cartel wants Tawanda settled. The violence keeps resources buried under bodies and blood."

"What can *I* do?"

"Nothing." Vanderhagen chuckled. "Thanks to you, I believe Franklin will owe me a favor."

James shook his head, got up, and walked over to the ever-ready chess game-table. "By the way, I've found another seduction expert." He pulled out a chair, sat, and looked at his watch. "We should know the outcome within the next 72 hours."

"A blind contract?"

"Just as we discussed."

The older man joined his son at the chess board. James moved his pawn to c5.

Vanderhagen said, "And so we begin."

Chapter 02▶Gramercy Avenue, NYC

Friday, 21 February
In the black and white tiled lobby of 215 Gramercy, Nikolai Zukov damp mopped the floor, straightened the furniture, and made a pot of coffee. As the concierge and maintenance go-to guy, he oversaw all the comings and goings in the three contiguous six story buildings, 213 to 217.

Christopher Gregory, owner of the complex, entered the lobby for their daily meeting. "How's it going?" Chris said, as he went to the coffee bar for his morning eye-opener.

Nikolai said, "No problems so far."

Chris walked across the room to lower his tall frame topped by sandy hair into the orange Eames chair. "What's up for today?"

"Renovating the kitchen in number three at 217 from ten to four."

"If you need another pair of hands, call me."

"My nephew is coming to help. Everything is good." Nikolai paused. "Oh, we got the permit to combine the entrances."

"Good. We can start when you're done with the kitchen."

"I think I will need to hire two people to support me if we are offering twenty-four-seven service to the tenants. I have two people in mind. I can set up interviews when it's convenient."

"You're the boss. I trust you."

"Then I will be supervisor with more responsibility."

Chris's eyes narrowed. "I see." He laughed. "Of course. It's been a while. How's twenty percent?"

"I am not offended. Thank you."

"Have you seen Rachel this morning?"

Nikolai shook his head.

Chris took a sip of coffee. "She seemed fine when we returned from Lake George. Now, two weeks later, she's lost her spark. Seems to think Ted Donovan's death was her fault no matter what I say."

"I am sorry she remains so troubled."

"I know. It's not good and I don't know what to do about it."

"Be patient. These things take time."

"The sooner the better," Chris said, "for her sake—and mine."

<~<~|~>~>

In her apartment, still in bed, Rachel Allen stared at her engagement ring, turning it this way and that, mesmerized by the light shards which once sent her into a panic attack. *This should be the happiest time of my life.*

Two weeks ago, at an isolated cabin, three stories above Lake George in New York's snow-covered Adirondack Mountains, she had conquered her biggest fear—going outside alone—for the first time since her campus rape eight years ago. Her bravery stopped the execution of forty Tawandanese diplomats, but to her horror, she killed a man in the process.

The smell of gun powder, the sound of Donovan's scream, and the crack of breaking bone kept her up at night and disrupted her throughout the day.

Presidential orders kept her story of those life-altering moments top secret. She had to live with it—live with the fact she murdered a man. An accident? A service to her country? Yes, all well and good. Yet, another truth, hidden from all, plagued her. No doubt about it, at that moment she wanted Donovan dead.

I'm Rachel Allen, former golden girl, rape victim recovering from PTSD, ardent human rights activist, Chris's fiancée, and stone-cold killer—just like Donovan.

Even last week's psychiatric counseling didn't help.

<~<~|~>~>

Dr. Ilse Younger, a woman in her early fifties, presented as a banker-hippy. She wore a dark pant suit, accented with a multicolored beaded necklace, and arranged her hair in a soft bun atop her head. Feathery tendrils framed her face. A warm, engaging smile counterbalanced her piercing gaze.

After pleasantries, Dr. Younger said, "What brings you here today?"

Rachel fidgeted with her fingers before returning the doctor's gaze and told her the story of Donovan's death. "Now, I have difficulty sleeping and concentrating. Simple tasks seem overwhelming. Worse, I can't get out of my own way."

"Anything else?"

"I can't concentrate, which means I'm not writing. I wish I could give it away. Hire a researcher, a ghost writer, and be done with it."

"You could do that."

"It's not me. It's not who I am. I love to get involved in my projects, lose myself in the process, find a workable truth."

"What's stopping you?"

Rachel blinked back tears as she struggled to maintain control.

Dr. Younger waited.

"I'm mad. Angry. Pissed off. And I don't know what to do with it."

"Angry about what?"

"Angry about being raped and what it did to me. I'm angry Donovan made me kill him, putting me into the state I'm in today."

"You did what you had to."

"No, I did more. I kicked him in his stomach with all the power I had."

"Was that wrong?"

"No. He deserved it."

"What do you think you might have done differently?"

"Maybe rushed him and grabbed the gun. Or thrown snow in his face. Or shouted to distract him so the FBI could have taken him. Anything to stop him from flying over the railing and breaking his neck."

"From what you've told me, it's not your fault he landed badly. In fact, with a little luck, he could have walked away from a soft landing without a scratch. None of which makes you a murderer."

"I wanted him dead. At that moment, I wanted him dead."

"That moment doesn't define you."

"Can you tell me what's wrong with me? Why can't I let it go? Get down to business and finish my book. Plan my wedding. Move on. Release all this, this anger?"

"I can't give you answers because I'm not you. I do, however, see two possible avenues of thought you might consider. We can talk about your conclusions at our next appointment."

Rachel remained non-committal, her eyes fixed on the psychiatrist. "Tell me."

"First," Dr. Younger said, "it's possible you're angry with Ted Donovan for dying and not giving you the chance to confront him about how he betrayed you."

"Perhaps."

"Second, it's possible you're afraid of your power. You never thought you'd be able to reclaim it and once you did, you used it, decisively, with force."

Rachel's jaw dropped. "What are you saying?"

"I'm saying you're a powerful woman. Circumstances caused you to doubt yourself, but when it counted, you rose to the occasion."

"I killed a man."

"Let's agree to agree Donovan's death was an accident. You saved the man you love by facing your worst fear. Not to mention you saved your own life."

Rachel swallowed. "I… I did save my own life, didn't I?"

"Not as typical as you may think."

"So why am I afraid?"

"It's not easy stepping into the life you've always dreamed about, the catalyst and game changer you wanted to be before your rape."

"Am I afraid to… change?"

"No, I don't think so. It's only been a few weeks. Try letting the anger go and deal with moving forward." Dr. Younger checked her watch. "It's time." She picked up her phone and tapped the screen a few times. "I have the same time available next week. Do you want to schedule now?"

Rachel shook her head. "No. I need time to process this session. I'll call you."

"Then call after May first, when I get back from vacation."

Chapter 03▶Gramercy Avenue, NYC

Friday, 21 February

Chris entered Rachel's apartment. "Rachel? If I find you in bed, move over."

"No. Wait."

Seconds later, Chris sat on her bed. "Did you say something?" He placed his hands on either side of her, leaned in to give her a kiss, and stopped at the crackly cellophane sound emanating from beneath the covers. He cocked his head and repeated his actions to reproduce the noise. Reaching under the covers, he brought forth a half-eaten box of Lorna Doones and held them in front of Rachel. "What's this?"

She retrieved the cookies. "Oh, thank God, I thought I'd lost them."

"Rachel, what's going on?"

"Come on, Chris. It's only a few cookies."

"It's never about the food."

Rachel laughed. "You're quite the interrogator, Mr. Gregory."

"Don't change the subject."

She pulled back. "The truth is I can't wrap my head around a big wedding right now."

He put the cookies on the side table. "You need to put Donovan behind you."

"He's dead because of me."

"He's a slug. Not worth your time. Remember, he tried to rape you."

"He was drunk."

"Don't defend him. I saw the tapes."

Rachel parried. "What about you?" She leaned toward Chris and poked him in the chest. "You shot a guy in the groin."

He took her hand and held it in his. "A mass murderer, on Donovan's orders by the way, came here to kill me at point-blank range. I didn't have a choice."

"Don't you feel anything?"

"I don't feel guilty if that's what you mean. Besides, Nikolai delivered the fatal shot."

Rachel nodded. "Maybe I'll talk to him."

"You don't have to talk to anyone. It was an accident."

"I'm not arguing with you. I don't have the energy."

"So don't use what energy you do have thinking about Donovan."

Rachel cupped his face in her hands and smiled. "Okay, Doctor Chris. How about October?"

Chris smiled. "Second weekend. The leaves will be in full color."

She said, "And because I'm such a mess right now, I'm going to turn the whole wedding over to my mother who absolutely loves this stuff. I won't have to lift a finger except to try on gowns."

"She can do it if she keeps my parents informed, the guest list even, and stays within budget."

Rachel erupted into laughter. "Not sure she can spell 'budget.'"

"I get your point. I'll be generous."

Chris stood. "I've got to get back to work. I'll be back at noon for our lunch and walk date."

"I'll be ready."

She watched him leave. Alone, Rachel fought the urge to dive under the covers and compromised by leaning against the pillowed headboard. She closed her eyes—the silence broken by the indistinct hum of the refrigerator, traffic noise from the outside world, and the roar of blood pumping through her system. A tear rolled down the side of her face into the curls at the nape of her neck.

Sensing the familiar, if distant, patterns of depression, Rachel jumped out of bed. She didn't want to go there. She had to do something. First, she dressed in her uniform—jeans and a T-shirt, then, she texted Nikolai. "*Where are you? Talk?*"

He texted back. "*Yes. #3–219*"

<~<~|~>~>

She walked into a maze of kitchen cabinets—patched walls ready for their skim coat and river-stone-pebble countertops gleaming under the lights. The place smelled of sawdust and wall compound. "Nikolai?"

He popped up from behind the counter. "Welcome to my kitchen makeover."

Rachel laughed. "Just like on TV."

"I would like to think it is better." He put his tools down. "What can I do for you?"

"I can't come to terms with killing Ted Donovan. I wanted to talk with you and maybe find out if there's a way to handle it."

"Perhaps a psychiatrist would be a better choice."

"I did that. I'm angry. Frustrated I wasn't better, smarter."

"You second guess yourself."

"All the time."

"And you come to me. Why?"

"You were a freedom fighter in the Bosnian War and killed a man in the lobby less than three weeks ago."

"This is true." Nikolai scratched his head.

"I can't forget the image of Donovan flying over the railing or the sound of his neck breaking when he hit the ground. When I took Karate, I never ever expected to use it to hurt someone, kill someone. I just wanted to feel safe."

"In the process, you learned to protect yourself and have confidence in your ability to do so."

"Did you train?"

"In a way," Nikolai said. "I saw so much horror by the time I picked up my weapon, the enemy lost its humanity. I didn't see people, I saw targets. I got many people to safety by not second guessing my actions. When the fighting ended, everything changed. The faces of the dead, friend and enemy, haunted me, my dreams, and… I… I said prayers for them. In my mind I buried each as they appeared. Over time, I have found peace. But it never goes away. It is always with me, a part of who I am. What you did, Rachel, will always be a part of you."

"But…."

"No but. Make your peace with Donovan if you must and live in the present. We don't have much time in this life. Be selective in how you choose to spend it."

The smell of coffee and fresh bread entered the room before the young man carrying the order. He set the box of food on the counter.

Nikolai smiled. "Rachel, this is my nephew, Tarik. He is working with me on this job. If I let him live, he will have the permanent assistant's job."

Rachel said, "Nikolai, thank you," nodded to the young man, and left.

Entering her apartment, she smiled at the sight of Chris, hanging out on the couch and working on his ePad. "This is a nice surprise. What are you doing here?"

"We're going out for lunch, remember?"

"I do. I just didn't realize the time."

"Where were you?"

"I went upstairs to talk to Nikolai. He's a very wise man."

"That's, in part, why I keep him around."

"You're a very wise man too."

"Better you know now," he said. "It'll make the rest of our lives together much easier."

Rachel smiled. "Don't count on it."

Chapter 04►New York City, NY

Friday, 21 February
Chris and Rachel ate at an outdoor café. Afterwards, they strolled hand in hand and paused here and there to engage in casual window shopping.

He said, "You seem to be feeling better."

She said, "Nikolai made me think about forgiveness."

"Nikolai never forgives. He's like an elephant."

"Very funny." Rachel gave Chris a hip-bump. "That's 'forget.'"

He smiled.

"Anyway," Rachel said, "he didn't actually use the word forgive. He said 'prayer.' Since I'm not religious, for me it's 'forgiveness.' So, when I get angry, I'm going to channel it into forgiveness and move past it."

"Angry at whom?"

"Me. The rapist. Donovan." She paused. "I know it doesn't make any sense. I can't seem to shake it."

"Donovan's death is still raw," Chris said.

"You know, before things got ugly, Donovan talked about patriotism and supporting the President."

"I can't believe he tried to justify his intent to murder forty people."

"It wasn't hard because he believed in the greater good. For that, I can find a way to forgive him."

"If it makes you feel better, Rachel, I'm all for it."

"You know, it's because of him I found the courage to go outside with you, without security."

"A good thing. His gift to us." He squeezed her hand. "By the way, have you gone outside by yourself yet?"

She said, "Don't push. I haven't built up the courage to face the crowded sidewalks by myself. The bumping and shoving send me into a panic. I think I'm always going to prefer staying home."

"We'll see."

She hugged his arm. She wanted to be brave for Chris. He'd broken their engagement because of her agoraphobic behavior. She struggled to break through in Lake George. And succeeded. However, old behaviors die hard. Although she never invented reasons to go out, she always said "yes" whenever Chris asked.

"Hey," Chris said. "Look what's going on here."

The surprise in his voice startled Rachel. She looked around to get her bearings. They stood on the edge of the park-like area of an animal shelter's adoption center. Dogs, eager for new homes, ran about in several enclosures and filled the air with yipping and barking, while shy animals huddled in crates or corners.

"Oh my goodness," Rachel said. "How cute are these little guys?"

Chris said, "I grew up with a yellow lab."

"Not me. I never had a dog."

A volunteer approached with a Chihuahua in her arms. "Would you like to come in and meet our furry friends looking for their forever homes?"

Rachel looked at Chris. In silent agreement and holding hands, they followed the woman inside. As soon as the dogs saw them, chaos erupted—barking, jumping, squeaking, and yipping—all saying the same thing, "Pick me!"

They spent time looking at each set of dogs. Rachel hung back as Chris interacted with them. She said, "You're quite at home with the canine set."

He smiled. "I admit I like dogs. Being here makes me wonder why I don't have one."

"Me too. You certainly know how to play with them."

Her gaze shifted from Chris to a caramel and white dog, lying by the shelter's back door, head on paws, and unresponsive to the controlled chaos. She said, "What's wrong with that dog?"

The volunteer said, "Zeus is a Staffordshire Terrier-American Bulldog mix. He's been with us for almost a month. His family had to move away, and they couldn't take him. Their little boy and the dog were inseparable, now they're both heartbroken. He's gentle but has not shown any interest in the families who want to adopt him. We get at least five requests a day, but he ignores any approach. It's too bad. If we can't find a home for him, he may have to be euthanized."

Rachel nudged Chris and they walked over to the dog. Zeus lifted his head and stared at Rachel who stared back. With uncharacteristic boldness, she sat down next to the dog, putting her hands in her lap. The dog extended his neck to check her out. She offered her hand, palm up. He sniffed and licked her fingers.

"What's your story, Zeus?"

Zeus's floppy ears pricked-up at the sound of her voice.

"Are you lonely, even with all these people around? I feel the same way sometimes. Are you afraid? I am, especially when I'm alone. I know it's not easy."

Zeus crawled closer to her and stuck his nose under her hand. She obliged and patted his head, her strokes getting longer with each pass, over his shoulders and on to his back.

"It's no fun being alone. You've got to make an effort to find another little boy or girl. They aren't going to be able to keep you here forever."

Zeus's tail tapped out a rhythm on the concrete.

"Good. We both have a job to do. And I think yours will be easier."

Zeus barked.

"You'll make your new human very happy. I know it."

Zeus whined and rolled over, exposing his stomach. Rachel laughed and stroked the smooth, soft skin. Zeus closed his eyes.

Chris said, "Who knew you're a dog charmer?"

She smiled and took the dog's face in her hands. "You're a handsome sweetie." After giving Zeus a few final pats, she said, "You'll be okay." Rachel lifted one hand toward Chris, and he pulled her to her feet. As they passed the volunteer, she said to Rachel, "So, you're taking him?"

"Who?"

The volunteer's gaze dropped to Rachel's side where the dog sat with his leash in his mouth.

Rachel backed into Chris and stared at Zeus. His head reached her fingertips. "Oh my God. I didn't realize he's so big."

Zeus moved until his body leaned into Rachel.

She looked at Chris. "What do we do?"

He shrugged and said, "What choice do we have?"

The volunteer waved the shelter manager over. He rushed over, carrying a manila envelope, and said, "I see you've met our prized boarder." He gave Zeus a pat. "He's a great dog, passed his "Good Citizen" training, and completed three-quarters of his service dog certification. I've enclosed all the information in his packet." He offered it to Rachel. "I think he's been waiting for the right person to help."

The remark caught Rachel off guard. "Me?"

"I don't know," the manager said. "Do you need help?"

Chris intervened. "We all do at one time or another."

Rachel smiled, letting Chris know she appreciated his intervention. She knelt and came nose to nose with Zeus. "Zeus, you're such a smart dog. I *could* use some help." She scratched him behind his ears and took the leash out of his mouth. He licked her cheek. She took his face in her hands. "That's it. You win. You're coming home with us."

Zeus barked as Rachel stood, leash in hand.

Armed with a doggie gift basket, Rachel, Chris, and Zeus began their journey.

After several blocks Rachel said, "I like this. Walking with Zeus makes me feel more secure."

Chris said, "Are you tossing me to the curb?"

"Never," she said and squeezed his hand. "I meant people don't crowd us as much."

"I noticed that also," he said. "Let's make arrangements to finish his training as a PTSD service dog, so he can accompany you everywhere."

"That's a great idea," Rachel said. "And I also hear a high percentage of couples contemplating marriage often start with a pet. It gives them time to get used to a family member who may not listen and has his own agenda."

Chris nudged her with his elbow. "After you, the dog will be a piece of cake."

Chapter 05►Soho, NYC

Friday, 21 February
Sybil Powell landed her dream job at age forty-nine. As the new executive director of PRAISE, Positive Response with Action to Insure a Safe Environment, she'd wield enough power to make definitive changes to insure basic needs and human rights for war refugees throughout the world.

"Stop daydreaming," Lidia Lundon said as she passed. "We've got to get these paintings unloaded and hung. We've only got two weeks before the opening gala. Everything has to be perfect."

Sybil smiled and said, "No problem." She'd loved watching Lidia move from the very first day they'd met ten years ago. They married four years later—the best decision she'd ever made. "I'm thinking about you."

Lidia came to her and gave her a big soft kiss. "Then I'm not angry."

Sybil picked up two paintings and carried them into the gallery. The white walls and moveable white panels glowed with their new finish. The graphics people were hanging the sign—The Lundon Gallery—and preparing the glass door for lettering.

Lidia, her artwork stacked beside her, said, "It looks good, right?"

"You amaze me. Tell me the story again about how you got this place. This time give me *all* the details."

Lidia tossed her head, and her perfect silky blonde hair sailed into a wave and settled over her eye. With a practiced move, she draped it over her ear. "I registered with a number of realtors. No matter what I chose, every place exceeded my price range or had accepted bids. Fed-up and exhausted, I went to the coffee shop down the street."

"I like that," Sybil said. "If you ignore it, it will come."

"That's exactly what happened. A real estate broker comes over to my table and introduces himself. He gives me his card and sits down. We talk for a few minutes, and he produces the prospectus for this place. After I looked over and he gave me the details, he asked me if it met my needs."

"Out of the blue? No flirting over coffee cups? No lip licking or finger wiggling?"

"Absolutely not." Lidia laughed. "After I reviewed it, I almost peed in my pants. Three floors—one for the gallery, one to live in, and one already rented art studio with living area plus a full basement for storage that we share with the other tenant."

"Nothing seemed peculiar?"

"What do you mean? I just won the lottery. I'm not about to blow it. So, I go with him for a walk-through. On the way, he leans close to me, like he's telling me a secret. He says if the owner's terms are acceptable, the place is mine. Sybil, I've got to say, my heart skipped a beat and I'd have fallen over if he hadn't caught me."

"Very dramatic, Lidia."

"Well, you wanted all the details."

"Somehow, for reasons I can't begin to fathom, you've gotten yourself the deal of the century. It's perfect for my PRAISE reception, and the invited guests are the perfect clientele for a successful gallery."

Sybil brought her arms up and Lidia stepped into them. The women hugged and kissed, lingering in their embrace.

Lidia said, "Come on. It's only a few more paintings. Once we're done, we can break for lunch."

"Afterwards, then?"

"Afterwards, I'm all yours."

Sybil smiled. "It's a deal. I'll finish emptying the truck." She left Lidia standing alone, biting her lip, and remembering.

The agent had brought her to this building, handed her the information folder, unlocked the door, given her the key, and disappeared.

Lidia went inside and saw a man facing away from her. She took a few tentative steps within the enormous empty space. The man never moved. She cleared her throat. "Excuse me. I'm Lidia Lundon."

The man turned and Lidia paled. "Mr. Vanderhagen. What are you doing here?"

"I've come to offer you a business arrangement to benefit us both."

"You know I can't. Sybil has expressly forbid any association with you."

"I'm saddened by my daughter's choice to remove me from her life," Vanderhagen said, his voice flat. "I hope you'll be able to see beyond her objections as I have many ventures which could make her life, and yours, much easier, comfortable and profitable."

"Sybil's made it on her own. I'm very proud of her."

Vanderhagen's smirk caused Lidia a microsecond of doubt about the truth as she knew it.

He said, "Miss Lundon, this agreement is between you and me. My daughter is not to be involved in any way. She will only know about it if you tell her."

"Umm. Mr. Vanderhagen, this feels wrong." She turned to the door.

Vanderhagen pulled out his phone and tapped "RECORD." He dropped the hand holding the phone to his side and put the other in his pocket. He said, "I don't think this is the time to stand on moral high ground."

Lidia froze.

He said, "I know your parents threw you out of the house as soon as they found out you preferred girls."

Lidia turned to face Vanderhagen. "That's none of your business."

He said, "For a while you stayed with friends, then ended up on the street. Not an ideal place for a pretty girl. After some time and a couple of arrests, you met an artist at a community center and traded sittings for lessons and a place to sleep. After several such arrangements, you got a scholarship to art school, graduated, and sold painted rocks at craft shows. You were selling your canvases for the first time when you enticed my daughter."

Lidia remembered the moment when the wiry yet sturdy woman with the pixie haircut stopped at her booth. She felt her presence before she turned, and when they locked eyes, her heart raced. "Sybil knows the whole story. So, you are wasting your breath."

"Nothing, and I mean nothing, ever really goes away, does it… Miss Lundon?"

Lidia took a step toward Vanderhagen. "Fuck you."

He said, "That's all old history, best left to the archives. Let's talk about your future."

"Don't you dare try to screw with me."

"Hardly. I'm prepared to ensure your name will be on the lips of art critics throughout the city and the international art world, your gallery opening will be covered in the *New York Times* and featured in magazines such as *Art in America*, *Artforum*, and *International Artist*, and any others you choose."

Lidia caught her breath. Her hand flew to cover her gaping mouth. "You can do that… for me?"

"I can. I can even provide you with a list of guaranteed buyers to your gallery opening. Your paintings will sell at prices befitting your new and elevated position in the contemporary art world."

"I… I can't believe it. It's what I've always wanted."

"And it's all yours if you agree to my contract and conditions," Vanderhagen said. "Miss Lundon, the whole building would be yours for a small monthly mortgage payment to satisfy my lawyers. In return, you agree to split the gross profits, placing my percentage into a protected offshore non-profit bank account."

Lidia turned. "I'd get the title to the building?"

"In five years, with the stipulation that if you breach our agreement, you'll lose the title, and we renegotiate the lease."

"What about structural issues, current and future?"

"Submit estimates and work orders. I will keep the building sound."

"And I get to be in all the arts magazines as the newest contemporary art sensation for my next three shows, and the Lundon Gallery shows will be featured for the next twelve months."

Vanderhagen cleared his throat.

"And," Lidia took a step closer to him. "I'll never tell Sybil."

He coughed into his fist, then said, "I agree, unless, of course, you break our agreement." Vanderhagen took a couple of steps toward Lidia. "Understand we are talking about your business and your chance to shine through your art. You don't need anyone else. You are perfectly capable of handling this transaction and meeting all the agreement points."

Lidia trembled with excitement—her struggles would be over. Yet, Sybil's caution lurked under Vanderhagen's offer. She had to be sure she wasn't missing anything and wouldn't be hurting anyone. Pulling herself together, standing tall, mustering her bravery, she laid it all on the line. "What do you get out of it?"

"You take an empty building off my hands and your donation will supply the necessary capital to make the world a better place by, in part, rescuing children from starvation, disease, and homelessness."

"So, our agreement would be for the greater good?"

Vanderhagen nodded, "Precisely."

Lidia clapped her hands and said, "Let's do it."

He ended "RECORD," and handed Lidia a pen. She signed the papers without hesitation.

Vanderhagen left. The recorded session found its way into his safe with all the other seduction conversations, leaving nothing to memory.

Workmen arrived the next day. All major systems were checked out and fixed where necessary. The "owner" apartment, above the gallery, underwent a total makeover under Sybil's practical eye. The women moved in a week later.

She shook her head to scatter thoughts of betrayal, lies, and poor decisions. She did what she did and had to move on. She had to trust it would all work out for the best.

She began placing the paintings around the room to create a flow based on groupings, color, and subject—the hardest part of any show. Lidia's eye never let her down and she went with her instinct.

"Wow," Sybil said. "I like it."

Lidia smiled. "Are those the last ones?"

"Yes."

"Excellent. Let's lock up. I'm starving."

<~<~|~>~>

The next day, Lidia hired two part-time assistants to help man the gallery and do the basic housekeeping for the set-up and the show. The interviews usurped most of the day. She checked the time. Sybil would be home in less than an hour.

Lidia leaned back in her chair and reviewed her checklist. She decided to take care of two phone calls and reduce her Thursday workload. She reached into her pocket and no phone. Sitting up, she didn't see it on top of her desk, so it had to be under the unsorted layers of bills, invoices, vouchers, and mockups.

Her hands patted the papers, feeling for the familiar bump and shape of the phone. Nothing. She slid fingers between the layers, searching. Nothing. *Fine. No shortcuts.* Lidia sorted the papers into piles and each pile into dates. In the grip of obsessive organization, clipped papers together by vendor, by date.

Done and proud of herself, she stopped mid-congratulations. Still no phone. Her scream of frustration died in her throat when the front door buzzer sounded. She flew out of her chair and found a stranger in the gallery.

"I'm sorry," she said. "The gallery's closed until…. Hey, how did you get in here?"

The man, sixty-ish, wore jeans, a sports jacket, and a gold chain around his neck. He held out his hand to reveal a phone in his palm. "Is this yours? I found it on the floor by the door."

Lidia ran over to him and said, "Yes. Thank God, you found it. My life is in there."

"Must have dropped out of your pocket." He handed her the phone.

"Thank you, Mister…."

"Gavin. My friends call me Gavin."

"You look familiar. Have we met?"

Gavin laughed. "I'm the potter in the third-floor studio." He held up his keys, the one for the front door between his thumb and forefinger. "Guess it's hard to recognize me without clay all over my face."

"Hmmm. Maybe. In any case, I'd like my key back."

He ignored her request and said, "I've been told I clean up well."

Lidia smiled. "Is there something I can help you with?"

"I'd like to confirm my show next month. I spoke to the owner to set it up. When I tried to discuss it with him yesterday, he referred me to you."

"Follow me and I'll make sure it's on my calendar."

In the office area, he sat in the guest chair, leaning back with his legs crossed ankle to knee. She went around the desk to sit at her computer. She brought up her calendar. "Let me see…found it. Gavin, your show is booked and confirmed."

"Good," Gavin said and pulled papers out of his jacket pocket and tossing them on the desk. "Here's some information for press releases—my card, resume, photographs, and reviews."

Lidia scanned the material. "Mr., I mean, Gavin, very impressive. Not only are your sculptures exquisite, they're in museums and private collections throughout the world."

"I work strictly on commission. The works for this upcoming show are prototypes, experiments with shape and glaze."

"I think it will be a great coup for my gallery. I'm honored."

Gavin smiled.

Lidia placed the information in a folder and labeled it. "Let's talk about promotion after the opening. If you have it in digital files, I'd…"

Gavin shook his head. "I don't. I'm technophobic." He uncrossed his legs and sat forward, elbows on the desk.

"Since I'm trusting you with my show, how's your accounting ability?"

Lidia answered his affront with a sharp challenge. "Are you asking me if I'm honest and you'll get your sixty-five percent?"

He smiled. "I meant no offense. I'm merely asking if you'd like help with your books. I'm a pretty good accountant and… available."

Lidia's voice remained cool. "Sybil, my wife, does the accounting around here. However, if I run into trouble, I'll let you know."

Gavin got up to go. "By the way, are you beefing up the security system?"

"I'm sorry. I don't see that's any of your business."

"What about a safe for cash deposits and payments?"

Lidia stood. "I think it's time for you to go."

Gavin faced her. "What are you doing about ID badges?"

Lidia pointed to the door. "Please go. I find your questions insulting and invasive."

He laughed.

Lidia folded her arms. "Gavin, what's really going on?"

Gavin sat on the corner of the desk.

She said, "Get your ass off my desk."

Gavin stayed put. "You should know I bartered my third-floor digs, studio, and basement storage in exchange for being the on-site consultant for the building and your financial consultant for the non-profit." He leaned closer to Lidia. "You and I are going to do great things together."

A chill ran down Lidia's spine. "We'll see." Before she spoke again, footsteps echoed from the floor above. She looked up before returning her attention to him. "Now, please leave."

Gavin got off the desk, gave her a salute, and took off.

Her phone buzzed. Sybil texted, "*I'm home.*"

"Coming."

Lidia locked the gallery and turned off the lights. In the darkness, she knew she'd crossed the line, ignored Sybil's wishes, and she'd have to deal with the consequences—Gavin. The man made her feel unclean.

Fuck.

Chapter 06►New York City, NY

Friday, 21 February

Dr. Ilse Younger pulled the cuff of her coat over the palm of her hand and polished the name plate on her office door. *Thank you, Mom and Dad.* They had supported her throughout her educational journey but didn't live to see her graduate with a Doctorate in Psychiatry. The daily ritual honored them.

Ilse's practice, articles, consulting, and high-profile clients had given her an elite standing in the medical community for over thirty years. Now, she luxuriated in a select clientele and scaled back schedule. She worked mainly from referrals and as a consultant to the FBI.

Her one appointment for today, "Just call me Gavin," cancelled. She used the time to finish file notes, clear her desk, and close up her office.

This would be her first vacation in years. Her job fulfilled her passion, and nothing made her happier than to be working. The award from The PRAISE Foundation not only included cash, but also an extended Mediterranean vacation, all expenses paid.

She never would have booked it herself, yet the announcement filled her with excitement.

Sybil Powell, her best friend who had just come on board as PRAISE's new executive director, stood by her side. The moment remained etched in her memory as a recognition milestone. Now, the time had arrived. Ilse smiled at the thought of trading in gray New York City for sun, blue waters, music, and culinary delights.

By early afternoon, she surveyed the office and pronounced it cleared. She called her phone service to let them know her office would be closed until May 1. Next, she changed the message on her phone. "Dr. Younger is not available. If you have an emergency, please call 911. If you need immediate help, stay on the line and you will be redirected to another physician." She did the same for her email "away" response.

She sent messages to her two children, one in California and the other in Denver. Done, she closed her laptop, put it in her briefcase, pulled out the wastepaper basket's plastic liner filled with trash and tied the end into a knot.

Her stomach growled. Lunchtime.

Ilse put on her coat and hesitated. Pulling out her phone, she called her best friend and confidante.

"Hi, Sybil. I'm walking out the door."

"Good for you. Have a great trip."

"I'll have pictures and stories for you when I get back."

"Miss you already."

Ilse put her phone away and picked up the plastic garbage bag. She debated taking her briefcase. At the last minute, she stowed it in the closet, walked out, and locked the door. She dropped the trash down the incinerator and took the elevator down to the parking garage.

Once in the cement maze, Ilse felt a sense of freedom that embraced her inner girl. No work. No responsibilities. She strolled to section B2 with a roll of her hips and bounce in her step. She used her gray sedan's keyless entry and got into the car. After placing her purse on the passenger seat and closing the door, she engaged the seat belt, and turned the motor on.

She paused before pulling out. A feeling. Something's off. Forgotten. Disturbing. Ilse went over her to-do list. *No. Not that. All done.* Did she forget to call someone? *No.* Leave something in her office? *No.* She sat for a minute, confused. There. An unusual earthy smell. The sound of another's breathing.

In a panic, she grabbed the wheel for leverage as her head pivoted over her right shoulder.

"Don't," said a voice from low in the back seat. "Eyes forward."

Ilse did what he said. She recognized the voice—a patient's voice. "Gavin, what are you doing here? You cancelled your appointment."

"We need to talk. Pull out of the parking garage."

"Okay. I've got some time. We'd have even more time if we stayed here. My plane isn't until seven."

"No. Not here. Start driving."

"I'd rather…." She stopped talking when she saw the knife in the rear-view mirror.

"Don't argue. I'm not in the mood."

As she drove, following his directions, she said, "What's happened? Are you in crisis?"

"Yes."

"I'm sorry to hear that."

"Want to know why?"

"Of course, if you want to tell me."

"I've grown very fond of you."

"It's called transference. We can work through that."

"You're leaving."

"I'm coming back."

"I can't wait. I love you."

Ilse's hands clenched, jerking the wheel. The cabbie alongside leaned on his horn, and she regained control. "My vacation won't change your feelings. When I get back, we'll have time to work through them."

"Our feelings, right Doc?"

"You know it would be unprofessional for me to fall in love with a patient. It wouldn't be fair to you or me."

"Do you love Sybil Powell?"

Ilse gasped and clutched the wheel.

"Take a left. I understand you two are very close."

Ilse's focus darted back and forth from the street to the face in the rear-view mirror. "We're friends."

"Friends who share family secrets."

Ilse's heart raced. "Let's pull over and talk."

"No. Keep driving."

After a few more turns, he said, "Stop here."

She did as he said and tried to get her bearings. The warehouses said port-side. The abutments indicated a bridge above. The piles of discarded bottles, cans, bags, and boxes screamed isolated. In a 24-7 bustling city Ilse had no idea such a desolate place existed. Her nerves tingled under clammy skin and perspiration bathed her upper lip, trickled at her hair line, and soaked her blouse.

She tried another tack. "You said you loved me. This seems hardly an appropriate place to talk of love."

He didn't answer.

"Perhaps a restaurant, a candlelight dinner, and a fine wine. I know just the place. We could...."

"No." He leaned forward.

Ilse saw his eyes in the rearview mirror. Then his arms. A twisted smile.

She pitched forward so she could turn to see what he was up to. The garrote caught her and jerked her back, hard, against the backrest. Her fingers fought the wire's death grip. Seconds later, her arms dropped, lifeless.

<~<~|~>~>

Gavin held the garrote tight. Pulling. Allowing the taut wire to do its work. Stretching her neck backwards until all signs of life left the body.

Hands covered with nitrile disposable gloves, he yanked the pendant off her necklace and stuck it in his wallet. Time to finish the job. He removed a contractor sized plastic bag from his pocket, placing it over her upper body. Once he had the bag secured, he moved her from the driver's seat to the car's trunk. He used another bag to cover her lower body and sealed the package with duct tape. Satisfied, he slammed the trunk closed.

Next, Gavin unscrewed the license plates and tossed them into the front seat. He retrieved her phone from her purse. He opened the back, pulled out the sim card, and broke it in half. He dropped the phone and pieces of sim card on the ground and smashed them with the heel of his shoe.

Her keys were still in the ignition. He used his knife on a second plastic bag and fashioned a poncho. Putting it on, he slid into the driver's seat and started the car. He spent a few minutes banging the car's body into walls, boulders, and cement abutments before driving to an auto junk pile. He wove the car into the wrecks, making it indistinguishable at first glance.

Before exiting he turned and reached for the container of accelerant and poured it on the back seat. By the time the car's interior temperature rose high enough to cause spontaneous combustion, he'd be far away.

He left the scene, license plates wrapped in the plastic poncho, his face hidden by the hoodie, and the purse tucked under his arm. He changed into his work pants and T-shirt, dumping the clothes into a collection bin for the needy, the plates into a garbage bin behind a restaurant, and the purse, sans ID, in yet another bin blocks away.

Chapter 07►Soho, NYC

Friday, 21 February
Gavin entered his pottery studio, which smelled of damp earth. He walked over to the kiln and dumped Younger's ID cards onto the fireproof shelf. He closed the door and turned it on. In less than an hour, paper and plastic would be ash. While he waited, he prepared tea, a ritual he performed after every kill.

Fifteen years ago, he frequented a Chinese restaurant which catered to the Asian community. One evening, the owner presented him with a gift of a special blend of tea, a practice revisited every so often. Tea became one of Gavin's passions.

In the kitchen area of the loft, he had an under-counter refrigerator, small sink, and apartment sized four-burner stove, populated with three different sized saucepans. Above the fridge, on the counter, sat a tea kettle and a ceramic cylinder full of cooking utensils.

Above the kitchen equipment, open shelving lined the wall and housed a limited collection of teas and several white porcelain teapots. His favorite was Silver Needle Tea steeped in his prized red Zhuni teapot.

As he prepared the tea, he remembered his father, Vincent Mansonati. After every job, he preferred drinking beer with his pals, needing the camaraderie of like-minded friends.

Gavin didn't have friends—he confided in no one. He applied a lotion to his hands, dry and cracked by the moisture robbing clay. At the kettle's low whistle, he turned off the gas. Picking up the remote, he pushed a button and the music of Gilbert and Sullivan reverberated through the studio. Listening to the Mikado Overture, he prepared the tea and let it steep in its lidded pot.

He removed two digestive biscuits from their package and placed them on a small plate, which he put on the tray with the teapot and cup. This simple fare was a long way from the bar snacks his father gulped down by the handful—popcorn, peanuts, and French fries, in fact, anything fried. The bullets killed him before the heart attack could.

Gavin pulled the wire clay cutter from his back pocket. Although he had several, this one had a thinner, longer wire. He had modified the wooden ends with shallow grooves for his fingers, guaranteeing a tight, non-slip grip—necessary for the extra tension. The wire did not cut through throats as easily as clay. The skin, cartilage, bone, muscle, veins, and arteries added resistance requiring more force. Vincent had told him about the time his garrote broke mid-kill. Gavin smiled. Forewarned was forearmed.

He cleaned the wire and cubed a block of clay from the feeder carton. Picking up a piece, he used his muscled upper body and strong hands to crush it into a rough ball-like shape. He walked over to the potter's wheel and dropped it on the center of the bat sitting on the potter's wheel and returned to kitchen.

He washed his hands and poured the tea. Cup cradled in both hands, he moved to the window to watch the boats on the Hudson River colored by the glow of sunset. With each sip, he rolled the hot liquid around his tongue, allowing the flavors to infuse his palate. The ritual slowed his breathing and relaxed his body. He leaned against the sill and closed his eyes.

"Come," his grandfather said. "Come with *Nonno*."

The little boy grabbed the big rough hand.

"We're going to play with the clay."

"Can I make snakes? And balls? And pancakes?"

"*Nonno's* going to let you do anything you want."

"A fire engine? Or a horse? Maybe a pick-up truck?"

"Or maybe N*onna* needs a new cup for her coffee?"

The boy clapped his hands. "I want to make a present for *Nonna*."

He followed his *nonno* into the pottery studio in the woods behind the family weekend and summer home.

In the quiet solitude, the boy learned the arts of transformation, concentration, and patience. Tiny chubby hands created dynamic shapes from blobs of moist clay and painted glazes. After two months, he had a presentable cup. N*onna* used it until she died.

Sighing, he washed and dried the teacup, rinsed and dried the teapot, and put them both back on the shelf.

Gavin stretched and sat down at the wheel, pulled Ilse's pendant from his wallet and set it on the table next to him, and shifted his focus to the clay. This piece would be for Ilse, a silent memorial, her pendant tucked inside. Like the others it would find a good home in a museum or private collection.

"A Wand'ring Minstrel I" floated in the air as he engaged the turntable motor. He wet his hands and placed them around the spinning material. As he centered the clay, watery slip oozed through his fingers until the mass spun true. Once again, Gavin closed his eyes as he repeated his *nonno's* words.

"The moment of perfect alignment. Experience it. Don't rush."

The hum of his fax machine—a necessary low-tech piece of equipment in a world of high-tech bugging—interrupted his revery. It sat on the counter below, to the right of the windows, under a poster announcing a past gallery show and his work schedule.

Gavin rinsed and dried his hands. He pulled out his phone, texted "*x*" to an unregistered number, and checked his Swiss bank account. The transfer went through. He read the fax to learn the name of his next contract before he crumpled and torched it.

Returning to the wheel, his serene face showed an inner truth--he loved the art of working with his hands

.

Chapter 08►Gramercy Avenue, NYC

Monday, 24 February
Rachel entered Chris's office.

He said, "You're up early."

"I got a phone call from Ted Donovan's lawyer."

"That man will just not stay buried."

"It seems I'm mentioned in his will. Do you want to come with me?"

"Absolutely. What time?"

"You pick. The lawyer said it would take less than thirty minutes, and he could fit me in anytime today."

Chris checked his calendar. "How does one sound?"

"Good. I'll let him know and ask Nikolai to watch Zeus."

<~<~|~>~>

At one-ten, Rachel and Chris were sitting in front of the lawyer.

He said, "I'll be brief. Theodore X. Donovan has named only two recipients to inherit his estate. The first is the PRAISE Foundation, to which he has bequeathed his investments. The second is you, Miss Allen. He named you executrix of his estate. You are to receive the monies in his bank accounts, the apartment and its contents, and his car. If there are any personal items in his PRAISE office, they're yours also. As executrix of his estate, he has designated the sum of one hundred thousand dollars for your time. Legal expenses and other expenses incurred with settling the estate will be borne by the estate."

Rachel looked at Chris and back at the lawyer. "I can't believe it. Why would he do that? Why me?"

The lawyer said, "He did not share his reasoning with me. He just asked that I execute his wishes." He pushed several papers in front of her. "Please sign these so I can begin the process. You'll need a Letter Testamentary to attest to your legal standing and be able to access his bank accounts. I'll take care of it immediately, and you should receive the documents within a couple of weeks."

Rachel signed the papers, and the lawyer placed an envelope in front of her. "In here you'll find what you need to access the apartment." He pushed another set of keys toward her. "You also get the car located in the building's parking garage."

Rachel turned to Chris. "What am I going to do with a car?"

"Learn to drive?"

"Right. It's the last thing on my list." She returned her gaze to the lawyer. "Are we done?"

"For now," he said. "Please keep me informed of anything you uncover affecting the value of the estate. Money will have to be set aside for state and federal taxes. My office will do the accounting. If any questions arise, I'll get in touch with you." He stood up and handed her his card. "Anything else?"

Rachel shook her head.

"Good. Call me anytime if you run into problems."

After leaving the lawyer's office, Rachel stopped and grabbed Chris's arm. "Chris, I killed Donovan. Do you think anyone's going to think I did it for the money?"

"First of all, you didn't kill him, and second, you had no knowledge of his intentions."

"You and I know that."

"And so does the FBI."

<~<~|~>~>

At the door to Donovan's East Side penthouse apartment, Rachel balked. "I don't think I can go in."

"Aren't you curious?"

"No, not really. The whole thing kind of turns my stomach."

"We don't have to do this."

"You do it," she said stepping aside.

Chris entered the apartment and said over his shoulder, "It looks like a hotel room that's just had maid service. No personal stuff. Nothing out of place. Do you want to come in while I look around?"

Rachel took a few hesitant steps into the foyer. "It doesn't look like anybody's ever lived here."

Chris laughed. "Exactly what I said. Somewhere between a furniture store and a hospital room."

Rachel walked into the living room. "Donovan certainly had a minimalist decorating style." She watched as Chris went through the credenza's drawers. "Any papers or files?"

"No, nothing."

She crossed the room and stood in front of the floor-to-ceiling windows. "This is an amazing view of the East River and the Brooklyn Bridge." She turned to Chris. "Wasn't there an explosion in this building the day Donovan died?"

"I'll check." Chris pulled out his phone and searched. "There was. In fact, it happened in this apartment."

"That explains why the apartment looks staged."

"But it doesn't tell us who or why."

"I'll find out." Rachel called FBI Special Agent Elizabeth Neilson and put her on speaker. "Hi Beth. Chris and I are at Donovan's apartment."

"What are you doing there?"

"I just found out I'm the beneficiary and executrix of Donovan's will. The apartment's part of the deal."

"That's quite a surprise."

"You have no idea," Rachel said.

Beth said, "Nice view."

"Come on, Beth. What's going on? We know a bomb went off in this place the day Donovan died. Today, it's pristine."

Beth said, "We found the shell of his safe bolted to the floor in the master-bedroom closet. The explosion not only incinerated the contents but blew off the door. Our best guess is that the failsafe mechanism triggered the blast when someone tried to figure out the combination. The evidence tells us that one person suffered severe blood loss and two others were present. They ransacked the apartment and removed all electronics and paper files. Our team is reviewing the building's security tapes, and the lab is processing the blood. We want to find these guys."

"My God. What was Donovan into?"

"Good question."

Rachel said, "Who did the renovation?"

"The building's manager insisted Donovan's estate fix it up as soon as possible to preserve the integrity of the adjoining units. When we finished our investigation, we turned it over to Donovan's lawyer."

"Funny, the lawyer didn't say a word about all that."

"The whole thing felt weird to me. However, without more evidence, we couldn't go any further," Beth said. "Oops. Got a call. Let's talk later."

Rachel put her phone away and looked at Chris, "So what do you think?"

Chris shrugged his shoulders. "I think there's a conspiracy to keep Donovan's personal and business connections secret."

Rachel laughed. "You see conspiracy scenarios in everything."

"That's my job," Chris said. "What do you want to do with the apartment? I'm guessing it'd be worth around eight million in today's market, if not more."

"I can't even think about it right now." Rachel stood in front of the windows, arms folded. "How does a person running a non-profit get to live in a place like this?"

"Apparently, he wasn't just running PRAISE—he supported it. He inherited money from his parents and enjoyed it. Not so unusual."

"Still, that's a lot of money. I bet all his talk of patriotism camouflaged a big payoff for the plane crash."

"You don't know that," Chris said. "But I wouldn't dismiss it either."

Chapter 09▶Gramercy Avenue, NYC

Monday, 24 February
That afternoon, while relaxing in Chris's apartment, Rachel got a call from the lobby. "Ted Donovan's associate is downstairs."

Chris said, "I'll go."

"No, I'll do it… with Zeus. Tarik won't let anything happen."

"True. Still," Chris pointed to his laptop, "I'll be watching you."

Rachel leashed Zeus and went downstairs to meet Mr. Smith. The man wore an overcoat and a fedora style hat, which he pulled so low it touched the top of his glasses. He said, "Miss Allen, I understand you've been designated executrix of the Donovan estate."

"I'm sorry. Do I know you?"

"Are you his executrix?" the man said with a touch of impatience.

Zeus moved from Rachel's side to an angled position in front of her, never taking his eyes off the visitor.

"Who's asking?"

The man took a step back. "Mr. Donovan wanted you to have this." He handed her a nine by twelve manila envelope and took off.

Rachel pet Zeus. "Good Boy. Let's go."

She returned to Chris's apartment. Zeus greeted Chris like he hadn't seen him for a week.

Chris said, "What's that?"

"Let's take a look."

They walked over to the kitchen counter. She opened the sealed envelope and let the contents slide out. Zeus lay down by her feet. "Another surprise from Donovan."

On the counter lay a set of car keys, a deed to a warehouse, a safety deposit key, the business card of a local bank manager, and scraps of paper.

Chris picked up the paper. "These are entry codes and passwords."

"For what?"

"I'm guessing your warehouse is a secure site."

"I wonder why the lawyer this afternoon didn't have these things."

"I bet he had no idea they existed."

Rachel stared at the contents strewn about the counter. "I'm calling Beth." She pulled out her phone. As soon as Beth was on the line and before she could speak, Rachel said, "Guess what?"

Beth said, "You and Chris have set the date."

"How did you know?"

"I guessed."

"You're right, so you get to be my bridesmaid," Rachel said. "Save the second week in October."

"I'm scheduling as we speak. What can I do to help?"

"Not a thing. I'm turning the whole event over to my mother."

"Interesting."

"I know it may not be the best solution, Beth, but I just can't deal with it now. Later, closer to the date, I'll get involved with the details."

"Sounds great," Beth said. "Work calls. Got to go."

"Wait. That's not why I called. Less than fifteen minutes ago some guy handed me the papers to a warehouse and another car."

Beth didn't say anything.

"Beth?"

"Wait a minute, I want Eric to hear this." Rachel heard her call out to FBI Special Agent Eric Jarrod, her partner in crime and life. "Pick up the phone. It's Rachel."

"Hi," Eric said. "What's happening?"

Rachel explained.

Beth said, "Rachel, we never told you our working theory."

Eric chimed in, "We think Donovan engineered disappearances spanning over thirty years. There may be supporting evidence at the warehouse. We need to get a forensic team over there. If we're lucky, we'll be able to give closure to the families."

Beth said, "Can we get the keys?"

Rachel said, "No problem. Come now and join us for dinner."

Beth and Eric arrived at seven. Rachel opened the door with Zeus by her side, his tail high, eyes bright, and nose working overtime as he sniffed the new arrivals.

Beth stopped in her tracks. "A dog? You got a dog?"

"Zeus," Rachel said. "We adopted him four days ago."

Chris laughed. "We didn't so much adopt him as he adopted Rachel."

Rachel patted Zeus's head. "He's my new shadow. Ignore him until he warms up to you. He'll come over for a meet-and-greet as soon as he's comfortable."

Keeping an eye on the dog, Beth and Eric entered with an overnight case. She wheeled the luggage over to the couch, tucked in the handle, and sat next to Eric.

Rachel said, "We didn't expect overnight guests although you're welcome to stay."

Beth said, "This isn't our stuff, it's Donovan's. His personal effects from Lake George. We've been over everything. Now, they're yours."

"I don't want any of it. Take everything back with you."

Eric got up and opened the case. He pulled out the computer and gave it to Chris. "Here. We've had our guys go over this, and they removed all items pertaining to Donovan's activities. If you find anything else, let me know ASAP."

"Sure. Nothing would make me happier than to help destroy Donovan's inflated image."

Eric reached in again and pulled out a wallet. "Rachel, you're going to need his credit cards to cancel his accounts."

Rachel shook her head. "I can't. I don't even want anything to do with his estate or his money."

Chris held out his hand. "I'll take it and see to the cancelations."

"Thank you," Rachel said. "Now put that stuff away, and I'll bring out the food."

<~<~|~>~>

After dinner, Rachel gave them the address, keys and codes. "You'll give us a full report?"

Chris said, "With pictures?"

Eric said, "Of course, if anything's worth seeing."

Beth said, "In exchange, I've brought you a gift." She opened her purse and produced a small bright pink leather diary with a brass lock. She handed it to Rachel. "I thought you might find this interesting."

"A diary?"

"The 1934 diary of a fourteen-year-old girl from Apalachin, NY," Beth said," a small-town west of Binghamton, on Route 17, just north of the Pennsylvania border."

"Where did it you get it?"

Eric said, "As you know, our first 'couple's project' is renovating an old row house upstate, in Albany. We were cleaning out the basement and found an exquisite hand-made oak safe hidden under the stairs."

Beth said. "We did a little research and believe we're working in an 1800's house built by a banker called D.C. Barnes. In his spare time, he had a talent for woodworking. He set up his shop in the basement, well away from his wife and five daughters."

Eric said, "We found pictures of his shop and his work in the library."

Chris said, "Did you bring any with you?"

Eric pulled out his phone and tapped the screen a few times. Rachel and Chris moved closer and watched the slide show while Eric narrated. He scrolled through the images. "These are shots from the library books. This is our basement. That's the safe. Here's me trying to figure out the locking mechanism. It took quite a few different approaches until we figured it out."

Beth pointed to an image and said, "That's the safe's interior. It's really a work of art." A few pictures later, she pointed and said, "That's the little suitcase we found."

Eric said, "Inside were newspaper articles, a few ribbons, a child's christening dress, some bits and pieces of jewelry, and the diary." He closed his phone. "You should have seen Beth. She set up a whole crime scene lab to record the contents and store them for fingerprint analysis."

Beth said, "I'm not apologizing. You never know."

Rachel giggled. "I can see you arranging the yellow tent numbers and rulers."

Chris said, "What, if anything, did you find?"

"She hasn't had time to run the tests," Eric said. "We found it this past weekend and have been inundated with work ever since. We're investigating the tri-state Necktie Serial Killer."

"So, to get your mind off Donovan, Eric and I decided to give you the diary. I know you love research, and this mystery will intrigue you."

Chris said, "Just what she needs. She's been complaining she's got a book due, and she's blocked."

"Temporarily blocked," Rachel said, shooting Chris a look of betrayal. "Beth, What mystery?"

"For us to know and for you to find out."

Eric checked the time. "We've got to go." He stood, helped Beth to her feet, and said, "Gallantry's not dead."

Beth said, "This time."

Chapter 10▶Gramercy Avenue, NYC

Monday-Tuesday, 24–25 February
After Beth and Eric left, Rachel and Chris walked Zeus. They returned to her apartment and spent the rest of the evening together, screening a movie and making love. Chris went home around midnight. It wasn't ideal. Her heart wanted him next to her, but reality made it impossible.

Ever since her nightmares began, Rachel's erratic sleep patterns ruled her nights. She had to keep her options open. Stay up. Read. Write. Pace. Snack. Watch TV. Workout. Shower. Her stress levels, already high, went through the roof when she also had to worry about disturbing Chris.

Alone, still warm from his touch, Rachel fell asleep without any problem. The dreams came later. Reality morphed into distorted apparitions, sounds, and smells. She relived an altered version of her struggle on the snowy precipice. She clutched the covers as her body twitched and tossed to fight off her demons. She formed words without sentences. Her

head jerked from side to side. And then, she felt
Chris. She leaned in for a kiss.

She opened her eyes in time to see a huge pink
tongue lick her from chin to nose. When she didn't
respond, Zeus did it again. This time she smiled,
scratching him behind the ears before wrapping her
arms around him. Zeus rested his head on her shoulder and never moved a muscle.

Rachel's clammy skin dried and returned to normal. The dog comforted her. She didn't have to explain, or complain, or defend anything. If she felt
good, he did too.

"Good boy, Zeus. Good boy."

She flipped the light on. "You woke me up from
the bad dream, didn't you?" Zeus got in two sloppy
face licks. His tail wagged. "You're so smart." Rachel
gave him a kiss on the nose and massaged his ears.
"What a good boy."

Zeus transitioned onto his back. Rachel scratched
his belly. "Chris didn't think we should be alone. I
disagreed because I knew you'd take care of me."

Zeus lay like a lump, eyes closed and just the hint
of a groan escaping from his mouth.

"It's almost six-thirty. Let me get ready and get
this morning started." Rachel stood and the sleeping
dog sprang to life and jumped to her, ready for action.
She laughed. "Okay. Okay. Let's do this."

<~<~|~>~>

Showered and dressed Rachel took Zeus into the
small grassy garden out back so Zeus could do his
thing. Afterward they went up to Chris's apartment.
She made coffee and poured herself a cup, which she
took over to the couch. Wrapped in one of the
throws, she curled up in a corner, Zeus on the floor

where her feet had been. After a few sips, she put the coffee down and fell asleep.

Chris woke at seven-thirty to find Rachel asleep in his living room. Zeus raised his head, then executed a full launch at Chris. The ruckus woke Rachel. He said, "Sorry. I had planned to let you sleep."

"It's okay."

"Bad dreams wreck your night?"

She nodded. "As usual. However, this time, Zeus changed everything."

Chris said, "Tell me while I make some coffee."

Rachel watched Chris as she related Zeus's hero-ism. The dog heard his name and snuggled against her. Rachel smiled and gave Zeus the attention he deserved. "I can't believe what a difference Zeus made."

Chris joined her on the couch and handed Rachel a mug filled with coffee. "Instead of milk, I topped it off with frozen yogurt. Tell me how you like it." While she did a taste test, he leaned over and petted the dog's head and sides.

She grinned and said, "This is delicious."

"You're welcome. I saw it on the internet and fig-ured it was worth a try. By the way, is Zeus also help-ing with your forgiveness process?"

"I wish he could," she said. "I'm still working on it. Ugh. I'm a mess."

Chris put his arm around her and gave her a hug. "I know you'll figure out how to find peace with your demons. I'm here to help no matter how long it takes."

Rachel kissed him and they sat in silence, taking in the moment.

Chris said, "Did you get a chance to look through the diary?"

"First thing on my list when I get back to my apartment."

Chris got up and said, "Eggs?"

"Yum." Rachel smiled.

Zeus's ears perked up.

Chris laughed. "Okay, some for you too, Buddy."

Chapter 11▶Gramercy Avenue, NYC

Wednesday, 26 February
Chris entered the lobby for his morning conversation with Nikolai.

Nikolai looked up and smiled. "You are too late."

"For what?"

"Rachel took Zeus for a walk to the corner and back."

Chris made a dash for the door.

"Do not worry. I have her on security camera. I am watching."

Chris executed a hard left and watched the video feed over Nikolai's shoulder.

His curly-haired fiancée hugged the building with her right shoulder and held Zeus's leash with her left. Rachel wasn't the slowest walker out this morning, if people using handicap walkers and canes counted. Zeus, despite the loose leash, stayed by her side. He walked with a purpose and people gave them a wide berth.

Chris said, "Good boy, Zeus."

Nikolai said, "She is taking a step away from the wall."

Zeus moved with her.

Chris said, "Uh-oh. What's she going to do at the corner?"

The men watched as Rachel made a U-turn before entering the crowd waiting for the light to turn. One minute she seemed fine and in the next she froze.

Chris grabbed Nikolai's jacket off the back of the chair. "I'm going out there."

"No, wait. Look at this."

Chris watched the monitor.

Zeus licked Rachel's hands and nudged them. He barked. He got in front of her and barked again. She reached out to him. He sat at her feet so she could pet him. She knelt and gave him a hug and a kiss. He gave her several licks in return. She stood, straightening her jacket. Zeus, on his feet, gave himself a good shake and took his position. She tossed her head, adjusted the leash, and they returned to 215, walking curbside.

In front of the building, she dropped the poop-bag in the garbage can and burst through the door. "Did you see? Zeus is amazing." Rachel patted Zeus and scratched him under his chin. He licked her hands, wagging his tail in every direction.

Chris said, "You took a big chance going out by yourself."

"Not so big. Nikolai promised he'd come get me if it all fell apart."

Nikolai said, "I did. I am glad I did not have to do it."

Rachel smiled at Chris. "Shall we go on a real walk now?"

<~<~|~>~>

An hour later, Zeus settled in his bed with his favorite chew toy. Rachel relaxed in her reading chair with a cup of tea, the rescued Lorna Doones, and the bubblegum pink leather diary. Inside she found a note from Beth clinging to the inside cover.

I tracked down the Tanner Family. The brother, Robert Tanner, still lives in the family home. He didn't want to talk with me and asked me to forget the whole thing. As far as he knew, his sister died years ago. I've also tracked the younger brother, the one who lived in the Albany home we're restoring, to a long-term care facility in New York City. Address also enclosed. I'd like to do more, but I'm too jammed to go any further. So, I'm turning the case, as it were, over to you. Enjoy the research. Let me know what you find out. Beth.

So, she couldn't just leave it. Rachel laughed. Once an investigator, always an investigator.

Beautiful penmanship filled the pages—letters more oval than round.

The first page declared, "Patricia Tanner, born 1920, daughter of Stella and Joseph Tanner, sister of Robert and William Tanner—Diary 1934."

The following pages revealed Patricia's difficult transition from child to teenager, her passions and dreams, and her harsh reality. The gifted child dealt with her classmates' bullying and outright ostracism. And if that wasn't bad enough, her body betrayed her. The pudgy child turned into a voluptuous teen without her permission. She did what she could to hide the transformation, yet boys teased her, and girls despised her.

Patricia's grades put her at the top of the class. Her violin mastery evoked plans as a concert violinist if she could ever get out of "this" town. Her parents had little time for her, absorbed in maintaining their

home and family in the midst of the depression. Although, to their credit, they did scrape together
enough money for her music lessons.

Rachel wondered what intrigued Beth. Several entries later, she found it.

April 1, 1934, Easter Sunday

Today Mother made me wear my cousin's too
frilly pink lace dress, too small straw hat with a pink
bow, and too big patent leather shoes to church. I
looked like cotton candy and felt ugly. My parents
said I looked beautiful. They must be blind. At
church, as I walked down the aisle to my seat, I kept
my eyes down. I couldn't bear to see anyone laughing
at me. I will, never, ever, ever live this down.

After services, Mother made ham, potatoes and
carrots, and for dessert, hot cross buns. My parents
invited our neighbors, Mr. and Mrs. Mansonati. They
brought lamb, lasagna, almond flower cookies, and
their children, Maria and Vincent. I ate a little bit of
everything, trying to match my portions with skinny
Maria. I failed. No wonder I still carry my baby-fat.
Mother promised it'd disappear this past year, but it
didn't. It better disappear by next year or no Sweet
Sixteen birthday party for me.

Will, Rob, and Vinny were excused to go out and
play while Maria and I had to clear the table. When
we placed the last dish next to the kitchen sink, we
decided to go outside and jump rope. Before we got to
the door, my father stopped me. He said, "Patricia,
will you please play your violin for our guests?"

I looked at Maria. She shrugged her shoulders
and went outside, closing the door behind her. I was
trapped.

My father handed me my violin and told the
Mansonatis I'd been playing for six months and al-

ready finished the intermediate course. I blushed from embarrassment. While I love playing, I hate being the center of attention.

My father wouldn't take no for an answer, so I retrieved the music stand and sheet music and placed it between me and everyone else. I played Mozart Symphony No. 40 (first movement), never looking up, ignoring the last repeat, and going directly to the end. I bowed to the polite applause, put everything away, and ran for the door.

Mr. Mansonati blocked my escape. He put one hand on my shoulder and told me my fingers danced over the strings with strength and purpose. I looked away before he finished. I think I mumbled "thank you."

He stepped closer—his hand on my shoulder, trapping me, and making me feel very uncomfortable. I looked to my parents for relief, but they seemed to be happy about his attention to me.

He looked at them and then at me. "My dear Patricia. We are both artists. You are only thirteen…."

"Fourteen in nine days," I said with a shake of my shoulder and a step backward. He did not release me. Instead, he smiled. "You are almost fourteen and yet, every note you played occupied a moment of perfect alignment."

He put his other hand on my other shoulder and squeezed. I stood there, straight as a board, silent on the outside—screaming on the inside.

He smiled, said, "Extraordinary," and released me.

As I ran to the door, he turned to my father and said, "Would you mind if I invited Patricia to my studio? I think working the clay would strengthen her fingers even more. It would be like one art form helping another."

I stopped and held my breath. It was the last thing I wanted to do. When Father shook his head and said, "She doesn't have time between school and music," my heart jumped for joy, and I ran outside to play with Maria.

Thank God my father refused. I don't want to be anywhere near that man.

Chapter 12▶New York City, NY

Thursday, 27 February
Rachel and Zeus entered The PRAISE Foundation offices. The receptionist peered down her nose at the dog and raised a doubting eyebrow.

"He's a service dog in training," Rachel said. "I've an appointment with Sybil Powell."

The receptionist made a call. Before Rachel could sit, Sybil came out of her office, hand extended. "I'm so glad to finally meet you. I've read your books and know we're going to get along famously." She addressed the receptionist, "Please bring us some coffee and nibbles from downstairs."

Returning to Rachel, she looked the dog. Rachel said, "This is Zeus."

Sybil smiled and led the twosome into her office. "Let's sit at the conference table. I've got papers for you, and we won't have to juggle coffee cups."

Rachel took a seat facing the windows, Zeus by her side. Sybil chose the chair next to the dog and said, "May I?"

Rachel nodded. "Say hello, Zeus."

Sybil held out her hand for Zeus to sniff. His tail thumped on the floor. Rachel said, "You've been approved."

Sybil scratched him under the chin and gave him a few pats on his shoulder. "Good boy. Nice to meet you."

Zeus licked her hand and snuggled by Rachel's feet.

Formalities over, Sybil said, "Welcome to the PRAISE board, Rachel, although I'm very sorry it's due to Ted Donovan's passing."

"Thank you. It's been something of a shock to find out I'm now responsible for managing his fortune."

"Did you know him well?"

"I thought I did. He saved my life almost eight years ago. I met him again this past fall, and we became friends. In the beginning of this month, we worked on a human rights initiative with a group of interesting people. Before we could finish our mission, Ted died." Rachel took a breath. "How did you know him?"

"I first met Ted in my late teens when my father invited him to dinner. We were close in age, but we never clicked. My father, however, seemed to adore him and treated him as a son."

"I didn't know. I'm so sorry."

Sybil laughed. "It's such a small world. Now I'm here, doing Donovan's job. In fact, he picked me when he decided to give up his position as executive director back in December. And now you're his proxy on all things PRAISE. So strange."

The door opened and the receptionist brought in refreshments, set them on the table, and left, closing the door behind her. The women each took a cup of coffee and agreed to split a lemon bar. Sybil took a bite and said, "Before we get started, I want to give you some material." She got up and retrieved a file from her desk, placed it in front of Rachel, and returned to her seat.

Rachel picked up the folder. "What's this?"

"It's a plan of action developed by Donovan. I revamped it and will present it to the board at our next meeting. This is your copy."

"Did you want me to read it now?"

"Not necessary. But when you do, please get back to me with any questions. I look forward to your impressions and suggestions on our future course."

"I appreciate your confidence."

Sybil reached over and closed the file. "Now, tell me about yourself. I like to know the people I work with."

"That's not so easy."

"Where did you grow up?"

"In Scarsdale. Went to college in upstate New York. I had to leave school just before graduation and began writing."

"May I ask why?"

Rachel contemplated her reply. Of the people who knew about her rape, only Chris and Beth were not family. She discussed it on-line within the safe confines of a rape victims' support community and with various therapists, but never in person with a stranger. Still, Sybil's immediate warmth and positive energy gave her the courage. Lowering her gaze to her hands, she said, "I was raped."

Sybil's hand covered Rachel's. Instead of withdrawing, Rachel raised her eyes to Sybil's and saw they were filled with tears.

Sybil cleared her throat and took a sip of water. "Me too."

"You?"

"I could say the same. You also look like an improbable target—confident and strong."

"Rape is all about the attacker's power and control. They're bastards. They get to walk away, and we're left to deal with the pain and reclaim our lives."

Sybil raised her coffee up in a toast. "Amen."

Rachel picked up her cup and tapped Sybil's. "To the survivors."

They sipped in unison.

Rachel said, "Did it change you?"

"Of course. I thought I controlled my life, my lovers, and my future. The truth terrified me. My reaction manifested in a fury I haven't completely dispelled. On the healthier side, I channeled much of it into my work—giving people back their power usurped by governments and human traffickers."

"Much like what I do for human rights with my books." Rachel smiled. "We are definitely kindred spirits."

Sybil laughed. "It'd be nicer if our reason wasn't so invasive and pervasive." She sipped her coffee and bit into the confection. "So, what's your situation now?"

"After a long recovery, I moved to New York. Met my fiancée, Chris Gregory, and now I've adopted Zeus." Tail bump. "I'd say I'm doing pretty well."

"What's holding you back?"

"I… I… uh… saw Donovan die. I'm working through the guilt. In fact, I saw a psychiatrist, Dr. Ilse Younger. She's good, so you might want to keep her name in the back of your mind, if you ever need someone."

"You're not going to believe this," Sybil said. "Ilse's my best friend." Her hand went to one of the pendants hanging around her neck. "We exchanged identical necklaces as a symbol of trust and commitment."

Rachel shook her head. "I don't think you should mention me. I've decided to put some time between me and our next session. She dug deep."

"Ilse's not one to pull her punches, for sure. I've always admired her for that. But don't worry, your secret's safe with me because I'm trustworthy and she's away."

"Yes, Ilse said something to me about not being back until May first."

"She's on a yacht touring the Mediterranean—a gift from PRAISE in appreciation of her work with trauma survivors. Donovan facilitated Ilse's trip before he died."

Rachel said, "I'm glad she benefitted from his largesse." She took a sip of coffee.

Sybil leaned forward, elbows on the table. "What are you working on now?"

"I'm working on another book and doing a little side detective work regarding an intriguing 1934 diary of a young girl. I'm researching what's become of her so I can return some of her things—if she's still alive. If not, maybe her family would like them. In any case, it's interesting and diverting."

"Because you're supposed to be writing?"

"Guilty…and blocked," Rachel said. "What about you? I mean, when you're not working here."

"In those ten minutes when I'm not working on PRAISE," Sybil said and laughed, "I live with my wife, Lidia Lundon, in Soho, above her new gallery. She's an artist and this gallery is her dream come true."

"It sounds lovely. I'm looking forward to meeting her."

"Maybe we can do dinner."

"Absolutely, I'd love that." Rachel got up to leave, paused, and sat down. "May I ask you something about PRAISE?"

"Of course."

"Every day, it seems, I find out something new about Ted Donovan. The FBI are going through his safe-deposit boxes and bank accounts. So far, they've found a significant amount of undocumented cash. I should know more within the next few weeks. Did you find any evidence of impropriety when you reviewed PRAISE books?"

Sybil's smile faded. "Why do you ask?"

"PRAISE was his whole life. He never talked about anything else. That makes me wonder, where did all the money come from? If not from the foundation, he may have had a covert side business."

Sybil opened Rachel's folder and pulled out the financial report, found the item she wanted, and showed Rachel. "Here's Ted's salary. Even at three-hundred-thousand, PRAISE administrative costs are less than ten percent of our total expenses. He worked out a policy where all functions and awards are underwritten by one or more board members, sponsors, or both. Donations go directly to projects."

"So as far as you and the PRAISE CPA know, all money has been accounted for?"

"Even if he had a slush fund of some sort, he'd have been too smart to set it up under PRAISE," Sybil said. "Still, I'll keep a lookout for any irregularities."

<~<~|~>~>

Sybil arrived home at dinnertime and found Lidia in the gallery, kneeling on the floor, painting panels. "I thought you were all done with this."

Lidia blew a strand of hair out of her line of sight. "Good to see you, too."

Sybil laughed. "Guilty." She re-enacted her entrance. "Hi, Babe. How's it going?"

"That's better," Lidia said. "I decided to paint them because I didn't like the color. My paintings are best shown on a chalk white background, and these panels turned out to be too beigey."

Sybil said, "If it makes you happy, I'm all for it. Personally, I don't see the difference."

"That's why I didn't ask you."

"Well, I've got something to ask you," Sybil said. "How about a little dinner party?"

"Are you kidding?" Lidia made a sweeping gesture encompassing the room. "Do you see what I've got to get done?"

"It's for a new board member—Rachel Allen. I met her today and felt an instant bond. I think you'd like her." Sybil paused. "And she has a dog."

At the word "dog," Lidia stopped painting. "I love dogs."

"I know. I'm buttering you up. She'd be a new friend for us as well as a big help with PRAISE."

"I guess I could whip up dinner for three without a problem."

"Four. She's engaged to a man named Chris something."

"Lovely. I bet he can't wait to sit around and listen to three women chatter away."

"True," Sybil said. "Maybe lunch would be better."

"Lunch or dinner, can we wait until after the opening?"

"Of course. I'll ask her which she prefers and set up date." Sybil pulled out her phone and added the invitation to her to-do list. "By the way, Rachel knew

Ted Donovan and thinks he may have a hidden slush fund."

"The guy who hired you? Your father's friend?"

"The very same. And you know, I would have dismissed her concern except for the fact he did work with my father."

"Are you sure?"

"Absolutely. However, since I hate him, we don't talk so I can't ask him."

Lidia winced. She could never tell Sybil the whole truth about the gallery. "Maybe you could ask your brother."

"Tweedledum?" Sybil laughed. "He's rarely help-ful."

"What about Peter? He could ask. You father adores him."

"Peter's in Cambodia. I hope he's far away from that man's reach."

"You do know he's only a phone call away?"

"Yet he never calls me."

"You're never around. He's hours ahead of us."

Sybil stepped around the panel to see Lidia's face. "How do *you* know?"

Lidia kept painting. "Peter and I talk, usually around three-thirty in the afternoon our time, and, mostly, when he can't get to sleep. It's all boring stuff. I don't think he has any close friends. I'm like a pen-pal except I'm a phone-pal. I listen to his impatience with practically everyone and everything at work, and he listens to me about my heretofore unchallenged life."

Sybil threw her hands in the air. "Why doesn't he call me? I'm a good listener. I'm great on feedback, strategy, planning, life changes, and problem solving."

Still painting, Lidia said, "He doesn't need any of that. And we both know if you can't fix it, you're listening tolerance might be two minutes."

"That's not fair." Sybil stomped off, stopped, and ran back. "Okay. Maybe that's true. Still, I'm his mother."

"And you're his go-to person when he needs fixes to his problems."

"You're saying he doesn't need me anymore."

"No. Just saying sometimes he needs to talk and for me to listen."

"So, you just sit on the phone, listen, and do what?"

"Doodle, do my nails, check my social media accounts—you know, all the things you hate when you talk to me. Sometimes I'll even have a drink. And you know what?"

"Tell me."

"I don't have many friends either. So, I'm more than happy to listen and help Peter get through whatever he's going through, whenever it suits him. Also, it's not often, he doesn't say much, and he's usually working on his fourth beer."

Sybil knelt and kissed Lidia. "Thank you for taking care of Peter."

Lidia sat back on her heels. "That sounds sarcastic to me."

"No. No. I mean it. You're a great friend, and I'm glad he has your support. Please keep me updated rather than in the dark."

"You're not mad?"

"No. In fact, I'm grateful. So grateful, I'll even help you paint."

Lidia smiled. "Sybil, you never cease to amaze me."

Chapter 13►Washington, D.C.

Friday, 28 February
United States President Franklin Taylor Sandford's months in office had aged him. At fifty-two, he might have been mistaken for a man of sixty. His dark hair had grayed at his temples. New furrow lines appeared between his eyebrows, across his forehead, around his eyes, and framed his mouth. He found out early in his administration that great responsibility carries great personal sacrifice.

Earlier this month, the Tawandian crisis, not known to the public, had robbed him of his vow to run the country free of manipulation by his wealthy and powerful donor. By holding himself to the highest standard of self-control in situations where it would have been easy to sacrifice his ethical and moral standards, he bypassed learning the tough and dirty tricks of the political trade. In the end, he made a deal with the devil.

President Sandford left the Oval Office, walking outside onto the veranda. He leaned on the balcony railing and watched his family below. He smiled and waved. The children waved back, urging him to join them.

He turned to the stairs, nodding to his security detail, and got about one-third of the way down when his phone rang. He pulled it out of his pocket, checked the ID, shook his head, and held the phone over the railing for a few tantalizing micro-seconds before he answered the devil's call.

"Good afternoon, Franklin," Philip Vanderhagen said. "Must be beautiful in your neck of the woods."

"It is."

"I'm in Philadelphia. If your schedule permits, let's have lunch in the next few days."

"I don't have my calendar in hand," Sandford said. "Is it something we can talk about now?"

"I'd like to ask you for a small favor, Franklin. The State Department has posted my grandson to a backwater far eastern country as some low-level Foreign Service go-for. He tells me his talents are wasted, and he's ready for a more significant posting."

"What's his name?"

"Peter Powell, my daughter's boy."

Sandford clenched his jaw. "Does he know where he might like to serve? As you no doubt are aware, prized postings are already assigned. Interference with the system at this point would have far reaching consequences."

Like an annoyed parent, Vanderhagen said, "Do not try my patience. You and you alone nominate ambassadors who are confirmed by the U.S. Senate. However, we are in a recess, and you are free to appoint anyone temporarily."

"Point made. What posting?"

"Tawanda."

"Philip, are you kidding me? Tawanda's as back-water as they come. It's a war-torn speck of African land populated by refugees, soldiers, and profiteers— including the government."

"My investor's interests are mineral. We need to have feet on the ground, and they can't be ours."

"Before I assign even one person to represent the United States over there, I'd have to recognize Ta-wanda as a country. I can't do that."

Vanderhagen's voice turned silky. "Franklin, my boy. We've come way too far for you to jeopardize your position."

"What does that mean?"

"It means I have damaging information that I am keeping under wraps to protect your image. I am not interested in jeopardizing your second term. All I'm looking for is a proactive strategy to advance our posi-tion in Africa. You're the President of the United States. You figure it out. I trust your judgement im-plicitly." Vanderhagen ended the call.

Sandford dropped his head and swallowed his an-ger. When he looked up, he smiled and threw kisses to his children. He returned to his desk and pressed a button on the desk console. "Nancy, get me Wendell Waters and ask Uriah to be on standby."

Unable to sit still, he paced as he waited. It didn't help his anxiety, so he walked over to the bar and poured two-fingers of Scotch. By the second sip, Wendell Waters, Chief of Staff, arrived—attractive, built like an aging linebacker, and dressed in a tai-lored pinstripe suit. He and Sandford were close friends. "Mr. President, what can I do for you?"

"Wendell, what's your take on putting one of our people in Tawanda?"

"Has our position changed?"

"No. It's an emerging nation, and perhaps our presence would keep us from being blindsided like before."

"President Okoro had a lot of nerve trying to extort the United States for millions of dollars."

"Yes, he did." Sandford took another sip. "Although we did an effective job of taking the wind out of his sails."

"I don't see any problem if you want to assign someone."

"You don't think it would be misconstrued as our recognition of Tawanda as a country even as it fights for its borders against the Democratic Republic of the Congo?"

"We do have representation in the DRC," Waters said. "Maybe it would be a good idea to monitor Tawanda as well."

Sandford nodded and walked over to the console. "Nancy, Uriah please."

To Waters, "Would you like a drink?"

"I'm good."

Uriah Henderson, Secretary of State, knocked and entered. "Good morning, Mr. President, Wendell."

Uriah rejected the offer of a drink, and they all sat down.

Sandford said, "I'm considering a person in some official capacity to be our liaison in Tawanda. What are your thoughts?"

"As we have already negotiated with Okoro, we have in essence acknowledged his existence. Therefore, I don't see any problem with an appointment."

"What would be your least invasive suggestion?"

"A consular agent. It's the kind of appointment I can make for locations where there are no current postings. It's immediate, doesn't need Senate authorization, and won't involve you directly."

"Wendell, thoughts?"

"Sounds good to me."

"So do we have consensus on the post?"

Heads nodded.

He handed Henderson a name on a slip of paper. "Assign this person."

Henderson read the name and gave Sandford a puzzled look. "Peter Powell?"

"Why? Do you know him?"

Henderson pulled out his ePad and after a few taps said, "He's a low-level assistant in the Cameroons."

"He feels he's destined to do greater things."

"Don't we all," Waters said.

Henderson said, "We've not seen extraordinary work from him. His records show he does show up and do his assigned work completely and accurately."

"Then it's settled," Sandford said.

"Sir, we do have better trained and more highly qualified people available."

"I'm sure we do. Make a list. We may have to replace Powell sooner rather than later."

Waters said, "And, Uriah, please send me a copy of the budget for the posting."

"Will do." Henderson nodded and left the room.

Waters turned to the president. "Who's Powell?"

Sandford took the last sip of Scotch. "Philip Vanderhagen's grandson."

Waters let out a long slow whistle and shook his head.

The president said, "I must be the most naïve man ever to grace this office. After studying all the mistakes of my predecessors, taking great pains to make my positions clear, and answering only to the American people, I'm still a pawn in the financial game of politics."

"I see you more as a knight, Sir."

"Vanderhagen may be the biggest thorn in my side, but he's certainly not the only one."

"Every president walks the thin line of satisfying workers, employers, and retirees so no one goes hungry or broke. You stepped up, and you're doing a great job."

"I hope that's true."

"In the scheme of things, Vanderhagen's request isn't going to impact our foreign policy nor step on anyone else's toes."

"At least as far as we know."

"Shall I let the appointment stand or get Uriah to hold off?"

"Let it stand and hope, down the road, it doesn't hit us where it hurts."

Chapter 14▶Yaounde, Cameroon

Friday, 28 February

Peter Powell took the call from Uriah Henderson's office, hung up, and called his grandfather.

"I got the posting," Peter said.

"Excellent. Have you done your homework?"

"I have, Sir. I'm fluent in Tawandanese, familiar with their customs and current export numbers. I've researched the government's role in the ongoing war with the Democratic Republic of the Congo and continuing negligence of the refugees."

Vanderhagen said, "Does the State Department know how prepared you are?"

"I don't think so. I've done the work on my own time."

"Now, Peter, you'll be in Tawanda as an agent of the government."

"I know that, Sir."

"However, if you find the time, I'd like you to stop in at our mine holdings. Do a walk through and see what's what?"

"As long as it doesn't interfere with my job."

"Of course," Vanderhagen said. "I'd never ask you to do such a thing. My sources tell me the Tawandanese government will be imposing new taxes on mined ore. I'm interested in ascertaining our current output's accuracy to evaluate the tax impact."

"I think that'd be okay."

"Excellent. When do you leave?"

"At the end of the week."

"Let me know your address. I'll send you a secure satellite phone."

"Will do."

<~<~|~>~>

At twenty-nine, Peter worked hard to personify average—average weight at one-sixty for his height of five ten, average countenance, made even more so by brown tortoise-shell rimmed glasses and bad haircut. He lived within his salary and adapted to the office culture of his co-workers.

However, behind his crafted facade, lay a handsome bachelor with a sharp analytical mind.

As a youngster, he spent hours with his grandfather who told him stories about the world and taught him how to play chess. During his tenth year, a major disagreement split the Vanderhagen family. The Powells moved to Portland, Oregon, and his mother forbade contact with his grandfather. Peter disobeyed.

He observed the Vanderhagen men discussing business, politics, and philanthropy. He had accompanied them to benefits where they gave large donations to organizations helping those unable to help themselves. He'd been taught by the best that privilege had responsibilities, and he intended to comply.

Following the path Vanderhagen laid out for him, Peter earned degrees in business, economics, and international relations, staying within the top seven percent of his class. This gave him entry to the jobs he needed to round out his education with real-world experience. He learned banking, local and global, and the protocols used in nation-to-nation exchanges. On the side, he took several Kidnap Prevention-Tactical and Bodyguard Training courses given by a crack team of Navy Seals.

<~<~|~>~>

Peter leaned back in his chair and, with fingers inter-twined, stretched his arms over his head. He rotated his shoulders, stretched his hands, and made the dreaded call.

"Hi, Mom."

"Peter! How're you doing?"

"I'm doing great. I've just been reassigned."

"Are you coming home?"

"No, not this time. I'm going to Tawanda."

"Africa? Isn't Tawanda still at war with the DRC?"

"That's the one. I'm excited. I'm finally going where the action is."

"And get yourself killed."

"I'm not doing any espionage work or joining the army, Mom. I'm just an observer."

"Observers get killed all the time."

"You know I can take care of myself. I've had the best training in the world."

"I know you're all knowledge and no experience. That alone could get you killed."

"I've also got compassion and a strong moral center thanks to you."

"You sound like a Boy Scout who thinks he's James Bond because he has a merit badge in 'Driving Cars.'"

"Come on, Mom. Don't over-react. It's a great posting."

"That's ridiculous. War zones are shit."

"You paid for my education, listening to me moan all the way. Now, be happy because it's paying off. I'm finally moving toward my destiny."

"I would prefer grandchildren."

"Don't worry. I'll be fine, Mom. Promise."

Chapter 15►Philadelphia, PA

Friday, February 28
"It's done." Vanderhagen shut the phone and addressed James, who sat across from him at the chess table. "Peter's going to Tawanda for the United States. If we can pull it off, this will be quite a coup."

James said, "Did you explain to Peter what has to be done?"

"He's on a need-to-know status."

"Not sure that's wise."

Vanderhagen's face hardened, and his eyes went cold. "Are you questioning my authority?"

"No, Sir. Just trying to have a strategy conversation."

Vanderhagen softened. "Strategy, huh. Get me a drink and we'll talk."

James put a glass in his father's hand before he said another word, and he sat down with his own. "Of all the mines we manage for the cartel, the diamonds are the most profitable. I'm concerned that without fore-knowledge, Peter will inadvertently cause problems."

"Because he's a white American man dealing with natives?"

"Exactly. If he even looks at them the wrong way, he could be lost in an abandoned mine for eternity."

"I think you underestimate how valuable our mine jobs are."

"Still…."

"My dear James, I'm not as concerned about the pilfering as I am about the new tariffs the Tawandian government plans to propose. If they do, in fact, require all exports to be in 'ready to use' condition, it will kill our black-market trade in quality rough diamonds because we won't be able to get them out of the country."

"Do you think Peter will be able to establish his credentials and reach the right people to stop the new amendment?" James took a sip of his drink.

"That's the million-dollar question, isn't it? Will the boy be able to use his government position to help ours?"

James coughed. "Peter's no Ted Donovan. I don't believe he'd be able to pull off the assassination of a government official, if that's what it takes, and get away with it." James sipped his drink. "What if he doesn't? I'm not willing to sacrifice his life for a handful of diamonds."

Vanderhagen said. "We can't afford to be short-sighted, sympathetic, or weak if we have to give up me, you, or Peter. Our decisions affect the entire mining industry in Tawanda."

James shot forward and put up his hand. "I…."

Vanderhagen cut him off. "That's why Lucy Kilmer is on board. She's had experience in Tawanda. Her flawless plan to seduce the Tawandian delegation to the UN by killing the engines and sending the plane into a death-dive over the North Sea might have solved a lot of problems if Sandford hadn't interfered."

James relaxed. "She can definitely pull it off without putting Peter's life in jeopardy."

Vanderhagen smiled. "Peter will bring the lamb to slaughter under the guise of cooperation. His sincerity would be real and therefore not questioned."

James picked up the queen. "And Kilmer's people would take care of the hit."

Vanderhagen looked at his son. "Does that work for you?"

James raised his eyebrows in surprise. "You're asking me?"

"You're the one with the problem."

Chapter 16▶Gramercy Avenue, NYC

Saturday, 1 March
Mid-morning, Rachel faced her computer, determined to finish a chapter in her book. Two hours later, she let out a scream of frustration. Zeus jumped to his feet, put a paw on her lap, and yipped. Rachel laughed and gave him a kiss on his head. "Zeus, nothing makes sense." At the sound of her voice, he relaxed, and lay down by her feet. "You're right. Time to stop." She saved her file, closed the laptop, and reached for the Tanner Diary. "Zeus, I'm going to get lost in someone else's life now rather than dwell on mine."

She moved to her most comfortable chair and opened the diary.

<~<~|~>~>

April 4, Wednesday
Father changed his mind and made arrangements with Mr. Mansonati for me to take pottery lessons on Thursdays after school. When I tried to refuse, Father

said Mr. Mansonati had powerful friends and I had to go. He scared me even more than I already was.

April 5, Thursday

I survived my first pottery lesson but just barely. For most of the hour, Mr. Mansonati showed me around his studio—where he stored the clay, drying shelves, the kiln, the glazes, the utility sink, and the potter's wheel and tools. I mostly followed him around and didn't let him near me. Suddenly he disappeared. Then, as if by magic, he stood in front of me with an apron in his hand.

He put the neck loop over my head and took the aprons strings, one in each hand, and stepped toward me. He reached around me to tie the knot. I felt his breath on my forehead and stepped back. I told him I could do it myself and I did. Creepy.

First, he had me sit at a table with a chunk of clay the size of a baseball and told me to knead it like bread dough. I tried. I even stood to throw my weight into it. The clay refused to yield. Mr. Mansonati dribbled water on the clay to make it softer. He'd told my father that the workout would be good for my fingers, and it was.

When he thought I'd done enough, he gave me a rolling pin and I flattened the clay. Next, he gave me a piece of 4x4 cardboard and told me to cut out five squares and put them together—a base and four sides. He showed me how to use liquid clay and a pinch technique to fuse the sides to one another.

Next, he gave me a wooden-handled tool with a wire at the end and told me to draw a decoration on each side. When I was done, I couldn't believe what I'd made in one afternoon. I wanted to take it home and show my family, but Mr. Mansonati said it had to dry before it got fired. Next week I'd be able to glaze it with my favorite color, pink, and take it home the following week.

I started to take my apron off, but Mr. Mansonati stopped me. He wanted to give me one more lesson before I left.

I watched as he sat down at the potter's wheel, turning it with his feet. The top spun like one of my father's precious records. He showed me how to wet my hands and center the clay, so it didn't wiggle or jiggle. Then, just by using his fingers, as if by magic, he drew the clay up and out to make a bowl. Before I could say or do anything, he squished it and pounded it into a blob. He said, "Your turn."

I sat down, wet my hands, and placed my fingers on the cool, slippery clay. My feet turned the wheel. I could feel the mass push and pull against my hands as I tried to center it. In frustration, I pulled my hands away. Mr. Mansonati said, "Don't give up. The first several attempts never work. Try again." So, I did.

When I still couldn't do it, Mr. Mansonati stood behind me and leaned over me, so his hands were over my hands, his head next to mine. He applied pressure to my hands which affected the clay. Slowly the wobble disappeared, and the clay centered. Amazing. It's only now I think about his presence—his body against mine, his arms around mine, his hands over mine. I guess I wanted to make the clay work so much I didn't want to think about how creepy he was. Or maybe I'm just being weird.

I turned to ask about making a bowl and saw my father in the doorway. On the way home Father asked if I liked it. I said "yes," and told him about my first project.

<~<~|~>~>

Rachel scanned the diary entries for the next several weeks until she came to this one.

<~<~|~>~>

June 7, Thursday

Today, when I spoke to Mr. Mansonati, he said, "Call me Johnny." I've never called an adult by his first name, except for Billy who sweeps and does odd jobs down at the grocery.

Johnny's so sweet. I've started wearing my hair up in a ponytail because I've had no time to sit for a haircut. Johnny says he likes it this way but prefers when I wear it down. I promised him I'd take out the ponytail before I left.

It's nice when he notices me since the kids at school ignore me.

The second potter's wheel arrived today. Now we can throw at the same time. I've become very good at centering because Johnny suggested I do it with my eyes closed so I can feel it—the moment of perfect alignment. He says to experience it, don't rush it, and it worked.

I'm now trying to make a bowl. It's harder than it looks. I've yet to finish one before it collapses, or Johnny shakes his head. I'm not really sure what he means when he does that, but I've narrowed it down to bad shape, bulky, or poor proportions. If I ask, he tells me I should know why by now. It's very frustrating.

Today, as I got ready to go home, I turned and found Johnny standing right behind me. He lowered his head as if to whisper in my ear and his lips brushed my cheek. Of course, it meant nothing. I mean he's as old as my father.

Rachel flushed with anger. She wanted to give a time-warp scream, "Get out of there." Helpless to change the past, she braced for the inevitable. Patricia filled the following diary pages with good-bye hugs, a kiss, furtive glances, hands touching, bodies grazing, until, at last, they had sex.

June 28, Thursday

Today's the best day of my life. I don't care if Johnny is forty, fifty, or sixty. He's my boyfriend now and forever.

At first, I wasn't sure I wanted to go all the way. I mean I've only heard about it from my girlfriends, and I know good girls don't do that sort of thing. But Johnny promised me he'd be sweet and gentle. He said I'd remain a good girl because nobody but us would know. I believe him.

He told me he loved me more than his skinny wife. He loved to touch my baby-fat and hoped I'd never lose it. Oh my God. I thought I'd died and gone to heaven. I love being in love with Johnny. We're going to do lessons at least three times a week, and he's putting a cot in the studio. I think I'm the luckiest girl in the whole wide world.

August 30, Thursday

I've missed two menstruations by now. I haven't told anyone because at this point no one can tell I'm pregnant. I check the mirror every day. I use a safety pin to close my skirt. I have to tell Johnny. If my parents find out first, I just know they'll kick me out.

September 1, Saturday

I went to the studio and tried to talk to Johnny today. He said he's closing for the winter and will only be returning once in a while when he can. When I mentioned the baby, he gave me a big hug and seemed excited. Suddenly, he pushed me away and asked me if he's the baby's father. That made me cry. He apologized, picked up a metal rod and offered to give me an abortion. My laugh turned into a scream when I realized he meant it. He calmed me down and we talked.

He wants the baby, but not me. He's married and that's that. He offered to pay expenses. I became hysterical. I told Johnny I loved him more than anything. Still, he pulled away. Told me to tell my father. Then he went into a corner and fiddled with a piece of pottery. When he returned, he had a wad of cash in his hand. He told me to take it and get rid of the baby.

I sat, frozen in place, cash in my lap, and trembling with fear.

When he started screaming at me, I jerked to my feet and ran. I heard the door slam shut on the pottery studio… and my future with Johnny.

So dear diary, this is where we part. I'm a girl no more. I've nothing to dream about, nothing to look forward to, and nothing to leave behind but you. I hope the future will be kind to us both.

<~<~|~>~>

Rachel closed the diary and held it to her breast because Patricia Tanner needed a hug. She started to cry. She needed a hug, too. It had nothing to do with time, or place, or inner strength. Vulnerability exposes weakness and the weak fall to the predator. *The rapist pounced on me. I pounced on Donovan. And the married potter pounced on Patricia. Fuck.*

Zeus bounded over to her, jumped onto her lap, knocking the diary out of her hands. He gave her a kiss. "Okay, okay. Thank you, baby. I needed that." Another lick. She hugged him, and said, "Off. You're just too big for this chair." He obeyed. "Good boy."

Picking up the diary, she noticed Beth's note sticking out of the diary pages. "William Tanner, Home for the Aged, North Broadway."

Rachel pulled out her phone and verified William Tanner still lived there. Next, she called Chris.

"Hi. Do you want to take a ride with me?"

"Lawyer's?"

"No, research."

"Do you need me?"

"I'd rather not go alone."

"If it's okay with you, call Jack. I've got a dead-line."

"It is. See you later."

Before she could get her coat on, Jack arrived downstairs. Rachel leashed Zeus. "I'm going to leave you with Nikolai."

In the lobby, Zeus bounded over to Nikolai who showered him with pats and scratches.

Rachel said, "I'll be back in an hour or so."

"No problem," Nikolai said. "Me and Zeus have things to do."

Outside, Jack held the door for her. She gave him the address and said, "You got here in record time."

Jack laughed. "All a part of our service." Once they were on the way, he said, "Chris hired J&J Security to be your on-demand drivers."

"He shouldn't have done that."

"He doubled our fee."

"You've stooped to bribery?"

"I wouldn't say 'stooped.'"

"Regardless, I'm glad you did."

<~<~|~>~>

The old man sat in a wheelchair, wore hospital garb covered with a standard issue robe and worn slippers. The oxygen nasal cannula did its job, giving Tanner the strength to sit.

"Mr. Tanner, I'm Rachel Allen."

He lifted his chin from his chest and stared at her. Squinting he said, "Who?"

"Rachel Allen. I'm a researcher trying to find your sister, Patricia."

"Who?"

"Your sister, Patricia."

He dropped his eyes to his hands. "Dead." The effort triggered a coughing and wheezing spell.

Rachel waited until he stabilized. "Can you tell me about her?"

"Sweet. Sad."

"Pretty?"

He nodded. "Smart."

"What about your parents?"

More coughing. "Dead."

"Were they nice?"

"Provincial."

He coughed and raised a hand an inch. An aide brought him a cup of water with a straw and held it as he sipped. When he finished, he appeared to doze off. The aide caught the cup before it fell off his lap and set it on the table.

Rachel persisted. "What happened after Patricia got pregnant?"

He shook his head and struggled to raise his hand.

"Will, did you know she was pregnant?"

Another shake. His hand gripped the arm of the chair.

"Your neighbor, Mr. Mansonati, got her pregnant."

The old man's eyes popped open. "Bastard." He gasped for more air and wound-up coughing and spitting. Only this time, it didn't stop.

A nurse came and touched Rachel's shoulder. "Time to go."

Rachel paused at the door and watched the aide wheel the old man away.

"Miss Allen."

Rachel turned toward the voice. It belonged to a sixty-something nurse.

"I've been here for a long time. I heard you ask about Mr. Tanner's sister." She handed Rachel a folded piece of paper. "In the past, a woman visited him a couple of times. Nothing regular and I haven't seen her for more than ten years. I copied the name down for you. I hope it helps." She turned and disappeared down the hall.

Rachel opened the note. It had to be Patricia because her *nom de plume* incorporated the names of her parents—Stella Joseph.

Chapter 17▶Gramercy Avenue, NYC

Saturday, 1 March
When she returned home, Rachel spent the next hour searching public documents from 1934 trying to locate a birth for Stella Joseph. She searched births in Vitalrecords.com. Nothing even close. After a moment's frustration, she decided to use the brothers' names—Willa Roberts or Roberta Williams. Nothing for the last name of Robert or Roberts. However, she struck gold with Williams—male, born February 3, 1935. The date fit.

She smiled. Patricia Tanner, now Roberta Williams, had a son. Now what? A young girl on her own could hardly support a child. She'd have to give him up for adoption or get married. Rachel decided she'd get married. So, she checked the Italian Genealogical Group's Brides Index.

Here she found no record for a Roberta Williams, so she tried Stella Joseph. Bingo. Stella Joseph Married in 1935. She clicked on "groom," and found out the groom's name—Henryk B. Zych.

A knock on the door and Chris entered. "How'd your day go?" Zeus ran over for his "hello" and Chris obliged.

Rachel said, "Interesting. I found more information on the Tanner girl."

"Did you realize it's seven?"

"What? No way."

"Did you feed Zeus?"

"He ate around four."

Chris said, "Finish up what you're doing while I take Zeus for a walk and pick up dinner."

He returned a half hour later with containers of Chinese and two beers. After a few bites, Rachel said, "What's the movie tonight?"

Chris swallowed. "I'm up for anything, so you choose."

She pulled out her phone and started scanning streaming movie lists.

He said, "I've been wondering. Whatever happened to Donovan's gun?"

Rachel never looked up so as not to telegraph her surprise at his question. "Why?"

"You seem to have everything that belonged to him. Was it in the overnight case Beth and Eric gave to you last evening?"

"Yes."

"A Chiappa, if I remember correctly. Are you going to put it up on eBay?"

"Oh, sure, and sell it to an international crime boss or local thug."

Chris laughed. "I think that's my first bad idea."

Rachel laughed. "You can keep the rest to yourself."

"Okay. Okay. What are you going to do with the gun?"

"I haven't given it a thought."

"Where is it?"

"In a locked box in my closet. Beth taped a note to the top to let me know that if I want to use it, I have to register it or I'll be arrested on felony charges."

"Maybe you should get rid of it."

"Or," Rachel said, "I can leave it where it is and do nothing. In fact, I'd forgotten I even had it until now." She tilted her head to the right and narrowed her eyes. "Chris, why do you care?"

He cleared his throat and said, "A few weeks ago you were stuffing yourself with cookies and now there's a gun in the house."

Rachel put down her fork and crossed her arms, elbows on the table. "I see. You've drawn some kind of connection between Lorna Doones and guns. Care to share?"

"You are still stuck in some kind of loop involving Donovan, death, killing, guilt, and…."

She said it for him. "Depression."

"Yes, depression. I doubt this is a good time to be fooling around with guns."

"You think I'm dangerous?"

"No, I didn't say that."

"You think I'm going to commit suicide?"

"Come on, Rachel. I…."

"You think I'm unstable. Incapable of holding myself accountable. A danger to myself and God knows how many others? Or don't you like the idea of women owning and being able to use a gun?"

Chris said, "You're deliberately misunderstanding my concerns."

"Tell me."

"I don't like guns, period."

"What about knives?"

"Knives?"

"Women and knives," Rachel said. "Maybe in my current altered state you should forbid me to use knives. Or razor blades. Or box-cutters."

Chris said, "Enough."

"Let me be clear," Rachel said. "It's not your decision as to what I can or can't do."

"I just want to keep you safe."

"Hey, I'm the one who saved your ass from Donovan."

Zeus moved to Rachel's side and put his head on her lap.

Chris raised his hands—napkin clutched in one—and surrendered. "I don't want to fight, and I don't want to lose you because you're playing around with a loaded gun."

"The empty gun's in the top drawer of a custom lockbox with a four-digit security code. The clip is in the bottom drawer with its own code. I don't know what I want to do with it, but I certainly don't want to hurt myself or anyone else."

"So, you're telling me I don't have to worry?"

"Absolutely." Rachel picked up her fork. "You never have to worry about me. I'm not going anywhere." She patted the dog's head. "Zeus's going to make sure of that."

<~<~|~>~>

Sunday morning, Rachel and Chris went out for breakfast, followed by a walk with Zeus along the East River. They were home by one. He had a client meeting, and she returned to her Tanner research.

From a myriad of sources, she pieced together the Zychs' life.

The bricklayer's priest asked him to care for the penniless young mother who had taken refuge in the church. In a short time, the kind young man married

Stella and adopted her son. The couple got by until the accident.

While Zych worked on the third floor, his scaffolding collapsed. He sustained a broken leg complicated by damage from the cascading bricks. The doctors saved the leg, which never healed properly. His ongoing surgeries and recoveries made it impossible for him to return to work.

While Zych watched the baby, Stella got a scholarship to secretarial school. Diploma in hand, she received a job offer from Zych's former employer, Pickens Construction, as a way to make amends. She took it. Over the next few years, she rose through the ranks to work for the company president, Thaddeus Pickens.

Zych spent his days caring for the baby and his nights drinking—in direct proportion to her overtime. One evening, after a long and loud argument, Stella sent him away. She found out the next morning, when the police came, he had walked onto the train tracks and charged, headfirst, at the oncoming engine.

<~<~|~>~>

After dinner, Rachel returned to her computer and the Tanner girl, now Stella Joseph Zych Pickens.

Searching through records, she found the Pickens address on the fashionable end of Park Avenue. Mr. Pickens's company achieved notable ratings…until it didn't. Soon after their marriage, Pickens's name started appearing in court actions and federal testimonies. The trade unions accused him of breaking contract rules by scaling back on wages and personnel. Customers accused him of using inferior materials and paying off building inspectors.

Soon, Pickens's name started showing up on transcripts of mob conversations reported by the news.

Forced to go to the mob loan sharks to pay court fees, he became entangled in their supply and labor chain. This further indebted him and undermined his credibility with his customers. In time, his company worked exclusively for the mob.

Four years into the marriage, one of his buildings collapsed. Thirty-nine people died. Pickens lost the business and their home. After that, the Pickens family vanished.

Chapter 18▶Damir, Tawanda, Africa

Sunday, 2 March
Peter arrived in Damir on Sunday. After a dusty ride
from the single-story airport terminal, his driver asked
which of the two sprawling European-style hotels he
wanted. The Damir Hotel Hawa, ahead on the rise,
with its manicured plants, gleaming white walls fes-
tooned with purple and gold banners catered to exec-
utives and honored visitors. The other, on his right,
didn't. Its lackluster façade, weed infested landscape,
and undisguised repairs, cried "unimportant."

He checked his documents. The State Department
must have chosen the lowest bidder. Peter had no in-
tention of living in squalor and walked through the
Damir Hotel Hawa lobby, his messenger bag across
his shoulders, and his suitcase in hand. The clerk at
the main desk gave him a quick glance and returned
to his computer.

Peter approached the desk. "Good day. I've a reservation."

With clipped enunciation, raised eyebrows, and half-closed eyes, he said, "Welcome to the Damir Hotel Hawa. May I see your confirmation?"

Peter pulled the paperwork from his pocket and placed it on the counter and slid it toward the clerk.

The desk clerk read the document and passed it back to him. "I'm sorry, Mr. Powell. This reservation must be turned in at the hotel down the street." The man turned to other pressing business.

Peter narrowed his eyes before raising his voice and feigning outrage. "You're kidding? Let me see that." He scanned the paper and waved it in the air. "I can't believe those airheads got this wrong. This isn't my fault. I filled out all their forms." Leaning on the counter, his hands clasped in prayer formation, he said, "Please, I can't…. I mean, is it possible… there's a room available?"

Shuffling through mail to avoid direct contact, the clerk said, "I am not at liberty to change your documents. You will have to leave."

Peter put his hand in his pocket, pulled out his wallet, and put a bill on the counter.

The clerk lifted his chin a fraction of a centimeter and peered down his nose at the offering. He didn't walk away. Peter added another bill. The clerk stared at it for a second and looked at Peter's wallet before returning his attention to the two bills.

At five bills, the clerk exchanged the money for a registration card, regarded Peter and said, "Do you have luggage?"

Peter nodded and pointed to the suitcase and duffle bag.

"May I have a credit card and your passport?" For the next few minutes, the man entered information into the data-hungry computer and returned the passport, credit card, and "229" room key. "Welcome, Mr. Powell. We hope you enjoy your stay."

A bellman, who said to call him "Bob," accompanied Peter to the room and showed him the amenities—bed, bathroom, closet, and air conditioner. "The AC will dispel daytime heat. At night, open the windows and use the fan." He pointed to the switch. Then he walked over to a painting on the wall. "One more thing," he said, as he pulled one side of the painting, "This is your room safe." He let the frame swing back on its hinges. "Inside are instructions on how to change and lock the combination during your stay."

"So, anyone can change it at any time?"

"No. It is Wi-Fi enabled and controlled through our security desk."

"So, security could get inside at any time?"

"Sir, I have been here a long time. None of our guests have ever had a problem."

Peter raised an eyebrow in disbelief. Bob didn't flinch. Instead, he walked over to the desk, opened a drawer, and pulled out a number of brochures. "These cover the main places of interest in and around Damir. If you'd like to visit or require transportation, call me." He handed Peter a card. "My contact information. Call me anytime."

He replaced the brochures, closed the drawer, and executed a slight bow with hand extended, palm up.

Peter said, "Thank you, Bob," and over-tipped him.

The porter smiled and left.

Alone, Peter upped the power on the AC, cursed at the imperceptible change in air quality, and called his State Department handler. "Made it. Room 229 at the Damir Hotel Hawa."

"Wrong hotel."

"Bad booking. I won't stay in fleabag hole-in-the-wall shanties."

"I'll convey your decision and make sure the right people know you're in town. The code will be a drink you can't get in Damir."

"So, hug the bar for now?"

"And sightsee. Get a feel for the people, government, media, resources, and needs. It'll be a while before you're contacted. Find out as much as you can so you'll be able to navigate without too much trouble."

"Done."

The call ended. Peter made another call.

"Hello, Sir. It's Peter."

"Peter, my boy. Where are you?"

"In Damir. I'll email the address to you. Just got in and getting settled."

"Excellent. I'll have James send you a SAT phone and letters of introduction to our manager of mine operations. Keep your eyes open, and don't do anything other than report back. We follow developments down there on the news. If you find things are contrary to what's being reported, tell us. Otherwise, have a good time. If you need anything, get in touch."

"I will."

Peter sat looking at the phone in his hand. "You want me to look around and have fun? Pretty much the same thing the State Department said." He frowned. "The Cameroon posting had more action than this." He threw the phone on the bed. "Two masters and no plan."

Chapter 19▶Damir, Tawanda

Thursday, 6 March
Peter strolled around Damir for days. He wore clothes
from the local shops, so he blended, more or less,
with the locals. Between forays, he read, sat by the
pool, took tours recommended by Bob, ate at local
restaurants, and watched soccer in the hotel bar.

Today, the empty bar's dark interior held no more
promise than all the yesterdays at the same time. He
ordered a local beer and sat outside under a frond
umbrella with his chair backed against a wall and a
sweeping Damir landscape in full view.

The three main roads were shared by walkers,
bikers, animals pulling or following carts, ancient
buses, military vehicles, police jeeps, and battered
used cars, some designated as taxis.

He sipped his beer and read the book he'd borrowed from the hotel's meager library. Two pages
into the story, a man appeared and sat down. Before
Peter could protest the intrusion, the tanned man,
who looked about forty, said, "Bet you'd rather have
a Samuel Adams."

Peter said, "How did you know?"

The man laughed. "You don't look African."

Peter smiled as the man threw his arm around the chair next to him. "I'm originally from Boston and looking forward to returning if I can ever get out of Africa. You remind me of home."

"Glad to be of service."

"Name's Sam. I'll be your tour guide and jack of all trades." He pulled a card out of his pocket and pushed it toward Peter. "My contact number. If you fail to ask me to meet you for a meal, I'll know you're in trouble."

"State Department?"

Sam shook his head, leaned in, and whispered, "And not the FBI either."

Peter started to guess other agencies, but Sam put a finger to his lips and said, "Not up for discussion. Just know I have your back."

"Don't get too excited. You're going to be bored out of your mind."

"Problems come out of nowhere," Sam said. "Got any questions so far? Anything you'd like to do? Places you'd like to see? We've got the time. Nobody rushes around here."

Peter laughed. "That's for sure."

"So, what'll it be?"

"Well, since I've been here, I've walked most of central Damir and been amazed at the clear demarcation of rich and poor, with nothing much between. It's evident in the buildings, the clothes, the food, and housing—or the lack thereof."

Sam said, "It's definitely a city of contradictions."

"I've done a lot of reading about the government and President Okoro. What can you tell me?"

"Okoro caters to his best interests. He takes a percentage of everything, and I mean everything, happening in Tawanda. Try to bypass him and you could wind up dead, or worse, banished into the hell of Forever Jail."

"What?"

"That's what the natives call it, Forever Jail, because once you're in, you're there…."

Peter shook his head, "Forever." He sipped his beer and said, "So any deal, of any kind, for any reason, must include kickbacks to him."

Sam laughed. "You're not as dumb as you look."

"So, I've been told." Peter spun the beer bottle. "Do I ever get to talk to President Okoro, and, if not, how high can I expect to get?"

"Okoro hangs out with his inner circle within the confines of the government slash palace. I hear there're beautiful gardens and fountains inside the walls, which are forbidden to uninvited guests. I doubt you're ever going to get to meet him."

"Even if I represent the United States?"

"The who?"

"Really?"

"Around here, the U.S. carries very little weight since it doesn't recognize Tawanda, blocks its membership to the United Nations, and withholds aid. That, plus your Consular Agent title, puts you at the back of the line."

"So, who do I deal with?"

"I'm guessing some low-ranking official who will carry your concerns up the chain of command."

"Then why are you here?"

"My job is to keep you out of trouble, which you *will* get into, and try to jump the line so you get to the people you must talk to."

Peter leaned back. "I can see we're going to be great friends."

Sam raised an eyebrow and said, "Yup, as long as you keep your nose clean and do what I say."

Peter shot him a wry smile. "Yeah, well, maybe just okay friends—acquaintances, even."

<~<~|~>~>

After lunch, Sam gave Peter a driving tour of greater Damir. From the hotel, Sam drove up the main road toward the Presidential Palace and government offices, circled the complex, and drove on. He pointed out the main military installations, the various business conglomerates, the wealthy neighborhoods, and the rest of Damir—a refugee village supplied by store owners eking out a living from threadbare stalls. As the car descended into the valley, the smell of sewage became overpowering.

Beyond the population center, the mining operations took over the landscape. Of all the companies represented, Mining International Non-Limited Enterprises (MiNe), Vanderhagen's group, dominated the installations.

Sam said, "Surprised?"

Peter said, "At what?"

"The size of your grandfather's operations."

"How...."

"I did my research. I have to know who I'm dealing with. Whatever happens, my agency will hold me accountable."

"I had no idea what to expect. I'm down here blind. I'm not part of Grandfather's business."

"Got to prove yourself first?"

"Maybe. However, first and foremost, I represent the United States. The mines will happen only if I have time."

Sam nodded. "Good to have your priorities straight."

At sunset, they returned to the hotel.

Just as Peter started to exit the car, Sam said, "Monday morning at nine, you have a meeting scheduled with a low-level advisor. Be out front at eight forty-five."

Peter gave Sam a thumbs up gesture, shut the door, and entered the hotel, going straight to the dining room. He spoke to the maître de and made a reservation for seven, allowing for time to shower and change.

He opened the door to 229 and dropped his keys into the ashtray, as he always did. This time, they clattered onto the wood. The ashtray had been moved. Peter surveyed the room. He checked closets and the bathroom.

Accustomed to the usual rearrangement by the hotel's maid service, he searched for other evidence of intrusion. In the closet, his clothes had been patted down because his careful spacing of the hangers had been disturbed. His stored suitcase now faced a different direction. Clothes in the drawers were no longer aligned.

He carried his electronics with him in his messenger bag, so they were safe. But that didn't mean he was. Peter checked every crevice, switch, outlet, and light for listening devices. He ran his fingers over the underside of all the furniture. He found the bug behind the headboard.

Leaving it for now, he opened the vents and ran his fingers over the wallpaper expecting to find a hidden camera. Nothing. Peter stomach growled. The clock showed six-thirty. Time to shower.

He arrived five minutes early for dinner.

Chapter 20▶Soho, NYC

Saturday, 8 March
Late Saturday afternoon, Sybil, arms full of packages, knocked on The Lundon Gallery door. One of the caterers let her in. The place buzzed with vendors setting-up—food stations, bars, flowers, and the sound system. This was not the quiet, elegant reception she'd imagined. She stopped in her tracks—heart racing, color draining from her face.

Lidia ran to her side. "Sybil," Lidia said.

Sybil stared back.

Lidia touched her wife's arm and gave her a kiss on the cheek. "Honey, what's the matter?"

"This isn't what we talked about. What have you done? We can't afford this."

Lidia laughed. "I'm glad you're surprised because I did it for you, honey. We're going to blow the roof off this town." Lidia turned to leave.

Sybil dropped her packages and caught Lidia by the arm. "Lidia, what's going on?"

Lidia jerked free. Hands on hips, she mounted her counterattack. "Not this time, Sybil. You're not going

to ruin it for me. I've got a guest list any gallery owner would kill for, and I'm going to milk it for all it's
worth. You'll be the center of attention tonight, while
I'll be the queen of the residual effects."

Sybil's face darkened and her lips tightened.
"What are you on?"

Lidia laughed. "Just enough to take the edge off."

Sybil put her arm around Lidia's shoulder and
steered her toward the stairs. When they passed one
of the assistants, she said, "Please get my packages
and bring them upstairs and leave them by the door."

Lidia broke free. "I can't do this now, Sybil. I
have to finish the gallery listings."

Sybil caught hold of her again and addressed the
assistant. "You know what to do, do it. Lidia will be
down in a moment."

Sybil dragged Lidia into their apartment. Lidia
wrenched her arm out of Sybil's grip and walked over
to the mirror, ran her fingers through her hair, and
checked the corner of her lips. "Let's make this quick.
I've got to get downstairs and put the finishing touches on everything. I want it perfect for you."

"Sit down."

"Sybil, I really don't…"

"Sit."

Lidia sat in an armchair, with one leg tucked under her and the other exposed halfway up her thigh.
She licked her lips and stuck out the lower one. "Baby, come to me and let me relax you the way you like
it."

Sybil stopped pacing. "I don't want to relax. I
want you to explain how you're going to pay for the
extravaganza downstairs."

Lidia lowered her chin and peered at Sybil
through her eyelashes. "I've got investors, Baby. Everything's okay. You'll be a star."

"Lidia, stop. I know you. This isn't about me. The gallery is filled with years of work you've displayed before and didn't sell. So, I ask you again, what's going on?"

Lidia examined her fingernails. "I thought you loved my paintings."

"I'm not talking about art. I'm talking about money. Now tell me, where's it coming from?"

"Well, if you must know, Miss Buzz-killer, I sold two paintings this afternoon."

"I'm not talking about today. What's going on downstairs takes pre-planning."

Lidia went over to the bar and poured herself a drink. "Want one?"

"No. Answer me."

Lidia turned, leaned on the bar, took a sip, and raised her eyes to Sybil. "The paintings sold for twenty-five thousand dollars each."

Sybil's mouth dropped. "You've got to be kidding."

Lidia sashayed over to the chair, sat and crossed her legs, drawing her skirt high above her knee. "It's true. I know you are more of a Classicist, but Retro is the new big thing. I'm going to be the hottest artist in the hottest gallery in the district."

"Bullshit. Tell me the whole truth, or I'm going to stick a knife through every painting downstairs."

Lidia popped out of the chair. "Okay. Okay. Okay!" As she walked toward the door she said, "I've hired several art critics."

In two strides, Sybil slid between the door and her lover. "Really? You bought reviews?"

"Well, not exactly. They're more like art advisors. They'll move through the show, point out the positive attributes of my work, and advise potential buyers of their necessary inclusion in any meaningful portfolio."

"You're going to scam PRAISE guests?"

"It's not a scam. It's true."

"Are you out of your mind?"

"Leave me alone."

"I want you to stop this immediately while there's still time."

"Sybil, I knew it." Lidia spun and marched to the middle of the room. Pulled tissues from her pocket and dabbed her forming tears. "You don't want me to succeed." She blew her nose. "You want to keep me in a box, playing with my paints, available to you whenever." She moved to Sybil and put her hands on Sybil's shoulder. "You have to let me do this." She rested her head on Sybil's chest. "Puleeeese."

Sybil pushed her away. "Impressive performance, Lidia. In fact, I'd say one of your best."

Lidia stepped backwards and picked up her drink. "I don't need your permission. I'm doing this. Although it'd be a lot more fun if you supported me."

"Lidia, I can't let you use people this way."

Lidia took a step closer to Sybil—their bodies within centimeters of full contact. "If you loved me, you would."

Sybil held her at arms-length. "This isn't about love, it's about money. And you know it."

Lidia twirled her hair around her finger. "I don't know what you mean."

"Lidia, come on. I take care of our finances. I know what you have, and you don't have enough to…."

Lidia shook loose from Sybil's grip and stuck her finger in her inquisitor's face. "You don't know anything." She snapped her fingers. "I have as much money as I want."

Sybil went rigid. "You what?"

Lidia's posture deflated. With head bowed, she murmured, "Have enough money to do...."

Sybil shoved Lidia backwards. "You fucking called my father, didn't you? After all the times I warned you the man's a cancer on this earth, you called him. Are you completely out of your mind?"

Lidia reached out to her. "No, no, I didn't. Your brother called to wish me good luck. Asked me if I, er, we needed anything."

"James?"

"Uh-huh. He offered us his full support. You know he's very proud of you."

"James is a nothing. He's Father's puppet." Sybil slumped into a chair and shook her head. "You have no idea what you've walked into."

"Come on, Sybil. Stop being so depressing. I'll be a success. Let me be a success... please."

Sybil, trying to hold back the floodgates of fear and frustration, said, "You are my everything, you sweet, wonderful woman. Things will be fine until the moment you realize they own you and every-thing you do or create from this day forward."

Lidia teared up, stamped her foot, and tossed her head. "You don't know that. You're just trying to manipulate me, kill my dream for some reason I can't begin to fathom."

Sybil stood up and hugged Lidia, who, rigid at first, softened and melted into the arms of her be-loved. Sybil said, "I'm sorry, sweetie. I just want to protect you. I wish you the best night."

"Really?"

"Go on. Do what you have to. I've got to get dressed and be ready to welcome the guests."

The women kissed and Lidia, after a final check in the mirror, raced downstairs.

Sybil walked to the window. She looked down at the street without seeing, pulled out her phone, and called her father. As soon as she heard his voice, she said, "You're a disease, infecting everyone I love. You knew I'd never become complicit in any of your schemes, so now you've targeted Lidia. I'm going to do everything I can to break your hold on her, old man. Count on it."

She ended the call, went into the bedroom, sat on the bed, and cried.

Chapter 21▶Soho, NYC

Saturday, 8 March

Saturday, after a training session with Zeus, Rachel worked on her novel. The Tanner diary distraction had given her the time she needed to let her novel gestate and take form. She now knew where it had to go, and her fingers flew over the keyboard. When her phone rang, it knocked her out of her zone, and she jumped. The ID showed, "Chris."

He said, "Ready for tonight?"

"No. Why? I'm working on my book."

"Your agent will be glad to hear that."

"Me too. It's finally coming together."

"Did you know it's five?"

"What? Are you kidding? Five o'clock?"

"I never kid about time. In fact, I think we have enough to…."

"No. I've got to finish this chapter while it's fresh in my mind."

"Well, you'd better get a move on because I'm bringing my dress duds down to your apartment, and we'll see what transpires."

"Nothing transpires before six. Get that. Nothing before six. Although, if you can take Zeus for a walk while I work, I could be ready by five-fifty."

"Be right down."

<~<~|~>~>

Jack drove and got Rachel and Chris to The Lundon Gallery by eight. They entered a room filled with delicious aromas, voices humming with conversation and laughter, and music with a rap beat.

Sybil called out to some unseen individual to lower the music, "I can't hear myself think," as she made her way across the room to welcome Rachel. "I'm so glad you're here." She turned to Chris. "Hello, I'm Sybil Powell."

"Chris Gregory."

"And I'm Lidia Lundon." She swooped into the conversation wearing a silk smock which shimmered and floated with her body's every movement. "Welcome to my gallery and the PRAISE reception."

Rachel said, "I'm very impressed. This is way beyond anything I expected. You've done a wonderful job."

"Oh, thank you," Lidia said, giving Rachel a quick hug. "I love raising the bar and waking this town up." She touched Sybil's arm. "I see someone. I'll be right back."

Rachel glanced at Sybil, who shrugged her shoulders and said, "Sometimes Lidia goes overboard, like tonight. One can only ride it out. I speak from vast experience."

"I think you're being too critical," Rachel said. "The exhibit looks great, the food smells delicious, and the ambiance feels elegant. Everyone will be impressed."

Sybil smiled. "Thank you for the reality check."

<~<~|~>~>

Rachel and Chris wove their way through waiters carrying either hors d'oeuvres or flutes of champagne. After taking a glass and sampling the offerings, they arrived at the food stations. Finger-foods on one table, a Viennese Table of sublime deserts, carved turkey or roast beef on half-sized rolls, and a vegan-vegetarian table. Something for everyone.

From the avant-garde to the tailored conservative, a steady stream of guests from PRAISE board members to the "A list" names from Lidia's black book, courtesy of Philip Vanderhagen.

The art advisors did their job. They toured the paintings with groups of two to six art aficionados, extolling the benefits of having one of Lidia's pieces in their collections. Lidia moved from the center of one circle to another, smiling and animated, basking in all the attention.

In a corner of the gallery, the DJ played to his audience who danced to the music, holding drinks in one hand.

All the gallery filled, Rachel and Chris found space in the doorway of Lidia's office.

Chris said, "So, how do you like Lidia's work?"

She said, "It's a little too sixties-psychedelic for my taste." She tilted her head. "Still, I do like the movement and her incorporation of images into the flow of color."

"Shall we buy one?"

"Sure, if you'd like one for your office."

"I'll see. I've got the brochure."

Rachel nodded. Chris put his arm around her and kissed her.

She snuggled into him and said, "I'm getting a headache from the noise and claustrophobic from the crowd. I'd like to go."

"Let's hope the formalities start soon so we can leave."

"What about me? Can I come?" The voice came from behind. They turned. The casually dressed man with a cocky grin and a gold chain necklace reminded Rachel of a snarky used car salesman. He said, "How come you two are on the side lines of this epic event?"

Chris said, "You're the one hiding in the office."

"Just taking a breather." He extended his hand. "I'm Gavin. The potter who lives and works on the third floor."

Chris shook his hand. "Chris and Rachel."

"Sybil's friend, Rachel Allen, the author?"

She said, "That's me."

"I've heard a lot about you," Gavin said. "I've got a show here next month. I'll make sure Lidia invites you. Hey, Chris, why don't you get us drinks, so Rachel and I can get better acquainted?"

Rachel felt Chris's hand tighten around hers. Before he responded, she said, "Chris, take me home. I've got to get out of here *now*." She stepped between the men and pushed Chris back a few steps.

Without taking his eyes off Gavin, Chris pulled out his phone. "Jack, we're leaving,"

Rachel said, "Do you see Sybil? I want to say good-bye."

Gavin raised his drink in a salute. "Nice meeting you. Look forward to seeing you again."

Rachel forced a smile to be courteous while Chris scanned the room. "I see her." He turned to Gavin and said, "Good night," and they walked away.

Rachel tapped Sybil on the shoulder. Sybil turned. "Having a good time? I can't believe how many guests we have."

Rachel said, "Beautiful event. Congratulations. Unfortunately, I'm not good in crowds, so we're taking off. Please tell Lidia how much we enjoyed her exhibit."

"I will. Thank you for coming."

Chris saw Jack at the door and gave Rachel's hand a tug. She looked at Sybil. "Bye."

<~<~|~>~>

On the way home, Rachel said, "Thank you for not pushing me to stay at the reception. It got so crowded I could feel people breathing down my neck and the smell, perfumes mixed with the odors of food, made my stomach queasy."

Chris said, "You probably saved me from an assault charge because I intended to use that jerk as a punching bag."

"I know. And while I think you would have done considerable damage, from my angle, the guy reminded me of a heavyweight boxer."

"Don't you think I could take him?"

"Only if your first punch was a knock-out."

Chris raised his fist and tightened it, flexing his muscles. "What do you think?"

Rachel felt the muscle in his arm. "Gavin had no chance."

"That's what I'm thinking." Chris smiled. "He's lucky we let him live."

Chapter 22►Damir, Tawanda

Monday, 10 March

Peter stood outside the hotel at eight-forty-five. The relative pre-sunrise coolness dissipated as the heat rolled in. Sam pulled up and he got in.

On the way, Peter said, "Someone went through my things and planted a bug while we were out yesterday."

Sam said, "First time?"

"If not, I didn't notice it before."

"Could be. Spies like to keep tabs on one another. It's all part of the game."

"I get that, but I'm not a spy."

"Perhaps I am."

"Are you saying guilt by association?"

Sam shrugged his shoulders.

Peter said, "Should I be scared?"

"No. Be careful."

Seven minutes later, Sam accompanied Peter into the governmental wing of the Presidential Palace. They presented papers to the guard at the reception desk who confirmed the information and appointment. A cadet, judging by his age, appeared with their visitors' badges and showed them to a visitors' waiting area.

Sam nudged Peter and shifted his eyes to the far corner of the room while reaching for one of the magazines on the table. A security camera swept the room in slow arcs. Peter pulled out his phone to check his messages. No cell reception.

A pretty girl in African dress brought tea and biscuits, set the tray on the table, and disappeared.

Over the next forty-five minutes, the same girl appeared several times to inquire about their comfort and needs. She never indicated when the scheduled meeting might take place. Frustrated with the long wait, Peter stood up to stretch and walked around the room. Mid-circuit, the girl entered the room and requested Peter, and only Peter, accompany her

He followed her down hallways, through galleries, up a staircase, and across an overpass. When she stopped with no warning, Peter had to step to the side to keep from crashing into her. Her fist rapped on the door in front of them, and he heard the Tawandian phrase for "Come in."

The girl held the door open for him and closed it once he entered.

"Greetings, Mr. Peter Powell," said the man behind the desk. "I am the clerk to the secretary of the counsel to the president. I am charged with taking down your information, so my superiors may make informed decisions regarding you and your presence in our country. Do you understand?"

"Yes," Peter said, and sat in the visitors' chair.

"Let us begin." The clerk verified all the information on Peter's request to enter the country, his passport, and his hotel registration. "Is there anything else you wish to add?"

"No."

"Now, please tell me the reason for your visit—the real reason." The clerk held his pen poised to write.

"I am a member of the United States State Department and here to keep my people apprised of your government's public announcements that may affect American business interests. Unofficially, I am a conduit for unofficial communications between our governments, which might prove to be less than ideal if they were found out to have been discussed directly between our leaders. I am to ensure deniability on both sides, should it become necessary."

The clerk finished writing, put his pen down, and stood. "Thank you, Mr. Powell. Enjoy your stay."

The clerk exited the room and the young girl returned. "Please follow me."

After what seemed a shorter, far less complex route, Peter arrived at the building's entrance. Sam leaned on the car in front of him. "How'd it go?"

"They know I'm here. Let's hope they're interested."

"Where to now?"

"Lunch, followed by a bike ride out to the MiNe main office."

"No need. I'll drive."

Peter said, "It's personal."

Sam said, "I don't care if it's sexual. People at the mines are renowned for their touchy dispositions. I'll have your back, plus I speak the language."

Peter didn't protest. "Okay, at least for the first visit."

<~<~|~>~>

An hour later, Peter and Sam entered the MiNe offices. Peter asked to speak with the Operations Manager, Musimbwa Bakama. He introduced Sam as his driver and interpreter and pulled out an envelope. "Here are the official documents to introduce me."

OM Bakama took the papers. After reading them, he said, "Mr. Powell, you are a representative of the owners?"

"Yes. Since I'm in Tawanda on other business, they asked me to take an informal tour of the open diamond mining operations."

"I see. Could you please be more specific?"

"The bulk of diamond mining scoops up dirt and sends it through closed computerized processing system. I'd like to walk the properties where the extraction still relies on human labor; in particular, the newly discovered kimberlite site. I want to become familiar with the day-to-day operations and how they are reflected in the monthly reports."

"May I ask, Mr. Powell, do you know why you have been sent at this particular time?"

"There's been some talk about new government regulations, one of which might eliminate the export of rough diamonds. The owners want to verify the potential impact on current extractions."

Bakama leaned back and stared at Peter for a few long seconds before he spoke. "So, you are here to merely observe."

"Exactly."

"You must give me time to set up a satisfactory tour."

"Not necessary. Please don't do anything special."

"I am afraid that will not be possible. My people have jobs to do and a schedule to keep. I cannot allow you to wander through the digging fields. It is both against company policy and dangerous because the mines, depending on which one you select, are vast tunnels, large deep terraced holes, or irregular hand-dug fissures. I cannot risk you getting hurt or lost without communication."

"I understand."

"I will check out your credentials with my contact. If they prove satisfactory, I will assign you a guide and interpreter. I will contact you if and when the arrangements are made."

Peter nodded and forced a smile.

<~<~|~>~>

By late-afternoon, while sitting at the bar, Peter got both phone calls in succession. The Counsel to the President invited him for tea at four the next day. Operations Manager Bakama confirmed Peter's authority and said they would be ready for his visit on Wednesday at nine.

He called Sam and said, "Life is about to get a little more interesting."

Chapter 23▶Washington, D.C.

Monday, 10 March
First thing, Wendell Waters walked into the Oval Office shuffling papers. When he looked up, he stopped in his tracks. "Mr. President, what are you doing here? You're supposed to be on Airforce One bound for Chicago."

"I'm fighting a monster head cold. I plan to alternate work and naps all day, take my medication, and be in perfect health tomorrow."

"It's a good plan, Sir. What about Chicago?"

"I've sent the Vice President. I'm sure he'll do a great job."

"I agree." Waters stepped forward to put a stack of papers on the president's desk. "Here are the first of your morning briefings."

"Good," Sandford said. "Nancy will be canceling my meetings today. It's not a good time for decisions."

"Understood. I will keep you apprised with updates. If you feel you must delegate, let me know. I'll be happy to carry out your orders."

"Thanks, Wendell. I appreciate all you do."

"Shall I send up some tea? Or maybe chicken soup?"

"Nancy's way ahead of you. It'll be here in a minute."

"Call me if you need me."

Waters turned to leave when Nancy burst in, all color drained from her face.

"M…M…Mr. P…P…President. Airforce One. Line one. The Vice President had a stroke."

<~<~|~>~>

Hours later, the president held a press conference and announced the Vice President's resignation. Afterwards, he met with his Chief of Staff.

"Damn shame," Waters said. "He did a good job, supported you, and didn't complain."

Sandford said, "I agree. Now who do we get to replace him?"

"I have a list of all the people elected to Congress who have similar qualities. I've crossed out all who are not members of the party, who are over sixty, or have not voted our way every time. Next, I eliminated those who represent interests counter to your platform and those controlled by lobbyists. After that, I reviewed the remaining candidates and thought about which one might be the strongest as a running mate for your second term."

"The suspense is killing me. Who do you think?"

"The new senator from Iowa, Sarah Mitchell."

"The young woman from the Midwest."

"I know she's only thirty-five, but John C. Breckinridge became Vice President at the age of thirty-six. And that's how old she'll be by the time Congress approves her."

"We'd be taking a chance."

"She's a Harvard Economics graduate and got her doctorate in Government from Berkeley. After her tenured professorship at Iowa State, she ran for office supporting jobs, education, health care, and, as she calls it, people's rights."

Sandford said, "You're saying she'd be picking up voters where I might need them?"

"Yes. I think you should meet with her."

"What about the other candidates?"

"Cookie cut-outs of each other. Not as interesting, appealing, or controllable."

"Because she's a woman?"

Waters smiled. "For the record, I mean, she's supported you on every piece of legislation."

"Okay," Sandford said. "Set it up."

Chapter 24►Philadelphia, PA

Monday, 10 March

The unregistered phone vibrated in Vanderhagen's desk drawer. He pulled it out and looked at the text message. "*VP vacancy established.*" He tapped the phone twice and deleted the info. Then he called James. "Anything?"

"Not yet. Sarah said she'd call if she heard anything."

"You're sure our man in the White House can do the job?"

"Don't worry," James said. "Got to go. Calls coming in."

Vanderhagen moved to the leather couch and turned on the TV news. The Vice President's stroke had the full attention of all the major networks—in words, pictures, and video. He flipped through the stations waiting for an assertion that the man had been the target of a terror attack or an act of sabotage. It never came.

He turned on his e-pad and searched social media for the same issue. Nothing.

James knocked, entered, and closed the door behind him. He sat on the edge of the couch, his phone in hand. "We did it. Sarah was just asked to step into the Vice President position."

"Sandford doesn't know?"

"If it's in the paperwork, it's hidden in the boring details. My source says Sandford has a dreadful cold and the medication hampers his inclination to read the fine print."

Vanderhagen allowed himself a partial smile and rubbed his hands together. "Excellent."

Chapter 25►Federal Plaza, NYC

Monday, 10 March
Beth met Rachel and Chris in the lobby of Federal Plaza. She escorted them to the office she shared with Eric. "Sit down. We want to tell you about the warehouse."

Eric said, "We don't have the whole story since the lab reports are not in yet."

"However," Beth said, "*We* are done with the space and can now turn it over to you." She handed Rachel the keys and codes. "And by the way, there's a beautiful BMW 650i Coupe Frozen Silver Edition waiting there for you."

Chris whistled. "That's a very nice ride."

Rachel said, "You want it, it's yours." She paused. "Okay, you two, tell us what you found."

Eric said, "It's not good, so prepare yourself."

Beth said, "Donovan designed the warehouse with great care and kept it as clean as an operating room. He kept a change of clothes in a small room and that was it. Nothing else. No documents or personal effects."

Eric said, "Except for this photo. The man could be anybody. We've got our face recognition people working on it as well as the image of the man who brought the envelope to you. Donovan covered his tracks better than most."

Beth said, "Despite his efforts to remove all trace of activity, we did find evidence in the two garages and downstairs in the dehydration chamber and crusher press. We have a pretty good idea of how Donovan operated."

Rachel said, "Operated? Did he have a business there?"

"Not exactly," Eric said. "Rachel, we have confirmation he murdered many people, who have been identified as killers themselves. We believe he killed the latest victims by injection."

Rachel stood shivering. Then she walked around hugging herself until she stopped and said, "Are you calling him a vigilante? Judge and jury?"

Eric nodded.

She walked back and forth, wringing her hands. "That sanctimonious maniac put his hands on me." She crossed her arm, protecting her body. "Are you sure? I'm having a really hard time visualizing Donovan down and dirty with hardened criminals. He seemed above all that." She stopped next to Chris. "Did you know? Is this what you tried to warn me about?"

Chris reached for her and maneuvered her back into her chair. "I had no idea. My background checks yielded sketchy information and inconsistencies about him. If I had any idea he murdered people, I'd have stopped you long before your limo arrived."

Eric cleared his throat. "During our research, prior to Beth flying up to Lake George, we came up with a number of missing persons we can attribute to Donovan because a significant percentage had a connection to PRAISE. If we're right, he operated undetected for over twenty years. In addition to death by injection, some had fatal accidents, and some just disappeared. We'll never know the true count."

Rachel said, "He certainly had quite the hobby."

Beth said, "I interviewed him, and I can tell you he controlled everything I observed and heard. It would have taken many more conversations to break through his façade. In the end, I'm not even sure it would have been possible."

Chris said, "Nice guy. Glad he's gone. Never liked him." He got up and walked over to the water cooler and took a drink. "Rachel?" She shook her head. He returned to his seat. "By the way, what's with the dehydration chamber and crusher?"

Eric said, "That's how he got rid of the bodies. Kind of a modern interpretation of the biblical 'ashes to ashes, dust to dust.'"

Rachel said, "That must have fed nicely into his God complex."

"There's more. Beth and I used your key and opened Donovan's safety-deposit box. We found some money, a list of bank accounts, letters between him and Brenda Underwood wrapped in ribbon, and a letter to you." He handed Rachel a large manila envelope. "This contains copies of the documents. We'll make arrangements with you regarding the cash."

Next, he held out a legal-size white envelope. "For you, Rachel. We decided to let you open and read it first. Regardless of what it says, he had far more money squirreled away than he ever reported. We are already at work trying to figure out where it came from."

Beth said, "Now you know the truth. It may not change anything regarding how you feel. I hope you now understand Donovan would have killed you or Chris in a heartbeat."

Eric handed Rachel the envelope.

Beth said, "Based on what we've found, it's possible he might have been a contract killer as well. We're sure he engineered the Imanuela Meyerson kidnapping and disappearance. We believe she was a political threat to Sandford's campaign."

Eric said, "And because of that, we are looking into other politically motivated deaths and disappearances."

Rachel, with Chris looking over her shoulder, flipped through the information. "These documents say he had a lot of money lying around, and by that, I mean a small fortune. He must have been very good at his job."

Beth said, "We have no proof regarding the source of these funds. As far as we know it's all legitimate." Beth pointed to the envelope. "One last piece of business."

Chris said, "You don't have to open it."

Rachel said, "I have to."

Beth reached into her pocket and put on protective gloves and opened a large plastic bag. She took the envelope from Rachel, lifted the flap, and pulled out a sheet of paper. After unfolding it, she slid it into the protective bag and closed the top. Then, she handed the sealed letter to Rachel, who read it out loud.

My Dearest Rachel,

If you are reading this, I am dead, and we never married. Both facts disappoint me. Still, from the moment we met, I've loved you with all my heart.

In considering all the things I've done in my life, the most important centered on making communities safer by eliminating their cancerous underbelly, which saved countless lives. For my passion, I offer no apology and have no regrets. No one should have to confront the loss I felt when Brenda died.

As for my work on the political front, those decisions were not my own. I had to trust the greater vision of those who knew far more than I and adhered to a master plan beyond my knowledge or understanding. I regret, in many cases, not opposing these forces. However, blinded by lack of insight, I did what I did on faith, in the belief my actions would make the world a better place.

No doubt you were surprised to be named in my will. Don't be. I couldn't think of a better person to continue my work. To that end, I have left you in charge of all my earthly goods to use as you see fit for the benefit of humankind. I trust you implicitly to do the right thing.

Love always and forever,

Ted

Rachel dropped the letter and put her hands over her mouth. She mumbled. "I'm going to be sick." She jumped to her feet and grabbed the wastepaper basket. Chris flew to her side, Beth grabbed some tissues, and Eric ran for water.

Rachel gagged several times without vomiting. The waves of nausea ended as quickly as they started. She straightened up. "I'm okay."

Chris put his arms around Rachel's shoulders. She rested her head on his chest. "I don't know why I'm such a magnet for the nut-jobs out there."

He said, "Am I to take offense at your generalization?"

"No," she said. "I'm the problem."

"If you, being smart, strong, funny, determined, and, at times, infuriating, are somehow a magnet for weak, dysfunctional lunatics, then a problem exists. However, it's their problem. You, Rachel, are fine."

She grabbed his arm and gave him a squeeze.

Beth retrieved the letter from the floor. "This may help us find who's behind the political killings."

Eric said, "At least now we know it's not some local small-timer. Donovan's referring to someone or some group with powerful connections. Identification will not be easy because such individuals and organizations maintain strict secrecy. The good news is Beth and I thrive on such challenges."

Beth smiled. "We'll get the bastards. And… er… Rachel, as Donovan's heir apparent, may we have your assurance you're not about to go out on a killing spree?"

Rachel didn't laugh. Donovan's words had struck deep. "Do you think he saw me as a vigilante?"

Chris took her hand and said, "No. He played you before, and he's playing you now. That's what he did. He's not a nice guy. He's a serial killer."

"You're right," Rachel said. "I know it."

Beth said, "For what it's worth, I think Donovan meant for you to carry on his philanthropic work and your fight for human rights using his fortune to make the impossible possible."

Rachel smiled. "Thanks, Beth. I'll make sure the money will make a difference."

Chris stood, pulled Rachel to her feet, and addressed Beth and Eric. "There's probably a ton of worthy uses for that building. Let's talk about it over lunch. I'm starving and I'm buying."

Chapter 25▶Soho, NYC

Monday, 10 March
The Lundon Gallery had closed for the day and interior security lights gave the space an ethereal glow. Sybil pulled out her keys and entered through the side door which led upstairs. After the first flight, she turned and entered the apartment, locking the door behind her.

"Lidia?"

No answer.

She opened the interior door to the gallery. Light streamed from the back office. She heard voices. Curious, she went down.

Sybil said, "Hi, honey, I'm home." As she rounded the corner, she saw the third-floor tenant standing over Lidia, seated at her desk.

Lidia looked up. "You remember Gavin?"

Sybil gave him a tight smile. She'd spent little time with the man and didn't like him—more instinct than fact. "I didn't realize you two had become friends."

Lidia said, "Gavin's helping me go over the sales from the weekend. He's got some accounting expertise, and we're organizing a system to handle all shows."

Gavin said, "It won't take too long. I'll give Lidia back to you within the hour."

Sybil said, "Not a problem. In fact, I'll stay and listen. I'd like to understand what's going on also." She sat down.

Lidia said, "Don't worry, I'll explain everything to you."

Sybil said, "I didn't realize accounting had magically become your strong point."

"Come on, Sybil. Don't be like that," Lidia said, "We agreed the gallery is my project. I'm handling it."

Gavin said, "She's a quick study."

Lidia said, "There, he said it. I can learn this stuff."

Sybil said, "Are you trying to get rid of me?"

Lidia shook her head. "Of course not."

"It's my fault," Gavin said. "I only work with owners."

Sybil resisted the urge to punch Gavin's smug face and forced herself to remain calm. She said, "You're in luck. As of Saturday, I'm an owner too. I advanced Lidia a substantial sum to cover her additional opening night expenses in exchange for a percentage."

Lidia said, "That's true. We shook on it."

Sybil caught Gavin's micro grimace.

"I see," he said. "Let's continue. Given the income...."

"Wait," Lidia said, handing Sybil a sheet of paper. "Here, look at this."

Sybil scanned the list of paintings sold and the purchase prices. "Are you kidding me?"

"I know," Lidia said. "It's amazing. Can you believe it? I'm a hit."

Sybil looked up. "This says you sold three-quarters of your exhibited paintings."

"I'm so excited. My work has found an audience."

"Who are willing to pay an average of…let's see…twenty-five thousand each."

"All those years of struggling and classes have finally paid off."

"It's true, yet I find these prices, well, surprising."

"Not so surprising," Lidia said. "Here." She handed Sybil a bound report. "It's the insurance company's appraisal. I had to ensure the show to open the doors."

Sybil scanned the report. The appraisal numbers matched the actual purchases. "Lidia, isn't the appraiser who signed off on this insurance one of the art advisors you hired for the opening?"

"Of course. Why wouldn't I? He loved my work."

Gavin cleared his throat. "Ah, ladies…."

Lidia ignored him. "Sybil, this means we have to pack the sold work and hang the rest of my work. Plus, I've got to get painting again. At this rate, I don't think I'll have enough work available for my next show."

Gavin took a quick peek at his watch and interrupted. "I have to be somewhere for dinner. Can we just go over the tax breaks? It won't take long." He looked at each woman for confirmation and got it. "Good. I've explained the favorable tax breaks incurred when Lidia donates part of the gallery income to a non-profit organization."

Sybil's face brightened. "Lidia, you're going to donate to PRAISE?"

Gavin said, "Not possible. It would appear self-serving. Not only are you the executive director but, as of Saturday, part owner of the gallery."

"What?" Sybil said. "Are you a lawyer too?"

Gavin said, "We've set up an offshore international 501C3 to distribute grants throughout the world."

"How does it work?"

"Pre-authorized individuals will pull money from the account to benefit humanity in keeping with the non-profit's mission. Very simple and straightforward."

"Lidia, are you donating a percentage of net-net profits?"

Gavin said, "No, she's decided to use the gross profit number to begin with. Once she standardizes the budget, net-net profit will be the way to go. She's also decided to use an accrual instead of cash system since art sales can be sporadic."

Sybil turned to Lidia. "You set this up without consulting me? Did you know all this when you sold $375,000 worth of paintings? How much are you giving away before expenses?"

Lidia's throat constricted in terror of the onslaught of disapproval. She whispered, "Half."

Sybil froze.

Lidia took a sip of water. In a confident voice, she said, "I'm giving away half. And don't yell at me. There are millions of people who don't have even one percent of what we do. If I can help, I want to."

"Lidia."

"Don't you see, Sybil? I want to be like you. For the first time in my life, I'll have money to do that."

Sybil wanted to strangle both of them but decided to back off for the moment. "You're a sweetheart, Lidia, and I'm very proud of you." She stood. "You two seem to have everything figured out. I'm leaving." She forced a smile. "Good night, *Mister* Gavin. See you in a few minutes, Lidia."

She strolled out of the room and walked up the stairs, as relaxed as possible, while her brain exploded. It all sounded so, so normal. Just a nice woman sharing her good fortune. If that were true, why did it feel so wrong? Sybil knew Lidia's naiveté made her a prime target. That much money going offshore would raise red flags at the Treasury, and it could cost Lidia jail time, or worse.

At the thought of losing the love of her life, Sybil picked up a pillow and covered her mouth. She let out a muffled scream of frustration. Twice. Done, she threw the pillow across the room, and poured herself a drink—one finger, no ice—and tossed it down. She took off her shoes and paced. It didn't help. She had a second drink in her hand as the door opened.

Lidia bounced in. "Rough day?" She walked over and gave Sybil a hug. "Me, too. Please pour me one." She kicked off her shoes and sat down, holding her hand out for her drink.

Sybil complied and sat down in the matching chair. "I'd like to make a toast to you and your great success."

"Thank you," Lidia said. "I love you too."

Chapter 26▶Damir, Tawanda

Tuesday, 11 March
At three-forty-five, Peter met Sam outside the hotel, and they drove to the government offices. When Peter opened the door to get out, Sam said, "I'll wait."

"Okay, no problem. See you later."

He walked up the stairs, into the building, and through security. The guard made a phone call and issued Peter a visitor's pass. "Turn it in when you leave."

Peter turned toward the seating area only to come face to face with the clerk from the morning meeting. He said, "Mr. Powell, please follow me."

Again, by elevator, stairs, and hallways, Peter had a tour of the government's physical labyrinth. This time, he marked points of interest with his phone camera, taking photos through his fingers. The clerk made an abrupt stop, turned, and led him through several rooms, depositing him in front of an ornate desk and vanishing.

"Welcome, Mr. Peter Powell."

He turned toward the voice. A man sat at a small conference table where tea waited to be served.

"I am Kwanh Ebu, cousin and chief counsel to President Okoro. Please join me."

Peter walked over and took the chair to Ebu's right. "Thank you for seeing me, Sir."

"I am interested in your presence here in our country." Ebu poured the tea and offered two trays. One had milk, lemon, and sugar. The other held an assortment of vegetables, fruits, nuts, and small, sweet cakes. "Please help yourself. All are delicacies of Tawanda."

Peter put a sugar cube in his tea and selected a pastry. "Thank you."

Ebu took a sip of tea. "So, I am curious. Why would the United States send an unofficial observer to Damir?"

"Your country is becoming a major player in the area. My government does not want to be the last to know about any changes Tawanda makes regarding your international position or dealings with foreign nationals."

"Does not the electronic media capture the up-to-the-minute coverage?"

"My government wants to be pro-active in this area, not re-active."

"Why did they not send an official representative?"

"My government would like to be in a position to offer help to your people, should help be necessary or desired, without arousing international attention."

"I see." Ebu took a sip of tea. "I presume you will not be sitting at the Damir Hotel Hawa Bar waiting for a summons. Active minds require activity." Another sip. "What are your plans during your stay?"

"While the bar will be my seat of operations, I do plan to visit the diamond mines. Musimbwa Bakama, the Operations Manager, approved my credentials and I begin tomorrow morning."

"And why do the mines interest you?"

"Controlling investors are concerned about a possible increase in tariffs and want to have a visual review of current operations. I am to be strictly observational."

Ebu nodded, encouraging Peter to continue.

"I also plan visits to local restaurants and cultural landmarks to learn more about the Tawandanese people, and maybe pick up rudiments of your language."

Ebu said, "Thank you, Mr. Powell, for sharing your information with me. It was, of course, none of my business. However, in return for your trust, I will let our vigilant police and security force know your intentions. It will limit their interference so you may move more freely."

"I appreciate your help."

"It does not come without strings, Mr. Powell." He took a bite of a pastry and washed it down with tea. "If, during your stay here, you find anything which might reflect badly on the Government's efforts to gain an invitation to the United Nations, I want you to come to me. Perhaps whatever it is can be fixed with a simple adjustment."

"Be your informant?"

"Yes, with American point of view. Much of what you may tell me will be, I am sure, a matter of interpretation. We will talk and I will explain."

"I understand," Peter said. "However, my usefulness might be compromised if I were observed coming to your office on a regular basis."

"I will resolve the issue, and Sam will let you know."

Peter nodded his head and said, "It seems we have an agreement."

<~<~|~>~>

Peter and Sam had dinner in the hotel. Private conversations were easier here than in the dark crowded native restaurants where you didn't know who could be listening. In the large well-lit dining room, tables had space around them, and the acoustics kept conversations down to a hum.

After ordering, Sam said, "How did it go with Ebu?"

"Nice guy," Peter said. "I'm impressed with his directness, and I think we understood each other."

"He's much easier to deal with than President Okoro…don't forget they're both seasoned politicians."

"I sensed Ebu favored the West."

"Definitely more than Okoro."

"Have you been inside often? I took pictures today and want to map the building."

"I'm surprised they didn't stop you."

"They didn't know."

"You took a dangerous chance because I have the building's schematics—far more thorough than the internet plans."

"Electronic or paper?"

Sam pulled out his phone, tapped it a few times. "Now you've got it."

Peter's phone buzzed and he checked the email. "Thanks."

"Now what are you going to do with it?"

"I have no idea. It's more of a comfort level than anything else."

Sam said, "What's up for tomorrow?"

"My tour of one of the mines. Have to be there by nine."

"Good. I'll pick you up at eight-thirty. Do you think they'll let me walk around with you?"

"I don't think so. Bakama doesn't even want me there."

"Should I be concerned they're going to drop you down a hole?"

Peter laughed. "I think they'd like to, but Bakama's not likely to put everyone's job in jeopardy by angering the owners."

"Don't count on it. Be careful and watch your back. Bakama is a powerful man who knows every facet of his job and rules his mine operations with an iron fist."

"Do I need a gun?"

"Not a good idea. I'll wait in the operations of-fice. If there's a problem, I'll know."

<~<~|~>~>

Back in his room for the night, Peter opened his computer and pulled up the MiNe map. They owned at least one in every major export—copper, cobalt, gold, tin, zinc, and the motherload: diamonds. He marked the entrance to each on his road map as well as Bakama's office. A major piece of missing information was how many sites sat behind each entrance. They could be underground, open-air holes, or formal terracing. He had no way of knowing until he got there.

He opened his messenger bag and pulled out the manila envelope from Vanderhagen. He read the reports and the handwritten note. "Enclosed are last month's reports. I did comparisons against similar extraction operations. While we have similar industry numbers, we are lowest on our non-mechanized excavations. I am concerned about production at the newly discovered kimberlite site. I think a smart operations manager would be turning out actual high numbers and pilfering to keep our numbers safely in the middle. While nothing may be amiss, I am confident your presence and keen observations will determine the truth in this matter. Above all, be careful."

Before going to bed, he forwarded the email from Sam to his grandfather with the message, "Best I can do. Hope it helps."

Chapter 28►Harrison, NY

Tuesday, 11 March
Lucy Kilmer returned to her home after her run-in
with the FBI. They caught her escaping to Canada
and held her for questioning in the kidnapping and
disappearance of a California family, in partnership
with Ted Donovan.

They couldn't prove their case. She had destroyed
all hard and thumb drives with links to the seductions
planned or directed by either Ted or her. The FBI
couldn't hold her based on one cell phone picture.
She walked, free for now. Of course, she'd promised
not to engage in any covert activities, be a good girl,
and an honest citizen. And she would… for a while.
Lucy shook her head. *People are so stupid.*

<~<~|~>~>

She wandered through the wreckage of her once beautiful home, torn apart by a thorough search team. Lucy smiled. All her doomsday planning had worked.
She'd be back in business within days, if not hours.

Using a throwaway cell phone, Lucy contacted a
local computer firm to set her up with a new equip-

ment, called to make sure her internet and Wi-Fi were on and working, and made arrangements to have her house cleaned top to bottom. She figured the FBI would bug everything electronic and even intercept the cleaning crew with their own people to go over everything again. Good. Their routine would make working around the obvious much easier.

Once she established "normal," Lucy retrieved her data storage from the various parts of her home's infrastructure—false beams and "extra" duct work in the attic, waterproof containers in the water tank, and compartments under the raised whirlpool tub and certain stair treads. She had gone to great lengths to ensure these spaces were undetectable. Utilitarian hiding spaces functioned, sounded, and appeared as expected. Nothing short of literally ripping the whole house apart would have exposed her hiding places.

For purposes of the real world, Lucy set up her new business—Kilmer Certified Actuarial Services. She'd earned her degree at Columbia and now it would pay for itself. Vanderhagen Financial Inc. turned out to be one of ten companies she contacted, and the first one to retain her services—exclusively.

The Vice President's stroke proved she could handle the most delicate of situations with the utmost discretion.

With her credentials re-certified, Lucy received the schematics of the Tawandian palace and government offices on her secure server. She got to work. Maximizing her talent and resources to make the world a better place gave her a high worth killing for.

Chapter 28►Gramercy Avenue, NYC

Tuesday, 11 March
Rachel, decked out in a gray sweat suit, sneakers, and red headband, crossed the black and white tiled lobby with Zeus beside her and headed out the door for their morning walk.

"Whoa," Nikolai said as he flew out from behind the desk. "Where are you going?"

"Tell Chris I'm going to the river walkway. Zeus and I have done the block for two weeks, and I'm ready to go further."

Nikolai raised an eyebrow.

"I'll be okay. Really. Don't be concerned. Zeus and I have this." Rachel pulled out her phone. "Look. It's on. I know you track it. And see, I've pre-set it to 'Nikolai' so one tap and we're connected."

"Still, I do not like this."

"Come on, Nikolai. A girl's gotta do what a girl's gotta do." With a broad reassuring smile, Rachel walked outside. Her bravado caused her heart to beat so fast she thought she might hyperventilate before reaching the corner.

Zeus whined and yipped. Rachel stopped, looked down, and smiled. "You know, don't you?" She gave the dog affection and their eyes met. "I'm depending on you."

His tail wagged.

"Don't let me down."

He barked.

Rachel crossed the street with the crowd and walked toward the East River. Alert and watchful, she felt confident as Zeus trotted beside her. She knew his unwavering gaze sent out a clear signal he would protect his owner under any condition and for any reason. They were an unassailable team and it calmed her.

For the first time, she began to observe her fellow walkers. Few made eye contact. Most seemed on a mission, walking as fast as their age permitted. Businesspeople and the casually dressed talked on cell phones, seeing only their destinations. Engaged in conversation or not, few were open to connections with others who crossed their path. If anyone happened to look their way, it was always about Zeus. It made her feel invisible and relieved her fearfulness all at the same time—a good thing.

She found a bench and sat so she could give Zeus some attention. "You're such a good boy." He licked her face.

Her phone rang. Chris. "So, you decided to take a long walk by yourself?"

"How did you know?" She watched the river and boat traffic as they talked.

"Nikolai," Chris said. "You okay?"

"Never better. I'm with Zeus and we're sitting on a bench admiring the view."

"I would have gone with you."

"I know. I wanted to expand my horizons on my own. Besides, Zeus's presence makes me feel brave."

"Glad to hear it. I've seen your panic attacks, and they're not pretty."

"Chris, don't worry. I'm fine. I'll call if I run into trouble. I promise."

"Okay. I trust you."

"Good. Be home soon."

"Call me when you get back."

"Sure." As she pocketed her phone, she heard her name. Rachel tightened the leash. Zeus stood, tense and ready for action.

"Rachel?" The man stood in front of her.

Zeus lowered his head and guarded Rachel.

She said, "Do I know you?"

"I'm Gavin," the man said. "The potter at the Lundon Gallery. We met Saturday night."

"Of course." Rachel nodded and patted Zeus on the head. "You weren't very gracious as I remember."

"I apologize," he said. "I may have had one champagne too many." He motioned to the bench. "Mind if I join you?"

Rachel stood. "You can have the whole bench. We're headed home."

"Sorry. I didn't mean to intrude. I'm just trying to be friendly. I've read your books and I'm intrigued. We're both artists, and I think we may have much in common."

"You're not intruding, I'm just ready to go home."

"Perhaps we can talk another time."

"Maybe. I'll talk to Chris and find out when he's available."

Gavin's smile faded. "I meant...."

"I know what you meant." Rachel stood. "And you know I'm engaged. So, it's a package deal or nothing."

Gavin's smile returned. "Chris is one lucky man."

"Take care, Gavin." Rachel left without looking back, Zeus trotting beside her.

<~<~|~>~>

She entered 215. Nikolai gave her a crooked smile and pointed to the ceiling—their code for Chris. "I know," Rachel said. "He called."

Nikolai shrugged. "Leave Zeus with me. He will be fine."

"Chris or Zeus?"

Without waiting for an answer, Rachel went up to Chris's apartment and found him sitting at his desk. Before he could turn, she ran to him and put her arms around his neck. "Hi, I'm back."

"I wasn't worried."

"You'll never guess who I ran into."

He swiveled to face her. "Who?"

"Gavin. The guy from the reception."

"I didn't like him. What did he want?"

"He wanted to set something up for coffee or lunch and talk art."

"I'll bet."

"I told him I'd check and see when you'd be free."

"Good answer."

She released him and went to the kitchen. She retrieved a couple of glasses from the cabinet. "Water?"

"No. I'm good."

"You know, I sense a certain arrogance in Gavin, reminiscent of Ted Donovan."

Chris said, "Then stay away from him. One Ted Donovan per lifetime is more than enough."

"Amen to that."

<~<~|~>~>

After she'd showered and changed, her phone rang. Beth. Rachel answered.

Beth said, "Are you up for lunch?"

"Sure. Where?"

"I'm in the lobby."

At Alfie's, the restaurant across from 213 Gramercy, Beth said, "I've been immersed at work and needed a break, so naturally I thought of you."

"I've been blocked and grateful for the diary diversion you dumped on me."

"Dumped? Never," Beth said. "I knew you'd be interested since your books are all about empowering women and the oppressed."

"I went to the nursing home and interviewed her brother Robert. He wasn't much help. It was one of the nurses who gave me the name of his periodic visitor… Stella Joseph."

"Her parents' names."

Rachel nodded. "However, no Stella Joseph gave birth in 1935. So, I tried a combination of the brother's names. A Roberta Williams delivered a son on February 3, 1935."

"Did you get his name?"

"No. The baby's recorded as 'male.' I decided New York City was not place for a destitute mother and child and checked the Brides Index. No Roberta Williams married. But a Stella Joseph did marry a Henryk Zych."

"Good work!"

"Yeah, but that's as far as I've gotten."

The waiter brought their lunch.

"I may be able to help. You know I've been working on the necktie killings. As it turns out, our killer is a copycat, mimicking the late Mansonati boys' modus operandi. In the course of assembling the family's information, I turned up Johnny Mansonati's daughter, Maria. She's 94 years-old and lives in Queens. Although she has no bearing on my case, she might know what happened to Patricia. If you're interested, here's her information. If you can arrange an interview, I'll tag along, you know, for protection."

<~<~|~>~>

Maria Mansonati lived in a two-bedroom condo located in one of the borough's better sections. Her aide answered the door and led them into the living room.

The ninety-four-year-old woman, wearing a floral kimono, sat in a wheelchair. Her white hair framed her face in soft rolls and a hint of rose lipstick covered thin lips.

Rachel stepped forward and introduced herself and Beth.

Maria glanced at her aide. "Who are these people?"

The aide said, "This is the young woman who called yesterday."

"When?"

Rachel intervened and said, "Maria, I'm doing research on Patricia Tanner."

Maria tilted her head from side to side. "Do I know these people?"

Rachel glanced at Beth and tried again. "Do you remember when you lived in Apalachin, New York?"

Maria stared at Rachel. "Grandfather's house."

The aide said, "She'll be fine now. The past she remembers. It's today that poses a problem."

Rachel thanked the woman and addressed Maria. "Who lived in your grandfather's house?"

"My parents, my brother Vinny, and me. Mama hated it there." Maria started giggling. "She'd scream,

'I'm no damn Snow White.'" Maria laughed, "It was hilarious."

Rachel said, "Did your papa like the woods?"

At the mention of the word "papa," Maria's face darkened, and her brow furrowed. "Papa was mean."

Rachel glanced at Beth and changed the subject. "Did you go to school in Apalachin?"

Maria brightened. "I loved school."

"Did you make any friends? Did you know a girl named Patricia Tanner?"

She searched the ceiling for memories and returned her gaze to Rachel. "Patricia lived next door."

"Were you best friends?"

"No."

"Did Patricia ever come over to your house?"

"Just for pottery lessons."

"Did you take lessons, too?"

Maria shook her head. "No."

"Did Patricia come often?"

"Mama hated it when Patricia came."

"Did your mother ever say why??"

Maria licked her lips. "One time, *she* screamed at *him*, 'What are you doing with the Tanner child.'" Maria closed her eyes. "That's when I knew *she* knew." Her face reddened.

Gently, Rachel leaned in. "Knew what, Maria?"

She looked at Rachel. "Knew what *he* did." Maria's jaw muscles twitched. "Knew what *he* did to me." She held her hand out. "Water." The aide brought over a small bottle of water. Maria took a few sips and gave the bottle back.

"What happened next?"

"I ran out of the room. The next morning, I could tell *he* beat *her* good."

Rachel wanted to reach out, touch the old woman, give her comfort, a hug, make her past hurt go away, tell her it wasn't her fault. Instead, she said, "I'm so sorry."

"It wasn't the first time nor the last," Maria said.

Maria dismissed the comment with a wave of her hand. "It was a long time ago."

Rachel said, "It must have been hard for you."

Maria said, "One time, I asked *her* why *she* didn't stop him. *She* said that despite the beatings, he made her happy."

"I said, 'What about me? He never made me happy.' Know what *she* said?"

"What?"

"He never beat you." Maria laughed without humor.

"Did you ever have a family of your own?"

Maria shook her head. "The bastard ruined me."

"Do you know what happened to Patricia after the summer of 1934?"

Maria shook her head again. "No."

<~<~|~>~>

On the ride home, Beth said, "Mansonati—not such a nice guy."

Rachel said, "I can't imagine growing up in that household."

"Agreed. I think Patricia did the right thing."

"You mean flee to New York?"

"You bet. From what we know, he probably would have killed her."

<~<~|~>~>

Beth dropped Rachel off at 215. Zeus greeted her as if she'd been gone a week. "How's my boy?" His tail alone could have powered electricity for an entire city.

Nikolai said, "He behaved like a perfect gentleman, and I walked him."

"Thank you." To Zeus she said, "Ready to go up?" As they left the lobby, she heard Nikolai letting Chris know she'd returned.

<~<~|~>~>

Chris burst into the lobby so wound up he couldn't sit. Walking in circles and waving his hands, he said, "Why didn't Rachel call me to say she'd returned? I've been stewing all afternoon. I worry about her, and she gives me crap for it. I just don't get it."

Nikolai said, "Are you asking me a question?"

"No, I'm letting off steam."

"Is it helping?"

Chris stopped at stared at him. "No. So, okay, here's a question. How do I care without creating havoc in our relationship?"

"A good question," Nikolai said. "What is it you care so much about?"

"She's putting herself into panic-inducing situations."

"Do you mean she is taking chances?"

Chris nodded. "I'm terrified I'm going to lose her, and she'll return to the withdrawn unapproachable woman who moved in here less than three years ago."

"The Rachel I see is pushing her boundaries, so she can become the person you asked her to be."

Chris opened his mouth, closed it, paused, and said, "I'm responsible?"

Nikolai raised an eyebrow and shrugged.

"Say it."

"Perhaps you still treat her as the woman who left for Lake George and not yet accepted her as the woman who came back."

Chris slumped into a chair. "I'm an idiot."

"No. I think you just forgot to change, too."

<~<~|~>~>

In her apartment, as soon as she kicked off her shoes, her stomach growled. She wrapped her hand around the refrigerator handle, opened the door, and surveyed the uninspiring choices inside. Nothing appealed to her. She shut the door and went through her pantry. Same results.

She poured herself a drink and laughed. She felt just like she did when her mother came home from shopping. She'd help unload six bags of groceries and put the food away. Afterwards she'd look for a snack, but nothing in all those bags ever measured up to the wonderfulness she wanted, needed, to wrap around her taste buds.

A noise at the door.

Zeus barked and Chris walked in.

She watched him cross the foyer to the dining table with a bag of take-out. Zeus pranced at his side, sniffing and licking his jowls.

Chris put the food down and turned to face her. "I worry too…."

She said, "I didn't call. I'm…."

They said, "I'm sorry," at the same time, and followed up with hugs and kisses.

Zeus's ruff-ruff turned their attention back to food. Chris scratched Zeus behind the ears and opened the bag. "Shepherd's pie from the pub around the corner."

Rachel smiled. "My favorite… and maybe Zeus's too."

"Good. It's hard to satisfy everyone."

"Don't worry about that," Rachel said, "you satisfy me."

Chapter 29▶East Side, NYC

Tuesday, 11 March

In the late afternoon at PRAISE offices, Sybil sat at her desk, feet up on a side chair, and played with a pen—clicking, twirling, and flipping it. Last night's meeting with Gavin bothered her. Why? She'd love to wipe the smirk off the bastard's face—the one he gave her when she started to question the money distribution. Her impeccable bullshit meter registered this guy in the red zone, and she wanted to know why.

Her phone beeped. An email. From ICU, Inc. She opened it immediately and read.

Dennis Gavin, age 54, DOB listed as November 15, 1966, no record of birthplace, mother, father, or schooling. Current Social Security records active as of 1990, received BFA, CPA from CCNY night school, potter by trade. No outstanding warrants, no record of arrests or any criminal activity. All U.S. taxes filed from 1990 forward. No property ownership. One vehicle: white van, registration current, insurance paid. No social media presence. Listing of major work in museums and major collections below.

Sybil closed her phone. The report verified everything he'd said. *Damn.* Still, he had to be somewhere before 1990. What happened in those first 24 years? What would be the value in getting a list of births with his birth date—which may or may not be real. Probably a waste of time and money. However, the fact that part of Gavin's life was undocumented supported her suspicions he had ulterior motives.

She opened her computer and googled "U.S. legal standing for offshore non-profit organizations," and found a paper by the American Bar Association. There, in black and white, it explained the illegality of the offshore money laundering schemes, verifying what she suspected all along. Lidia had gotten herself into a serious situation without understanding the ramifications.

Now what? She, a chess master, felt out of control. Gavin may be good, but she's better. She had to find the ideal strategy to make sure there'd be no way in this world he'd be able to call checkmate.

She got up and grabbed her coat. She needed airtime to think.

Sybil knew how to play the part of social butterfly, all the while loathing the superficiality of the role. As a consequence, she had many acquaintances and a few close friends. Her father trained her to keep all personal information close and share little else unless necessary to control the conversation. He advised it would keep her in control and in an enviable position during any negotiation. Much as she hated him, he'd been right about that.

As a result, Sybil kept her own counsel—Ilse being one of the few exceptions. She pulled out her phone and called Ilse. Maybe she'd answer while she tanned on the Mediterranean cruise ship's deck. No answer. She was on her own. She lifted her head, squared her shoulders, lengthened her stride, and marched home.

<~<~|~>~>

"Lidia? Are you here?"

No answer.

Sybil pulled out her phone and called.

Lidia said, "Hi, Sybil. What's going on?"

"Where are you?"

"In my studio. Where are you?"

"Upstairs."

"I'm conceptualizing. Be up soon."

"Do you want me to start dinner or order out?"

"Casserole's in the oven. Turn it on to 350, and we'll eat when I get there."

Sybil shut the phone, walked into the kitchen, and followed Lidia's instruction. After changing into jeans and a T-shirt, she returned to the living room, poured a bourbon, grabbed her phone, and sat on the window seat. She liked winding down by watching the street change from day to evening. The descending darkness obscured the uncontained trash. The signs outside the buildings glowed brighter with each passing minute, and the lit interiors revealed a hidden world, giving the street a whole new dimension.

She watched and sipped, unable to shake the knowledge she had to do something, or Lidia would land in jail, or get hurt, or both.

Sybil figured she had three options. She could call and report the scam to the Internal Revenue Service— that'd shut it down fast, except she didn't know the name of "it," and if she did, Lidia might get incarcerated in the process.

Option two. She could talk with Lidia about refusing to participate and put their relationship on the line. Lidia would see it as an intrusion on her ability to manage her own affairs. Ever since the gallery deal,

Lidia had talked only of her impending great success and elevated visibility on the local, national, and international art scene. Even if she'd give up the off-shore non-profit, she'd never give up the promised notoriety.

Or she could talk to her brother. Sybil took a gulp of bourbon. The whole idea made her stomach turn. Still, James wasn't her father—only his puppet. If she could gain his sympathy, even a little, he might be able to speak on her behalf and get her father to look elsewhere. What could happen? If he said "no," she'd be pissed but it wouldn't change Lidia's current position, and maybe he'd say "yes," and free Lidia. No downside.

Who was she kidding? Of course, there was. She'd owe him—just for listening, and even more if he actually did make a difference. The Vanderhagen men thrived on indebtedness—it provided the necessary leverage to control every single business deal—it was their Samurai katana.

Sybil stared at the phone in her hands. Calling James did have another downside—it might make her father furious, and that man always got even. To save Lidia, she'd have to chance that. She opened her phone and called.

James answered on the first ring. "Sybil."

"James. Do you have time to talk?"

James paused. "Not for long. My meeting's in ten minutes."

"It's about Lidia."

"Your paint-by-number girlfriend?"

A snappish and defensive Sybil said, "Wife and artist, and you know it." She heard herself and softened. "I'm sorry, James. I don't want to fight with you." She cleared her throat. "I understand you gave Lidia money for the gallery opening."

"I did advance her a large sum of money."

"Why?"

"She's doing us a favor, needed the money, and I helped her out."

"What favor?"

"She set up an offshore non-profit and gave us sole access to the money. She will donate a percentage of her sales, for which we will supply most of the buyers. Through her largesse we will channel contributions to global projects supporting prevailing effective governing policies."

"That sounds like insider jargon to me, James. Tell me the truth."

"Sybil, it takes a lot of money to make sure global economies run smoothly. The offshore non-profit will be a tremendous help to advance our interests."

"Please, James. Do it without Lidia."

"It's too late."

"If you don't stop this, Lidia might wind up in a federal penitentiary."

"She knows what she wants and is ready to do whatever it takes. Don't get involved."

"I love her. I'm already involved."

Her brother didn't respond.

"James, did you hire Gavin to do Lidia's books?"

"Um…. Look Sybil, if you want Lidia free of our agreement, you'd have to work with us. Be our new Ted Donovan. Set up and control your own account from which you would oversee politically necessary adjustment operations for our group."

Sybil caught her breath. Rachel was right. Ted Donovan did hide great sums of money, laundering it through PRAISE. Son-of-a-bitch. "James, I would never work with you."

"You wouldn't have to do anything, just manage it. We have operatives in place to do site work."

"No."

"I thought liberating Lidia is why you called."

"You mean it's either her or me?"

"Unless you want to negotiate with Dad."

"No."

"I remember when you and he were inseparable."

"Before you went off to school," Sybil said. "You weren't around when he found out I had a boyfriend at fourteen. In our huge house, I only saw him in his study or the dining room except when he hosted a party. Then, one day, he walked into the basement playroom and caught us having sex."

"Did he hurt you?"

"No. He pursed his lips, shook his head, and closed the door behind him. We never talked about it. Two or three boyfriends later, the night of my sweet sixteen birthday party, after everyone had gone, he asked me into his study. I danced in, excited, expecting an extra special gift, something between father and daughter to treasure for the rest of my life. Instead, he sold me out—literally.

"He wished me a happy birthday and congratulated me on becoming a woman. He offered to pay for college, gave me a cash gift of five thousand dollars, and sat me down to explain the facts of life.

"His facts were that I had underage sex with my boyfriends, and he was prepared to publicly accuse them and have them tried for statutory rape.

"I couldn't believe he would throw them in jail and ruin their lives. He said he had mourned my lack of restraint and had gotten over his initial desire to kill the boys. With time, he had figured out a way to harness my sexual energy to serve the family business.

"I jumped to my feet and called him disgusting. He didn't even flinch. He said I was to make myself sexually available to the men he chose for me who were rich and had eligible sons for whom they picked the wives.

"I told him he was out of his mind, and I would not take part in his insane scheme. He said I do it or the boys go to jail, and I'd be cut off without a dime. When I protested and called him despicable, he called me a whore. He said he planned to get me married off to the wealthiest and most influential individual he could find.

"In the end, he smiled, a half-smile, maybe more a smirk, when he said I'd get the life I'd grown accustomed to, and he'd get the inside track to the power he needed—a win-win."

James said, "You knew he'd do something. Did Mother know?"

"No. I don't think so. Unfortunately, she found out one night at an intimate dinner party for ten. She saw me get up and leave with one of the guests. She asked me to stay. Father, at least one drink over his limit, told her I worked for him. And for that matter, she did too. Mom jumped from the roof that same night."

"Not true."

"Less than a month later, that pillar of society arranged my marriage to Brian Powell, the heir to a lumber conglomerate based in Oregon, and wouldn't take 'no' for an answer. I fought the arranged marriage to the altar.

"In the end, I was lucky. Brian turned out to be a gentle man with more principles and ethics than anyone Father had met before. When my husband refused to put his workers at risk or his reputation on the line for one of Father's 'business opportunities,' I could feel the anger 3,000 miles away. Brian died in a car crash 90 days later."

"That wasn't Dad's fault."

"Yes, James, it was. Nice day. No traffic. No skid marks."

"Not true."

"It was our anniversary. Brian was on his way home to me and Peter when Father had him murdered."

"No. No. Not true."

"Believe what you want," Sybil said. "Now, you tell me how I'm supposed to 'talk' to him when I can barely speak his name."

"I'm sorry, Sybil, Lidia's decision stands."

The dial tone drowned her hope. She was on her own.

Chapter 30►Gramercy Avenue, NYC

Tuesday, 11 March
Rachel texted Chris. "*Ice cream?*" at nine PM.

He answered. "*In 20.*"

She frowned. Twenty-minutes. With her visit to Maria Mansonati fresh in her mind, Rachel decided to find out what she could about Johnny Mansonati.

Public information confirmed he'd been detained for questioning in the November 14, 1957, raid, led by a local police officer and New York State Troopers, at the home of Joseph "Joe the Barber" Barbara, McFall Road, Apalachin, New York. He worked as a hitman for the mob.

She googled "Mansonati" and researched several promising sites. She also went to the federal trials in the National Archives and checked out lawyer and witness statements. Next, she googled the identified lawyers and, without giving it a second thought, the FBI Records via FBI's online resource, Vault.

Time and stimuli evaporated while she immersed herself in the data. She never heard the door open or sense Zeus's excitement. Chris walked in and said,

"When you didn't come up, I figured I'd come down."

Rachel jumped at the sound of his voice. "What's going on?"

He handed her a large cup filled with ice cream and hot fudge.

Rachel grinned and accepted the dessert. "Just what I needed."

Zeus barked, tail wagging.

Chris said, "Okay buddy. I didn't forget you." He placed a bowl of vanilla ice cream on the floor and returned to Rachel's side, holding his cup. "Hey, what's that?" He pointed to the monitor. "That's big-time mob stuff. What are you doing?"

"Nothing. Research." She thrust a big spoonful of ice cream into her mouth and shrugged her shoulders. "I simply searched on mob hit-man and pedophile, Johnny Mansonati."

"On the FBI's site?"

"It's public. Not a problem."

Rachel's phone buzzed. "It's Beth. She's downstairs."

Rachel texted, "*My apartment.*"

Beth walked in with an overnight bag. "I see I've interrupted something."

"No," Rachel said. "I'm just doing some research."

Beth said, "On Johnny Mansonati?"

Rachel nodded "How did you know? Am I in trouble?"

"No, you're fine. Because of the similarity in modus operandi, the FBI has any reference to Mansonati flagged. We just want to know who's looking. You've done nothing wrong. However, I noticed you came up on the list of users, and I needed a place to stay tonight. So, I'm here."

Chris said, "Ice cream?"

Beth smiled. "Absolutely."

Rachel said, "Do you really think someone has gone to all the trouble to track down and use Mansonati's modus operandi? It seems too improbable to even consider."

Beth said, "On the surface. However, we do know his son, Vinny, followed in his father's footsteps and died in a shoot-out at a local restaurant. Tony, Vinny's son, a twenty-something kid at the time, saw the whole thing. He testified in closed court and went into witness protection with his family until his mother, Gabriella Mansonati, found out her mother lay on her death bed. Gabriella opted out and returned to her family's home."

"What happened to Tony?"

"He vanished. Tony could be dead or living under an assumed name. If he's alive, he could be our killer, even though he'd be in his mid to late fifties."

Chris got up and went into the kitchen.

"Is Mrs. Mansonati still alive?" Rachel said and pulled out her phone. "Gabriella, right?" She typed in the name and found the address. "She's about an hour away. I'd love to interview her."

Beth raised an eyebrow. "I don't know. I'm not sure how the diary from Apalachin got mixed up with my murder case, but I think maybe it's time you backed off. Your writer's block must be over by now and the diary can wait."

"Are you kidding? You have to know I'm not going to let this go. My first book, *Rape: Power, Control, and Healing from a Woman's Perspective* is all about empowerment. If I can help Patricia Tanner-slash-Stella Zych Pickens or her family come to terms with her rape and subsequent issues, I want to, no, I *have* to try."

"So, you're not giving up?"

"Mrs. Mansonati may have a clue as to what happened to Patricia," Rachel said. "I have to find out. It's an old missing person case, and the people involved are dead. What bearing could it possibly have on a current serial killer?"

"Well, let me talk to my supervisor," Beth said. "I know Mrs. Mansonati's been interviewed and not under investigation. She's had no connection with Anthony for over thirty years."

"If it'll help, tell them you'd come with me."

"Don't get your hopes up until I get back to you."

Chris returned and handed Beth a bowl of ice cream. "I don't want to leave you out of our party."

Beth smiled. "This is just what I needed."

"Enjoy." Chris pulled out his ePad. "You girls catch up, I'm going upstairs." He looked at Rachel. "Come up when you're done."

Rachel turned from Chris to Beth and the overnight case.

Beth said, "Eric's pulled an all-nighter, and I wanted company so…."

Rachel said, "Say no more." She stood up, hugged Chris and gave him a kiss. "How about we come up for breakfast in the morning?"

"That works. See you around seven-thirty."

After Chris left, Beth said, "Tell me what you found out about the Tanner girl."

Rachel showed her the file as she explained. "So that's it. I'm now on the hunt for Mrs. Stella Pickens and researching what happened on the Mansonati side."

Beth said, "Reconsider a book deal. This might be a page turner—fact or fiction."

"Maybe. I am getting a firsthand look at the struggles of women during the thirties. When I compare it to today, I'm not sure we've come as far as we think."

"I agree, although some days are better than others."

"Beth Neilson, are you complaining?"

"No. I'm exhausted. I'm not sure I can reach into my purse." Beth over-acted the effort to do just that, "…and show you this." Beth held up her left hand adorned with a one carat solitaire diamond ring. "Eric and I are engaged!"

"Oh my God. How wonderful! I'm so happy for you. When? Where?"

"Just after we left the other night. I didn't call because I wanted to tell you in person."

Rachel said, "Come, let's go tell Chris."

"How about we tell him in the morning?"

"It's a plan."

At bedtime, the women climbed into Rachel's king size bed and Zeus pushed his nose between them.

Beth giggled. "You want a hug?"

Zeus's tail shifted into high gear.

"Here you go, big boy." Beth put her arms around his neck and her hands fondled his ears. She got a big kiss in return. "Is this big guy helping you get through the night?"

"You bet. He seems to sense the change in my breathing or something and calms me down before I enter extreme panic. He's the best."

Beth laughed. "And in Eric's absence, the greatest goodnight kisser—ever."

Chapter 31▶Damir, Tawanda, Africa

Wednesday, 12 March

Peter strode into the hotel bar. Sam, sitting at their corner table, raised a beer. Peter nodded, got his own bottle, and joined him. Throwing his gloves on the table, he said, "A day at the mines turned out to be even less interesting than I expected."

Sam said, "Dirty. Dusty. What else did you think you'd find?"

Peter dropped his hat on the gloves and sat. "I didn't get a chance to find out anything. They gave me the whirlwind tour and showed me the door. Hell, they didn't even give me time to call you. MiNe transport brought me back."

"You're not an insider."

"Even so, I figured there'd be time to ask questions. I wanted to learn about the process. Get a feel for the operation. Talk to staff and workers."

"Unrealistic. You're a nobody. They have no reason to impress you."

"Then my guide did a great job. He showed me everything and nothing.'"

"You wanted more depth?"

"I think I anticipated a sense of pride."

"American enthusiasm?"

Peter nodded. "It wasn't there." He took a sip of beer. "Guess I'm way out of my comfort zone. Still, the guide's overly solicitous behavior tells me he concealed critical information."

Sam raised his beer bottle in a salute. "Good instincts, Peter. An excellent trait for interpreting Tawanda's political world."

"Anyway, I'm here to represent the U.S.—not become involved in the mining company."

"Good decision. Use the same logic in your meetings with Ebu. Let the State Department guide your response and use me as a resource for any immediate action."

"That's my revised plan."

The men clinked bottles.

<~<~|~>~>

After dinner, Peter passed through the lobby on his way to room 229. Bob approached. "Mr. Powell, a package has arrived for you. Shall I bring it up to your room?"

Peter turned to the desk clerk who had disappeared and back to Bob. "Sure. Thank you." Avoiding the gathering at the elevators, he took the stairs. Before he closed the door, Bob arrived, holding the package like a bejeweled king's crown on a velvet pillow.

"Great service," Peter said, taking the wrapped box and giving Bob a tip.

"Thank you, Mr. Powell. Have a nice night."

Closing and locking the door, Peter placed his keys and the package on the table and did a full room search. Finding nothing, he put his back to the camera in the headboard and opened the package from his grandfather—a SAT phone and an audio jammer. Now electronic eavesdropping devices would be useless.

He turned on the jammer and called his grandfather on the SAT phone. "Reporting in, Sir." Peter went on to explain his day at the MiNe site.

Vanderhagen said, "Did you read the reports I sent you last week?"

"Of course. As soon as I got them."

"I'd hoped you'd prove my suspicions baseless, but you've only supported them."

"Proceed carefully, Sir. The men down here are very protective of their operations."

"Not their operations. My operations. The cartel's operations. If something's going on, I bet it's not in the company's best interests."

"I'm sorry I didn't have better news."

Vanderhagen cleared his throat. "Um, Peter. Do you have time for another visit? I will make a call and insure you get the, shall we say, executive tour."

"As an observer?"

"For now. We need to keep it low key and not arouse any concerns until you can identify specifics. I'll talk to Bakama first thing tomorrow. I'm sure he'll be more than accommodating."

<~<~|~>~>

Mid-morning the next day, Sam drove Peter to the Operations Manager's office.

"Good morning, I'd like to speak to Musimbwa Bakama," Peter said to the young woman at the desk.

A door opened and Bakama appeared—a false smile frozen in place. "Mr. Powell, welcome."

Peter overlooked the lie. "Thank you for setting up this second tour."

Bakama said, "You may send your driver home. I've arranged for a guide who is also an interpreter."

Peter texted Sam, "Don't wait. Come back later."

A tall thin African man entered Bakama's office.

In Tawandanese, Bakama said, "Is everything prepared at site 3?"

Peter kept busy with his phone so as not to telegraph his understanding of the conversation.

The man nodded.

In English, Bakama said, "It is all arranged. Mr. Powell. This is Wembe.

Wembe said, also in English, "I am pleased to show you around, Mr. Powell."

"Excellent. I'd like to see an open dig for diamonds. Do you have a map?"

Bakama and Wembe exchanged furtive glances. Bakama snapped his fingers and the secretary brought in a map. Bakama handed it to Peter. "Will this do?"

Peter examined the possibilities, his finger tracing the sites, and said, "Mine number five."

Bakama said, "It is far."

Peter said, "Is that a problem?"

Wembe threw a sideways glance to Bakama and said, "No, Sir."

<~<~|~>~>

The ride to number five took an hour on the main road and forty-five minutes bouncing over a dirt road. By the time they arrived, Peter's clothing stuck to his body, and dust covered his exposed skin. In the nondescript parking area stood a numeral 5 sign.

"Mr. Powell, you may wash off here." Wembe stood by a trough of water and ladled the liquid into a bowl, which he placed on a table. A clean towel hung over the back of a rusting folding chair.

Off to the left stood a brand new ten-by-twelve tent—the packing creases sharp and new. Underneath the canopy, a table and chairs, unmarred by use, waited for people.

Wembe said, "Come. Let us sit in the shade."

Peter said, "I didn't see a tent like this yesterday."

"The tents are being assembled one at a time. Every site does not have one."

"Is this the first?"

"I do not know," Wembe said. "The workers will come here for water breaks. In time, we will add a food service truck for midday meals."

"When?"

"Mr. Bakama can give you the details." Wembe produced two bottles of water and gave one to Peter. "May I take you to the dig?"

Peter nodded. "Let's go."

On foot, they reached the site in ten minutes.

The large pit looked like long tapered fingers had plunged into its sides and base. Each indentation proved to be a digging site. Workers terraced each hole as they dug.

Wembe explained. "Our dig supervisors have strong boxes. When a worker finds a diamond, he raises the stone. The supervisors keep count. On each break, the workers turn in their bag of stones. If the count is off, the workers lose part of their commission or worse. They could be dismissed."

"What about the buckets?"

"Those go to the washers. They take the filled buckets to the river and wash the dirt. This way they filter out the stones. Our washers are trained to tell which are diamonds. It is a system that has worked for many years."

"I count six supervisors standing around the rim and about thirty workers."

"Each supervisor monitors five to seven diggers and washers."

"What do the workers earn?"

Wembe cleared his throat. "Our workers are paid one dollar and five cents per day. Other employers pay less than a dollar. For every pound of rough diamonds, they get a twenty-five-cent commission. More than fair."

As Wembe talked, Peter watched the men at work. Not one acknowledged him, although there were side glances to each other. Peter couldn't tell if they understood English, reacting to Wembe's information, or they were uncomfortable with his presence.

"Where do the workers live?"

"We provide a tent city. Most of our people are refugees who were living in Damir. We offer them food, shelter, and a job. Our rehabilitation program meets government standards."

"And other employers?"

"Their workers live way below poverty level in shanty towns, where the sex trade flourishes, and the infant mortality rate is high."

Workers' body and eye movements cast a shadow of suspicion that Peter couldn't ignore.

Wembe snapped his fingers at one of the supervisors. The man yelled in Tawandanese, "Fifteen-minute break."

All the workers stood up and faced the supervisor. The man said, still in Tawadanese, "Follow me to the tent. Give your pouches to your counter. Hold your heads high. We have water. Drink one, take one. Eyes forward."

The workers moved off in silence.

Peter turned to Wembe. "Can you show me how to dig? I'd like to experience the effort firsthand."

"If you like. Please follow me."

The two men climbed down a nearby hole. Wembe picked up a shovel and handed the pick to Peter. "You loosen the earth. I will put it in this bucket."

They filled the bucket and took it over to the nearby stream. Wembe selected one of the small handmade screen boxes. "Mr. Powell, empty some dirt from our bucket into the screen." Peter did as told. Wembe wet the dirt and shook the screen until only pebbles remained.

Wembe ran his hands over the pebbles. "No diamonds." He tossed the stones onto a pile. "Now you try."

Peter rolled up his pants and took his sandals off. He waded into the stream and took a box. Wembe filled it with dirt. Peter washed the mass over and over, as Wembe did, until there were only pebbles.

Wembe said, "Bring it here."

On dry land, Peter watched as Wembe's nimble fingers and practiced eye surveyed the stones.

"There." Wembe's fingers pointed to a rock.

Peter picked up the half-inch sized rough diamond. "Really?"

"Your first find, Mr. Powell. Keep it as a reminder of your tour. When we return to Mr. Bakama's office, he will authorize it, so you are not accused of stealing." Wembe held out a small leather pouch. "Put it in here. I will hold it for you."

Peter gave him the stone and said, "These men work very hard for their money."

"We all do, Mr. Powell."

He rolled down his pants and put on his sandals, once again presentable. The workers returned, holding water bottles in their hands. They scampered into the pits and got back to work.

Peter stroked his chin. "I'd like to see site four."

"Today?"

"Right now."

"I have to call Mr. Bakama. He pulled out his phone. In Tawandanese he said, "The man Powell is insisting I take him to site four. Sir, four is not ready." Wembe listened and said, in English, "Mr. Powell. We cannot go there today."

Peter took the phone. "Mr. Bakama, what's the problem?"

"Ah, Mr. Powell. I would be happy to grant you access. Unfortunately, the site is closed for the rest of the afternoon due to an unfortunate circumstance—a worker has died."

"Then, I'd like to go site six."

"Mr. Powell, it's been a long day for all of us. Let us schedule for tomorrow."

"I'd prefer now."

"Let me speak to Wembe."

After the call, Wembe turned to Powell. "I may take you up on the hill, on the rim, but not into the dig."

Peter nodded. "Let's go."

<~<~|~>~>

From his vantage point above mine site six, Peter had a view of the workers down below. Even at this distance, the activity level put the last dig to shame. Talking, shouting, digging—a discordant symphony. Then the wind changed. A putrid odor filled the air.

Peter rotated his head to determine the source of the stench. He saw nothing out of the ordinary. He took several steps until he could see over the hill. The workers' wretched quarters stretched out before him.

As he turned to Wembe, he felt a blow. The soil slipped from beneath his feet. Arms flailing, Peter fell into the dig. He bounced and rolled from one plateau to another until he found a hand grip that held and stopped the momentum. He got one glimpse of the clear blue African sky before the trailing rain of dirt and rocks hit him. His training kicked in and he rolled onto his belly, got into a turtle position, and covered his neck and head with his hands. He leaned into the step riser for protection and to save as much air as possible. Then he lost consciousness.

Chapter 32►Damir, Tawanda, Africa

Wednesday, 12 March
"Wake up, Mr. Powell. Wake up."

Peter opened his eyes.

"I am so glad you are still with us," Wembe said.

"Where am I?"

"In hospital. We removed you from the pit and transported you here."

"How long...." Peter struggled to sit up.

"Three hours," Wembe said. "The doctors think you may have contracted an illness from the water."

"Illness?" Peter's hand went to the bump on his head. "I got hit from behind."

Wembe said, "You are mistaken. The illness made you dizzy. The bump is from your fall."

Peter flashed a twisted smile and raised eyebrow. "I'm not going to argue." He sat up, legs over the side of the bed. "Where are my clothes?"

"The doctor must check your condition before you can leave. I have explicit orders."

"No dizziness and nothing feels broken. I'm fine."

Wembe said, "The illness is common to visitors. It will leave bruises where capillaries have burst. Your body will turn interesting colors over the coming days."

Peter did a quick scan of his extremities. "Nothing yet." He turned to Wembe. "Tell me about what I saw before I… er… collapsed."

"The pit?"

"No, the sprawling encampment that smelled of rotting garbage and shit."

"I am not permitted. It is a way of life closed to outsiders."

"Is it Tawandanese policy or company policy?"

"Again, I am not permitted…."

"So, they're complicit."

Sam and the doctor materialized at his bedside. The doctor leafed through his notes and said, "Your x-rays and blood work are in order." He presented a small envelope. "Inside this packet are painkillers to get you through the night and ten days of antibiotics."

Peter accepted the medication. "Thank you."

"Take care, Mr. Powell."

The doctor left and Wembe stood. "Your driver is here. I will go." He turned to leave.

"Wembe, wait," Peter said. "I still have questions."

"Contact Mr. Bakama if you would like another visit." With that, Wembe disappeared.

Sam took a seat. "You look none the worse for wear."

"I could use a long hot shower."

"What were you two discussing?"

"Hand me my clothes and get me out of here. We'll talk in private."

<~<~|~>~>

By the second beer at the Damir Hotel Hawa bar, Peter said, "I smelled the fetid odors before I saw the worker's quarters. They live in a garbage dump. Far worse, if that's even possible, than the refugee encampment circling the city."

"Ah. I guess not part of your tour?"

"Correct. Apparently, it's a dirty little secret." Peter laughed without humor. "An economy to maximize profits for the companies and payoffs to the government."

"You do know it's business as usual?"

"I do now, and I'm ashamed my family has anything to do with it."

Sam said, "While I empathize, you're here to keep an eye on the government's plans and keep the State Department updated. Don't let this issue sidetrack your focus."

"I can't ignore it. The situation sucks. Not just for the workers. Their families live in that filth twenty-four-seven. It's Tawanda's dirty little secret. I'm sure the government looks the other way to protect their tariffs."

"Still, not directly affecting the U-S-of-A."

Peter said, "I'm not going to sit here and do nothing."

"You have to. The American government can't get involved, mainly because it has no jurisdiction, no enforcement, and no plans to go to war over African refugees."

"Disenfranchised people."

"Forget it for now," Sam said. "Go take a long hot shower and rest." Sam rose and pushed his chair in. "Don't do anything stupid while I check to see what, if anything, can be done. Agreed?"

"Agreed." Peter said and pulled out his phone and held it in the palm of his hand. "Wait. Look at this. Perfectly clean. No sand or dirt. No finger-prints."

Sam said, "Do you think it's been hacked and synced to another other phone?"

Peter nodded. "I didn't fall by accident. Someone hit me and pushed me over the edge."

Sam said, "Don't do anything until I get back to you," and rushed out.

Peter held on to the phone and went up to his room and locked the door and slid the dresser in front of it for extra security. Peace of mind restored, he smashed the phone and retrieved a new one from his cache. He stripped, going over each piece of clothing for electronic bugs.

After showering, he lay on the bed, hands clasped behind his head, staring at the ceiling until his eyelids, heavy with exhaustion, closed.

Two hours later he sat up. He held his head, as if it were too heavy to hold up straight. He stretched his arms and legs, wincing as his muscles flexed. He dressed and checked the time—five PM.

He tapped his phone and texted Sam. "Going for walk. Meet you at 7. Usual place."

<~<~|~>~>

The angle of the sun caused long shadows that creat-ed a secondary landscape on the roads and park areas. It made detecting surveillance impossible. Peter re-laxed and ambled through the city's inner and outer markets, to the edge of the refugee camp. He leaned over and picked up a handful of dirt, letting it sift through his fingers into the breeze. The particle trail left no doubt. He stood upwind.

With the exception of well-worn paths, the camp looked like a clothesline with flat rooftops as sheets.

The paths, named like streets, stretched as far as the eye could see. Peter stood at an intersection. People of all ages sat, bored, hungry, exhausted - movement only gifted to the young. If he entered, he'd be out of place.

Peter returned to the main street and flagged a cab. "Take me around the encampment."

"It could take some time."

"How about a ten-block square?"

The cabbie nodded, and Peter got in. As he put the car in gear, the cabbie said, "What is it you want to see? Perhaps I can be more of service."

"I want to see how the refugees live. Compare it to the mine workers."

The cabbie said, "Here, water is trucked in two times a day. People fill their cans. Then the truck moves on. In the mining camps, it is different. A central trough is filled each evening. The people must share. If not, some get none."

A water truck pulled into a street ahead of them. As the taxi passed, an endless line of refugees formed as if by magic.

"If you look between the streets, you'll see the ditches filled with waste covered with lime. There are no pipes. Everything seeps into the soil. There is small coin to be made by those who clean the ditch. They are paid by the government officials offended by the smell—when the winds change."

Peter pulled a handkerchief from his back pocket and held it over his nose.

"Here." The driver reached over the seat and handed Peter a small green jar. "Camphor. Put some under your nose."

Peter twisted the cap off. "Whew. It smells like Vicks VapoRub."

"Straight camphor. Less expensive."

Peter hesitated.

"Problem, sir?"

"No. No problem. I want to remember the smell and that people breathe this air every day."

"One can get used to anything with regular exposure and enough time."

"I don't believe that for one second."

The driver said, "The smell in the miners' camps is worse. No government people to clean up the solid waste."

Peter dipped his finger into the gel and smeared it under his nose. He handed the jar back to the driver and kept his handkerchief in hand.

<~<~|~>~>

By seven, Peter sat at the back corner table in the hotel bar, keeping tabs on all entrances. Sam joined him on the hour, stopping to talk to the bartender first.

He arrived at the table and said, "Feeling better?"

"Sore. Walked some of it off."

Two beers arrived, and they placed their dinner order.

"I've spoken to our friends," Sam said. "You're not to get involved in any way. No waves. No accusations. No suggestions. No threats. No promises. Nothing. Nada. Comprende?"

"Got it. Sleep in my clean bed, breath fresh air, and enjoy modern conveniences, fresh food and clean water." Peter gave a hollow laugh. "I'd say seven thousand miles, more or less, warps Washington's perspective."

Sam took a long swallow of beer and set the bottle down with a gentle thud. "Yep, that about says it all."

"The human rights violations are appalling."

"Not your call. Not your job."

"Sounds more than a little self-serving to me."

"Peter, I'm telling you to let it go."

Peter set his jaw and shook his head. "My mother, the family humanist, would be appalled. She could not let this go on. She'd do something."

"She'd be stopped," Sam said. "These conditions have existed since the war in 2003, and no one wants to take responsibility or provide the resources necessary for refugees without a home, who won't move unless they go back to the home they came from. It's the same all over Africa and the Near East."

"Just because it's pervasive doesn't make it right."

"Be careful. Interference isn't tolerated very often, if at all."

Chapter 33►Washington, D.C.

Thursday, 13 March
Wendell Waters and Uriah Henderson sat in the Oval Office waiting for the President. Sandford entered followed by staff carrying in plates of sandwiches and crudité for lunch.

"Thank you for joining me. I wanted to discuss several issues off the record."

President Sandford had his usual turkey, bacon, lettuce, and tomato. He dumped carrot sticks and yellow peppers onto his plate and grabbed a glass of water. After finishing half his lunch, he began. "How are we doing with Sarah Mitchell?"

Waters said, "The party supports her. Her strong voting record and interviews have shown she knows her stuff. If she's caught off-guard, she admits it, promises to research the topic and to follow up— which, by the way, she does."

"Are there any weak links we have to shore up?"

"Don't think so. We haven't heard any negative uprisings from the opposition. My sources tell me her reputation for honesty and fairness carries a lot of weight."

"Excellent. When do you think we can expect a vote?"

"Within the month at most, and hopefully, within two weeks."

nodded his head. "Good."

"Uriah, what's happening with our man in Tawanda?"

"Good question, Sir." Henderson wiped his mouth with a napkin. "We know he's there, staying at the Damir Hotel Hawa, and taking tours of the city, mines, and government. Getting his bearings."

"Anything to report?"

"Monday Peter met with Kwanh Ebu, Counsel to the President, and established himself as a facilitator to assure understanding between our two countries. We also know he's being watched. He found a bug in his headboard, and his belongings have been disturbed every day. He's being careful. I'll let you know as soon as I know more."

"If Ebu decides to use him, it may turn out Vanderhagen did have our best interests at heart—but it's too soon to tell." Sandford walked over to the bar and poured a finger of Scotch.

"Wendell, is everything set for this evening's address on my energy initiatives?"

"The fossil fuel people are up in arms, their messages to you warn about lower profits, layoffs, and rising prices."

"They've had years to change their energy concentration to eco-friendly alternatives. The announcement tonight won't catch them by surprise."

"They say they're not ready."

"No one's ever ready for change, unless they sit at the low end of the totem pole, and sometimes, not even then."

Chapter 34►East Side-Soho, NYC

Thursday, 13 March
Sybil sat in her office reviewing PRAISE grant applications, each one accompanied by her standard checklist. If an applicant missed an item or didn't meet her standards, the whole package went into the circular file. At the end of the process, she'd reassess those remaining and present her final choices to the board.

By four, exhausted, she couldn't read another word and went home.

The apartment was quiet. Sybil dropped her bag and briefcase on the kitchen counter and went into the bedroom. There, she changed into jeans and a T-shirt. Grabbing a bottle of water from the fridge, she went downstairs into the gallery to look for Lidia.

She found her partner in the adjacent studio, slumped in an upholstered slipper chair—crying. An unfinished canvas perched on the easel while paint tubes and brushes lay scattered on the table.

Sybil handed her a box of tissues. "What's going on?"

Lidia got herself under control and said, "I can't paint a fucking thing. *That's* what's going on."

"Well, we both know *that's* not true."

"For fuck's sake, stop denying me my truth."

"Okay. All right. Tell me."

"I've always used my emotional wreckage as inspiration and dumped my frustration on canvas. Brush strokes and color came from my subconscious—bold strokes born out of pain and anguish."

"You don't think a Master's in Fine Arts had anything to do with it?"

"I mastered taking it in and spitting it out like the rest of them. I'm the poster child for sucking-up."

"All your shows. What about them?"

"My work went largely unappreciated. Most of the paintings sold for around $250—when they sold. Nobody got me except you, Sybil. You understood."

"And since then, your work has changed. Not so much anguish. Not so dark."

"It's true. I found light and tempered it with darkness—my emotions always raw and evident on the canvases."

Sybil walked over, kneeled on the floor next to Lidia. She put her arms around the suffering artist. "What's different now, baby?"

"I'm an empty vessel. No guts. No emotion. No fucking passion."

"What about happy?"

"Nobody wants 'happy.'"

"I get it," Sybil said with mock seriousness. "You don't want to be happy."

Lidia giggled. "Stop that. Don't make me laugh. I'm serious. I don't have anything to shout, scream, or cry about. I don't know how, nor do I want, to paint fucking happy."

The room went silent. Sybil caught her breath. Lidia froze. Then they both broke out into hysterical laughter, tears running down their faces.

Sybil stood and took Lidia's hand. Pulling her to her feet, she said, "Let's go upstairs."

<~<~|~>~>

An hour later they were eating their way through Chinese take-out.

"So," Sybil said, "is it really true the only emotions you can paint are negative?"

"So far, positive hasn't worked for me."

"Validating the public perception that only wretched starving artists paint the truth?"

"No one would believe it if it weren't true."

"I don't think Picasso ever said it, and he did okay."

"Sybil, listen to yourself. You're comparing me to Picasso."

"You're getting twenty-five thousand dollars a painting or more. Who should I compare you to?"

Lidia's mouth dropped.

Sybil grabbed the clicker, turned on the TV, and put on the news. "While you may not have any more personal demons, the world is filled with voices that need to be heard. You can speak for them because people are now listening to you."

"Oh my God. Oh my God." Lidia leapt to her feet arms stretched toward the TV. "How could I be so stupid, so… so egotistical? All I could see were my own problems. My issues are a drop in the ocean of humanity. I have the power to change the whole world." She twirled in the center of the room. "People are depending on me to tell their story, and that's what I'm going to do." She ran to Sybil and gave her a bear hug. "You're my inspiration and my heart."

Lidia ran to the door and jerked it open. "Don't wait up for me. This may take all night."

When the door closed, Sybil poured a two-finger bourbon. She took a long sip, filling her mouth with the liquor before swallowing. Shaking her head, she walked into the bedroom and stared into the mirror. "I wonder," she said aloud, "if it's going to be easier living with a prophet than an anguished painter." She waited for a sign. Finished her drink. No sign. She smiled and said, "I don't think so either."

Chapter 35▶Gramercy Avenue, NY

Thursday, 13 March

Beth arrived at Rachel's apartment by six-forty-five, fifteen minutes late for dinner. "I'm so sorry. It's been a crazy day. I've been running on hi-test since this morning."

Rachel said, "Take a minute and catch your breath. Chris hasn't come over from the office yet. I'll let him know you're here." She pulled out her phone and sent a text. "What can I get for you?"

"A beer would be perfect."

Before Rachel could start quizzing Beth about Mansonati, Chris arrived. "I've brought a banquet from the health food store."

Rachel said, "We've decided to try to eat healthier without actually cooking."

Beth said, "You let me know how that works out."

"Ladies," Chris said from behind the counter, "come taste your culinary delights."

The variety of cold salads and hot pot concoctions smelled great. They filled their plates and moved to the dining table.

When she finished, Beth pushed her plate away and said, "I happened to be in my supervisor's office as he considered your request to talk to Mrs. Mansonati when phones all over the building started ringing. Ilse Younger...."

"The psychiatrist?"

"Yes. Did you know her?"

"I saw her for a session in February. Why?"

"Someone garroted and dumped her in the trunk of her car. Been there almost a month. It wasn't pretty. We believe she's a victim of the Necktie Killer."

"How come it took so long to find her?"

"Everyone knew she'd gone on a Mediterranean vacation, so no one missed her. We found out from one of our informants who works for a chop shop. As part of the crew hauling cars away from an illegal dump, he found the body and called it in."

"And like the others, it duplicates the late Vincent Mansonati's modus operandi," Beth said. "So, we're dealing with either a copycat, or, as I'm beginning to believe, his grandson, Anthony."

In the ensuing silence, Chris put the news channel on TV and watched the report.

Beth said, "The FBI will not interfere with you setting up an interview. They don't want to pester the woman since everything she's told them has checked out. There's no reason to believe she has anything to do with her missing son. Just in case, however, I'm to go with you as a friend. No badges. Nothing official."

"Wonderful." Rachel pulled out her phone and held her hand out to Beth, who pulled a piece of paper from her pocket and dropped it on Rachel's palm.

"So," Chris took a sip of beer, "you two plan to walk into a killer's home and have tea with his mother. Am I right?"

Rachel said, "It's not his home. It's his mother's."

"And," Beth said, "she's eighty-five. Lives there with day help."

Rachel said, "Sounds safe enough, Chris, if that's your worry."

Beth raised her hand. "Um, FBI here. I think I'm more than capable of handling an old woman and her aide."

Chris said, "What if the aide happens to be the killer?"

Beth said, "I have a trained stoic face and Rachel," she looked at her friend with a behave-yourself stare, "will act like nothing's out of the ordinary."

Chris laughed. "Rachel has the most expressive face of anyone I know. Don't count on her."

"Don't listen to him," Rachel said. "I can do this. We'll be fine."

She entered Mrs. Mansonati's number in her phone and walked into the next room. Upon her return, she said, "All set. She remembers Patricia and would be happy to talk about old times. We're meeting her tomorrow morning at ten."

Chapter 36►Soho, NYC

Friday, 14 March
At midnight, Lidia left her studio and climbed the stairs to the apartment. She found Sybil sleeping on the comforter. Lidia bent to give her a kiss. When Sybil didn't respond, Lidia nudged her shoulder. "Wake up, honey. Time to go to bed."

Sybil moaned and stretched. "Wow. I must have been exhausted. What time is it?"

"After midnight. I got some good work done, thanks to you," Lidia said as she walked over to the TV and turned it on to watch the late news—their nightly ritual. She turned to Sybil, who had curled into a ball. "Come on, Sybs. You've got an early start."

Sybil got up, disrobed, and hung up her clothes. About to remove her under garments, she froze at the report of Ilse's murder. As the words sunk in, she screamed and collapsed into a chair.

Lidia ran out of the bathroom. "What? What?"
"Ilse's dead."
Lidia. "Oh my God!"

Sybil burst into sobs.

"I'm so sorry." Lidia dropped to her knees and embraced Sybil, repeating, "I'm here. I love you."

When the initial wave of horror passed, Sybil sprang to her feet. "This isn't an accident."

Lidia, still on her knees, sat back on her heels. "The police said murder."

Sybil said, "Everyone I'm close to… dies. My mother's suicide. My husband's accident. And now, Ilse's murder."

"I'm still here. And so is Peter."

"He's got Peter in Africa and you tied to a money laundering scheme. Since he can't control me, he gets to the people I love." Sybil turned to Lidia. "I don't mean he actually did it. He paid someone to do it."

Lidia said, "Who are you talking about?"

"My fucking father, that's who."

"Your father knows who the Necktie Killer is?"

Sybil grabbed Lidia's shoulders. "Haven't you been listening to me?"

"I have no idea what you're talking about." Lidia pushed Sybil away and stood up. "The police say the Necktie Killer murdered Ilse."

Sybil took a deep breath and covered her face with her hands. Moments later, she regained control. "I bet if he doesn't know this Necktie Killer, he knows someone who's imitating him."

"Sybil, why would he do that?"

"He's sending me a message."

Lidia walked over to Sybil. "Honey, do you hear what you're saying? You're just upset. Grasping at straws because you've lost Ilse."

"He wants me to know I'm vulnerable at all times. I have to do what he says or face the consequences. If he can get to Ilse, he can get to Peter, or…."

"Or what?"

"He can get to you."

"Come on, Sybil. You're just upset. None of this makes sense."

Sybil said, "Yes, it does. You see, he knows I asked James to remove you from the offshore non-profit. I checked. It's a money laundering scheme that could land you in jail."

"That's ridiculous. You know I'd never agree to something illegal."

"Absolutely… if you knew."

Lidia got busy straightening up the room.

Sybil watched and heard a sniffle. "Are you crying?"

Lidia shook her head but didn't turn.

Sybil walked up to her. "Look at me." When she did, Lidia's reddened, blotchy skin gave her away. "What's the matter?"

Lidia swallowed and said, "I'm afraid. If you're right, we're both in danger and it's my fault."

"Listen to me. You didn't know."

"Do you think he'll come after me?"

Sybil embraced Lidia and held her tight. "I won't let him. He'll have to deal with me first."

Lidia sniffled. "You're the best." She stepped away and said, "Get into bed. I've got just the thing to calm us both." She disappeared for a few minutes and returned with hot chocolate. She handed Sybil one of the cups. "Here, this'll make you feel better. Drink slow. I spiked it with vodka."

Lidia went around to her side of the bed and slipped under the covers, next to Sybil. In the evening quiet, they sipped their bedtime cocktails.

<~<~|~>~>

Sybil's phone rang at six. She went on full alert. Calls at this hour meant trouble. She didn't recognize the ID.

"Hello?"

"Mom, it's Peter."

"What's wrong? Are you okay?"

"I'm okay, Mom. I'm sorry to wake you so early, but I've been up for hours and couldn't wait any longer."

"I understand. Tell me."

"There's a human rights crisis here, and I've been ordered not to interfere."

"Tell me. I'm listening."

Chapter 37▶Washington, D.C.

Saturday, 15 March

At a knock on the door, President Sandford looked up from his computer. Secretary of State Uriah Henderson walked in and placed a folder on the president's desk. "Here's the report on Peter Powell. We have a man watching him"

Sandford stood, picked up the report, and sat down on the couch. He read the report and said, "What are your concerns?"

"Although Powell established conversation with the Tawandanese government, he appears to have his own agenda."

"Explain."

Henderson said, "He doesn't keep to the hotel. He seems to be familiarizing himself with the city and the outlying mining operations."

"Seems reasonable. What's the problem?"

"He's aware of the inhumane conditions at the worker encampments and Damir's refugee village."

"Come on, Uriah. He's not the first. Why do we care?"

"My contact's afraid Powell will make an effort to modify the situation regardless of my explicit orders to stand down."

"Do you think he'll jeopardize our government?"

"No, Sir. He's smarter than that. He won't involve us."

"So, again, tell me why it's a problem."

"At the moment, all business profits related to the mines are figured on the cost of doing business. If human rights become an issue, it will affect the price of goods by thousands of dollars per ton, which will affect big business, our donors. The collateral damage would be layoffs of the U.S. workers, which goes against our goal of full employment."

"And what about the African workers?"

"Their encampment is a just a place to sleep. The owners supply food and water."

"Do the workers complain?"

"If they do, Sir, they lose their jobs."

Sandford said, "What do you suggest?"

"Reassign Powell. Perhaps order him back to the States for a job in Washington and keep him off foreign soil altogether."

"Don't engage. Is that it?"

"The alternative may cause us unimaginable consequences."

"That means turning a blind eye to the plight of the Tawandian people."

"They are not our people, Mr. President. Not our problem."

"Uriah, it's a distinct possibility we have kept our hands off Africa for too long. The problem in Tawanda is mirrored in war-torn Africa and similar situations all over the world. If we can figure out a way to help, we'd have a model to repeat elsewhere."

"Sir, you don't want to start a war with the African countries."

"No, I don't. But what if we could enforce our current policy, and perhaps update it, to clarify our displeasure with population dehumanization. Unwillingness to adhere to the policy would carry repercussions."

"It'd be easier to bring Powell home."

Sandford nodded. "Do you think we should?"

Henderson shrugged his shoulders.

Sandford said, "Bring me the human rights policy we attach to our international agreements along with a revised version addressing young Mr. Powell's concerns."

"Yes, Sir."

"We'll present it to Wendell and see what he says. When can I see it?"

"You mean today?"

"I'd like to stop Mr. Powell from overplaying his hand with some concrete assurances. If you could get a rough draft to me by this afternoon, I'd appreciate it. By the way, let Mr. Powell know we are considering his report."

Henderson nodded, "I'll take care of it."

Sandford waited for the man to leave, pulled out his phone, and summoned his Chief of Staff. Waters entered the Oval Office less than three minutes later.

"Good morning, Sir. What can I do for you?"

"I'm thinking of strengthening our human rights policies that we attach to our agreements with other countries."

Waters said, "The policy and enforcing another country's compliance are two different issues."

"I would like to have controls in place that make compliance a non-issue."

"A lofty goal, Sir."

"Henderson will have a rough draft of a stronger policy on my desk this afternoon. I haven't given him much time on purpose. I'd like to get a first round of input quickly, so he doesn't waste his time on a document too far away from our intent."

"Is there's something else driving the time frame?"

"Vanderhagen's grandson. Here's the report. You can take it with you." Sandford paused while Waters scanned the document. "We advised him to ignore the issue, but we don't think he's going to listen."

"We could talk to Vanderhagen and ask him to get his grandson under control because it'll affect his Tawandian holdings as much as anyone's."

Sandford said, "Asking Vanderhagen for a favor is like dealing with the devil. There's always payback, and it's always expensive."

"That's true."

"If we can get a new policy in place before we have any formal dealings with Tawanda, it will not be seen as directed toward any one country."

"How about we spin it so it tags you as the 'Human Rights President?'"

"Good idea, Wendell."

"Sir, may I suggest a companion policy applicable within our own country? I don't think it would be good press to throw stones when we have our own issues with homelessness and hunger on our doorstep."

Sandford nodded. "Do it."

"I'll get something in writing ASAP." Waters got up. "Sir, I think we are in for some interesting times."

The President said, "Interesting *and* long overdue."

Chapter 38►Gramercy Avenue, NYC

Saturday, 15 March

Rachel finished dressing and checked the time. Beth would be downstairs any minute to pick her up for the interview with Mrs. Mansonati. Her phone rang. The ID showed, "*Sybil Powell.*" She answered.

"Good morning, Rachel. I know it's early, but I'd like to get your thoughts on an issue before I involve PRAISE officially."

"What issue?"

"It has to do with your book, *Women and Human Rights: Not an Option,* in which you address the problems of war refugees. You wrote that several years ago. The situations you talked about still exist. I'd like your take on possible current solutions to present at the PRAISE board meeting for their consideration."

"Sure. Go ahead."

"I'd rather not do it on the phone. Do you have time to meet this morning?"

"Sorry, I'm going out. However, I expect to be back this afternoon. Can it wait until then?"

"What time?"

"Say three at PRAISE?"

"No, not there. I'd like to keep this just between us."

"Okay. Come over to my apartment. We can talk freely."

"Good. It's a date. I'll see you later."

<~<~|~>~>

Beth drove them to Mrs. Mansonati's. She lived on a street populated by Tudor-style mansions. "Nice neighborhood," she said.

Rachel agreed. "I guess the mob took good care of her."

Beth's phone buzzed. She pulled over and read the text. "The FBI van just passed the house. Their infrared scan showed two people on site. No service vehicles in the area besides a flower delivery truck two streets over."

"So, we're good to go?"

Beth nodded and drove up to the gate. She pressed the guest button, and the gates opened.

They were met at the front door by a woman in her mid-fifties wearing a nurse's outfit—floral top with solid pants and blue patent slip-ons. She said, "This way," and led them into the parlor where Gabriella Mansonati sat straight-backed on a Victorian sofa.

Rachel said, "Good morning. I'm Rachel Allen and this is my friend, Beth Neilson. Thank you for agreeing to meet with us."

Mrs. Mansonati said, "Please sit." To the nurse, she said, "Bring the tray."

The old woman appeared to be in remarkable health—gray hair coiffed, delicate facial features accented by make-up. She might have been a model under different circumstances. She wore a dark pleated skirt with a beige sweater set reminiscent of, if not actually from, the fifties. Over the cardigan, with the top button closed, a delicate pearl necklace encircled her neck along with a thin gold chain supporting a small gold crucifix.

The nurse returned with tea and a plate of assorted cookies. She set them down. When she offered to pour, Mrs. Mansonati shooed her away. Rebuffed, the woman disappeared down the hallway.

Rachel said, "May I take notes and record our session?"

"Yes."

"Mrs. Mansonati, did your husband ever say anything about the Tanner family, his family's neighbors from McFall Road, in Apalachin, New York?"

"Very little."

"In particular, Patricia Tanner. She played the violin."

"Maria's friend?"

"Yes. I understand she took pottery lessons from your father-in-law. I'm trying to locate her."

"You're not looking for my son, Anthony?"

"No. I'm only interested in Patricia."

"Vincent never talked about her." Mrs. Mansonati reached for the tea pot. "Tea?"

Rachel and Beth glanced at each other, nodded, and accepted the woman's offer. After a few sips, they split an almond horseshoe cookie.

Rachel took another sip to clear her throat and said, "Did you happen to overhear anything about Patricia?"

Mrs. Mansonati pursed her lips and stared, unseeing. Moments later she said, "Vincent told me his father searched for the girl when she disappeared. He found her married to some bricklayer and made her pay for taking his son away from him."

"Pay how?"

"None of my business. I did hear the bricklayer died, her second husband went bankrupt, and she married some big fancy financial consultant. Last thing I remember is that she moved somewhere south of here. We never talked about her again." Mrs. Mansonati picked up the tea pot. "More tea?"

Beth shook her head, and Rachel said, "No, thank you."

"It's nice to get visitors. I've outlived my friends and relatives."

Rachel said, "I'm so sorry."

"Even my son avoids me."

Rachel and Beth exchanged glances. Beth said, "I'm sorry."

"Don't be. Good riddance to bad garbage."

<~<~|~>~>

After the women left, Gabriella Mansonati didn't move, waiting for the nurse to remove the tray. Noises in the kitchen caused her to call out. "Come get the tray this instant."

A figure entered the room and said, "It's me, Mother." He handed her a bouquet of flowers.

Without looking at them, Mrs. Mansonati dropped them on the floor and said, "Lovely."

The man walked over to the couch's side table, reached behind a photograph, picked up a phone, and turned it off.

"What's that?"

"A smart phone, Mother."

"What's it doing here?"

"I used it as a microphone. I listened to your whole conversation as I sat in my van."

"Hrumph," she said, raising her chin just enough to register her disapproval before she called out. "Nurse."

"I've taken care of the nurse, and I'll take care of you tonight." He picked up phone, opened it, pulled out the sim cards, and broke them into pieces. "I must say, this transmitted the whole conversation with amazing clarity."

She said, "They asked about Patricia, and I told them. They won't be back."

"Are you sure? This is the second time you've had visitors in less than two weeks."

"Unrelated."

"Yet strangely coincidental, don't you think?"

"I'm too old to think. Get the nurse. I want her."

"She's indisposed. Too bad she saw me when I walked in."

"I did what you asked. Now leave."

"They'll be back, Mother. Again, and again. They'll never stop trying to use you to get to family secrets—to get to me."

"A waste of time."

"I can't take another chance you'll slip up."

"I've endured a life cow-towing to thugs and murderers, listened to their whining and complaining, been brutalized and raped by my own husband, and I'm the one left standing."

"I've always admired your resilience, Mother."

"Do what you have to do. I'm eighty-five and not afraid of you or death."

"Mother," he said, the bloody garrote behind his back, "you're the best."

Chapter 39▶Gramercy Avenue, NYC

Saturday, 15 March
Rachel returned from a walk with Zeus to find Sybil in the lobby chatting with Nikolai.

"I'm so sorry," Rachel said. "I didn't think I'd be late."

Sybil said, "You're not. I'm early. Nikolai has been kind enough to entertain me with stories from the old country."

He said, "My pleasure."

Rachel said, "Thank you, Nikolai." Turning to Sybil, she said, "Come on. Let's go upstairs and chat."

In the elevator, Rachel said, "I'm so sorry about Ilse Younger. I want to offer my condolences. I know she was your best friend."

"I used to talk to her about anything and everything. I will miss her terribly." Sybil pulled out a tissue. "Lidia's being very supportive and helping me deal with it."

"Let me know if I can do anything."

<~<~|~>~>

Once in the apartment, Rachel gave Zeus a pre-dinner treat and served Sybil cheese and crackers. Drink in hand, Sybil relaxed. They nibbled on the food and sipped while they danced around the purpose of the visit.

"So, tell me what's going on."

Sybil paused as if organizing her thoughts and then spoke. "I had a call from my son early this morning. He's checking on mining operations for his grandfather's company when he's off duty. His real job is working for the State Department as an observer—in Tawanda."

Rachel smiled. "You're not going to believe this, but I happen to know a great deal about Tawanda. It was to be our, that is, President Sandford's, think tank's working model. Only a couple of months ago, Ted Donovan, several others, and I were up in Lake George devising strategies for emerging countries."

Sybil took a sip of her drink. "That should come in handy."

After a prolonged silence, Rachel said, "Sybil, spit it out. You're killing me."

"Peter has seen the refugee camps and living conditions for the mine workers. The situations are beyond appalling, yet he's been told to step down on this issue. He said visuals can't convey the intolerable conditions for those intergenerational encampments."

Rachel said, "It's the same situation throughout central Africa."

"I would like to propose PRAISE take an aggressive lead in obliterating this affront to humanity in Africa and anywhere else these conditions exist."

"You're talking about mobilizing people who ignore the reports of genocide of one culture by another. You read my book. I live in disappointment."

"If it's okay with you," Sybil said, "I'd like to outline a plan of action and run it by you. I think we can come up with an effective informational campaign, and motivational incentives that will pressure governments to act. Then we can present it to the PRAISE board."

"How could I possibly say no?"

Sybil laughed. "I didn't want 'no' to be an option."

"When will you have a rough draft?"

"In a couple of days," Sybil said, "or sooner, if I can manage it."

"If you need anything, call me."

Sybil stood to leave, hesitated, and turned to Rachel. "There is one thing I need to disclose. It may change your mind."

"I doubt it," Rachel said.

"There are powerful interests at play in Tawanda, one of which is my father's company. If we attack the status quo, there might be serious reprisals from ruthless operators."

"Will we become targets?"

"It's possible, but…."

Before Sybil finished her thought, Rachel jumped to her feet—the heretofore comatose Zeus by her side. She paced the room while Zeus stayed with her, thrusting his snout into her hand and applying body pressure to her leg. He didn't let up until she stopped. Her hand moved to his head and started scratching behind his ears. She kneeled down and accepted his kisses. "Thank you, Zeus. I'm fine."

Sybil said, "What just happened?"

Rachel said, "I…can't put myself in such a vulnerable position—again."

"Again?"

"When my second book, *Women and Human Rights: Not an Option*, came out, I made the Ayatollah's hit list because I had references and examples to current Islamic beliefs regarding the treatment of women. After his death, I was downgraded, and eventually forgotten." Rachel sat down, and Zeus dropped to the floor by her feet. "For a while, I lived in terror." She leaned down and caressed Zeus's ears. Straightening, she said, "Sybil, I don't want to, can't, go through it again."

"I understand. Let's keep this between us for now. Let's not upset anyone for no reason. When it's time, we'll make sure we have our bases covered and our interests protected. I also promise to leave your name out of it."

"If you'll do that, I'm in."

Sybil said, "Thanks. I'm glad I have someone to share this with. I don't have many go-to-people." With a big smile, she continued. "Saving the world can get to be such a burden."

Rachel laughed. "Not if we do it together."

Sybil smiled. "Before I leave, what's the update on your side project? You know, the diary you mentioned."

Rachel said, "I'm making progress. I should have answers in a few days."

<~<~|~>~>

After Sybil left, Rachel picked up her notes from the morning interview. She read them several times and jotted down her impressions as they flooded back. Satisfied she caught the critical nuances, she opened her laptop and began typing the interview for the record and to share with Beth.

Halfway through, Chris burst through her door and put on the TV.

"Don't say anything, just watch and listen."

Rachel saw a reporter standing in front of the Mansonati home in Newark. Yellow caution tape crisscrossed the screen and prominently stretched along the property borders.

The reporter said, "…Neither the FBI nor police are confirming or denying cause of death. All we know at this time is that two women, identified as Gabriella Mansonati and her nurse, were found dead. Authorities began their investigation when the nurse's family reported her missing."

Chris turned the TV off and said, "Your handi-work?"

"What?"

Chris motioned to the TV, "Did you two do the deed?"

Rachel's eyes went saucer wide. "Are you kid-ding?"

"I thought you said it'd be a piece-of-cake-interview. Go in, get the info, get out. No problems. No trouble."

"The interview went fine." Rachel said. "I can show you my notes. We talked. Had tea. All very straightforward. Mrs. Mansonati seemed genuine enough."

"But?"

"No buts. She gave me some new information about the Tanner girl and that was it, except for a parting sentence when she made it clear she had com-pletely severed ties with her son, Anthony."

"What did you make of that?"

"At the time, Beth and I were surprised she men-tioned him without any prompting on our part. May-be she tried to tell us something."

"What did Beth say?"

Rachel's phone buzzed. Beth texted, "*Downstairs.*" Rachel released the door and within ninety seconds

Beth burst into the apartment, "You'll never guess...."

Rachel said, "Garroted?"

"How did you know?"

"Guessed. Seems to be the recurring theme."

"Well, it may be her son. According to our expert's preliminary examination, the two women were strangled in the same way as Younger."

Rachel said, "Do you think the murderer hid in the house while we were there?"

"No. I watched Mrs. Mansonati. No nervousness or hesitation. She didn't act like someone who knew she was in imminent danger. I had no sense she was stressed in any way."

Chris said, "She may not have known. There are a number of ways someone could listen without being inside the house. In fact, it wouldn't be hard to set up a phone as a mic and tap into the whole conversation from a distant location."

Rachel said, "I didn't see a phone of any kind, anywhere."

Beth said, "Me neither."

"It could have been on the floor, behind the couch," Chris said. On or off, it doesn't matter. If the connection's in place, you can listen."

Zeus stood, stretched with a whine, tail wagging, and full of expectation.

Rachel laughed. "Dinner time. I guess he doesn't care we're in the middle of two mysteries."

Beth said, "I can't stay. I'll be back between ten and eleven to sleep. Rachel, where does this leave you with the Tanner research?"

"With Mrs. Mansonati's revelations, I've hit the end of the Mansonati connection...at least for now. After fathering her child and possibly causing all the grief in her first two marriages, I don't think Mansonati bothered her once she left town."

Chris chuckled. "He did more than enough to her while she lived here."

Rachel said, "I didn't mean to dismiss him. I just meant when he was done, he was done."

Beth said, "It did sound like it ended. In fact, I got the sense Stella's third husband may have had the power to threaten Mansonati if he persisted."

Rachel said, "Maybe. I intend to find out. Tomorrow I'm going to pursue the financial advisor. I believe the bankruptcy proceedings mentioned his name."

"Good. We'll touch base as soon as either of us has any information." Beth took a few steps toward the door, hesitated, and turned. "Rachel, I think Chris," she flicked her eyes to him and smiled, "has a right to be concerned. It's possible our inquiries are somehow intertwined. Please be careful and don't go anywhere near the Mansonati family."

Rachel nodded. "No problem. I'm done."

Chapter 40▶Damir, Tawanda

Monday, 17 March
Peter walked in the morning coolness, returning to the hotel bar for his second cup of coffee. He sat and watched the Tawandanese news station with English subtitles.

The anchor said, "In other government news, the Minister of Mines has announced a proposed amendment to the current laws to bring Tawanda in line with surrounding countries. It will increase the State's compulsory shareholding in registered mining companies from the current 3% to a maximum of 35%. The change is to be achieved by increasing the government shares by 5% with each mining permit renewal. This process will now be required every three years, reduced from ten. Further, companies will be limited to exporting 'ready to use' products.

"In a phone conversation with a mining executive, who refused to be named, the government's aggressive approach will adversely affect the ability of mining companies to attract investors. In addition, it has failed to take into account the appalling lack of energy supply, a government responsibility, which companies must have to meet the export demands."

Peter caught the bartender's attention. "Is that report on-line?"

The man shrugged.

Peter pulled out his phone and googled the station, found the announcement, and sent it to his grandfather and the U.S. State Department—in separate emails. Almost immediately, his phone buzzed. A text message. Kwanh Ebu wanted to see him at eleven. He texted Sam.

At ten-thirty, he approached the hotel's front door and called Sam's number. He heard a phone ringing as he stepped outside.

Sam, leaning on his car, said, "Ride?"

<~<~|~>~>

Counsel to the President Ebu greeted Peter. "So kind of you to come on such short notice."

"I'm honored."

"I expect you are somewhat troubled because I did not alert you to the news affecting our mining industry."

"I must admit the news surprised me. It puts additional hardships on the mining companies and their countries of origin."

Ebu said, "I have been in endless meetings with the president and the mining and public affairs ministers. I understand you have concerns for those living in refugee and mining camps, concerns we have been living with for some time. With these new proposals, we can raise the necessary capital to improve the lives of the impoverished."

"Does that mean you'll direct the money to your people?"

"An adequate percentage."

Peter's face remained impassive. "Enough to address housing, food, medical care, jobs, and end the sex trade?"

"That is our plan."

"And the war?"

"Sadly, we must defend our borders as long as they are threatened. Therefore, a percentage will be directed to supporting and enlisting troops for the army."

"Will the government make these allocations public?"

"Mr. Powell, you cannot be so naïve as to think we would reveal our plans until we are able to implement them. It would open us up to all kinds of scrutiny and oversight which would hinder our ability to govern with autonomy."

"What do you suggest I do with this information?"

"It would help us a great deal if your president understood our position and supported our efforts in conversations with American businesses that have holdings in Tawanda."

Ebu's phone rang. He took the call. "I am afraid my next appointment is here. We will have to leave the rest of our discussion for another time."

"I understand. Until then."

<~<~|~>~>

Peter strode out of the government offices, jerked the handle on the car, got in, and slammed the door shut.

Sam said, "Tough meeting?"

"I hate being played." Peter stared out the window. "Ebu expects me to believe, on his say so, the government will use part of the increased tariff profits to benefit the war refugees."

"You think it's a cover-up?"

"You bet. My bullshit meter reads way past the red zone. Ebu never mentioned the actual apportionment, so who knows how much will line private pockets, including the President's."

"What did he really want?"

"Me to convey Tawanda's intent to Sandford and enlist his help to control any adverse corporate pushback.

"And will you?"

Peter said, "I think it's a lie. What would you do?"

"It's your job to act as intermediary, not interfere with policy."

"I've nothing concrete."

"That's Henderson's job."

Peter pulled out his phone and made the call. When he finished, he asked Sam to drive him back to the hotel. "I've got some business to take care of. And then I'd like to talk to Bakama. Can you pick me up later this afternoon?"

Sam nodded.

<~<~|~>~>

In his hotel room, Peter turned on the audio jammer, picked up the SAT phone, and called his grandfather.

"Peter, my boy. How are you?"

"Fine, Grandfather. Did you get my email?"

"We are studying it now to determine our course of action."

"How can I help?"

"Do nothing. We'll take care of it. Thank…."

"Wait a minute, Grandfather. I want to talk to you about the horrendous conditions in the workers' encampment."

"Ah. I didn't realize you were escorted so far afield."

"I smelled it by accident. It's worse than a garbage dump. When I walked to the top of the hill, I saw it in the distance. It even looked like a garbage dump. Since I'm sure you'd never approve such conditions, I'm telling you so you can address the situation immediately."

Two heartbeats of silence passed before Vanderhagen said, "I'm glad you told me. We have no true understanding of the social and societal makeup of our workers. We made the decision to leave that situation to the on-site Tawandanese managers."

"I don't think you understand. Human beings are living in shit. Literally."

"They live as they've always lived."

"If you saw what I saw, you'd know that's not acceptable."

"Peter, I've been the go-to guy for the cartel since before you were born. I've learned not to micromanage situations in foreign countries. I suggest you learn the same."

"But…."

"Changing the subject, Peter. Have you observed any mining operations which affect the low numbers we're experiencing?"

"I don't know. The raw diamonds found in the open pits pass from the workers to the supervisors to the operations manager's safe. At the end of every day, the stones are sorted and recorded before MiNe security collects them for final processing."

"I see."

"I'm going to ask Bakama for his daily and monthly reports and compare them to those you sent me."

"If Bakama says he needs authorization, tell him to call this number 32-555-0101"

"But...."

"Thank you, Peter. We'll talk later."

The call ended. Peter's muscles tensed in rage. He fell to the floor and did push-ups, followed by stretches. Several repetitions relaxed his body and calmed his mind.

<~<~|~>~>

Peter arrived at the MiNe office around one in the afternoon.

Bakama's secretary said, "I'm sorry. Mr. Bakama does not see anyone without an appointment. He is busy all afternoon and tomorrow. If you leave your name and purpose of your visit, I will ask if he can find time...."

The operations manager's door opened. "No need to be so formal," Bakama said to his secretary. "Mr. Powell. It is good to see you have recovered from your mishap."

"Thank you," Peter said. "I've returned to finish my review for the company."

"I'm not sure what more I can tell you. However, come inside," he said, motioning Peter into his office and toward the guest chair, "We will talk."

Peter took a seat and said, "The owners have asked me to find out why the figures on the open mining operation are the lowest in the region. Nothing I saw explains it."

"I did not know about such a problem," Bakama said.

"How do you get the field information to compare to the sorting room tally?"

Bakama stood and went into an open vault. He returned with several ledgers. "Here, check them yourself."

"Check what?"

"The supervisors bring the raw diamonds into the secure room at the end of the hall. Using wall charts for grading and size, they record their finds in these ledgers and place their packets in a lockbox. Guards transport the lockbox to the company's official counting room, from which comes the official reports."

"So," Peter said, "the ledgers and the reports should be the same."

Bakama leaned back. "Precisely."

Peter selected one ledger with dates corresponding to the reports he had in his ever-present messenger bag. "May I take this ledger back to the hotel to compare to my reports?"

Bakama smiled. "I cannot let the actual ledger leave. However, if you supply the dates of your report, I will have the pages photocopied for you."

Peter gave him the dates. Bakama summoned his secretary, gave her the information, and asked her to prepare the copies. While they waited, Peter said, "One more thing. Do you keep the daily slips from each supervisor?"

Bakama hesitated a beat too many to say *no*. "Let me see what I've got." He walked into the vault and came out with a small packet. "I believe this falls within your dates."

When the secretary returned with the ledger and copies, Bakama exchanged the documents with the slips. "And these too, please."

Peter called Sam. "Hey. If you're not busy I'd appreciate a pick-up."

Sam said, "Roger and out."

Peter put his phone away and waited in the uncomfortable silence for the secretary to return. When she did, she handed the slip copies to Bakama and left. The Operations Manager put the originals on the desk and gave the duplicates to Peter.

A car arrived. A door opened and shut. At the sound of Sam's voice in the reception area, "I'm here for Mr. Powell," Peter stood. "Thank you, Mr. Bakama, for the information." As they walked out of the office, Bakama followed. He nodded to Sam, and then said to Peter, "I will see you in the morning."

Peter said, "Yes, first thing," and exited the building. "Come on, Sam," without looking back.

Sam caught up and said, "What...?"

Peter said, "Not here. Let's go."

Once they were in the car and the motor was running, Peter said, "I have information Bakama was reluctant to share. I didn't want to take the chance he'd stop me."

As Sam drove out of the parking lot, Wembe stepped out of the shadows, face grim, and kicked the dirt with his foot. A breeze caught the dust cloud, and it danced along the ground.

<~<~|~>~>

President Sandford read the Tawandanese report from the Minister of Mines twice. Once for content and once for the sub-context. His intercom buzzed. Nancy announced Secretary of State Henderson, who then entered the Oval Office.

"Mr. President."

"Uriah, come in. What have you heard from Tawanda?"

"Powell had a meeting with Kwanh Ebu. According to Ebu, Okoro's plans are to use part of the additional revenue to improve living conditions for the war refugees."

"I see," Sandford said. "A blatant attempt to make human rights a non-issue."

"Yes, sir. Powell's thought as well."

"And will our man back off?"

"He said he would do as we asked and not put U.S. policy to the test. He agreed to continue to monitor the situation and keep us updated."

"Good."

Henderson cleared his throat. "Sir, are you aware Powell's mother is the Executive Director of PRAISE? He's asked her to look into it from a non-profit humanitarian perspective."

"Theodore Donovan founded PRAISE. Who's behind it now?"

"Sybil Powell is Executive Director, as I mentioned. The board runs it, and Rachel Allen controls Donovan's interest."

"Hmm. Wendell knows her. I'll take care of it. Anything else?"

"Not now."

Sandford said, "Keep me apprised. I don't want any surprises."

Chapter 41▶Soho, NYC

Monday, 17 March

The Lundon Gallery buzzed with activity. In the front room, Lidia removed the sold paintings and replaced them with others from her collection. She took each purchased work back to the storeroom and prepared it for shipping.

Moveable wall panels provided Gavin with a staging area out of the public view. He brought up boxes from the basement for his upcoming show. After opening each one, he confirmed its contents and scribbled notes on his ePad.

The artists managed to crisscross paths without colliding or connecting until Lidia made it a point to enter the hidden alcove and check out the potter's progress. "Hi, Gavin."

Gavin jumped at her unexpected interruption and bumped into her. "Sorry."

"No problem. Is everything okay?"

"You caught me imagining the whole show in my head and noting key ideas."

Lidia smiled. "Which will probably change hourly until the day you actually arrange the show."

Gavin laughed. "True, still, I'm not taking any chances."

Lidia pointed to a box. "May I?"

Gavin slid it toward her. She picked it up and she peeked inside.

He said, "I can do better than that." He pulled the sculpture out of the box and set it on a pedestal. "Now, what do you think?"

"Your work is beautiful," she said. "Have you figured out which one will be your front-and-center piece?"

"Not sure. I have three in mind. I'm trying to visualize the lighting and considering gels to wash the wall."

"Hmm. Interesting. Let me know when you're ready to experiment and I can help."

"Thanks," Gavin said and lowered his ePad. "How's your painting going?"

"I'm blocked, hence the housekeeping."

"What's the problem?"

Lidia said, "I'm trying to merge my breezy style with social commentary. I thought it'd be easy, but it's not. To say I'm more than a little discouraged would be an understatement."

"Art is hard."

"Not for me. Not when I have a vision. There's a satisfying flow and rhythm from the first brush stroke to the last."

"And that's not happening?"

Lidia shook her head and said, "I've got the pieces floating around in my head. It's the whole picture that eludes me, at least for now."

"The process is frustrating."

"Maybe I'm thinking too much."

Gavin nodded. "Over-thinking is the creative's curse."

"You're right. You've made me feel better."

He said, "How about an exchange? You help me with my set-up, and I'll critique your paintings."

"Absolutely," Lidia said. "That's just what I need. A fresh eye. Sybil doesn't have the artist's eye and doesn't understand people like us." Lidia retreated to her office.

He called out, "Where're you going?"

"I'm getting my clip board. I like to doodle while I think."

<~<~|~>~>

Sybil approached the gallery. Through the window, she observed Gavin and Lidia's intense conversation. Her lips pursed and her jaw clenched. She withdrew into the shadows and watched. In her heart, evidence or not, she knew he was toxic and his growing closeness to Lidia scared her. She had no actual proof Gavin worked for Vanderhagen, just James's hesitation. Yet it seemed as soon as Lidia closed on the space, Gavin appeared and set up the offshore non-profit. A coincidence? Probably not. Gavin and Vanderhagen had to be connected.

She used the side entrance and went up to their apartment, hung up her coat and put her bag, briefcase, and laptop on the dining room table. She got a drink from the bar to ease the knot in her stomach and retrieved her laptop to review Peter's research. She felt sure she could help her son—Lidia not so much.

Sybil set her drink down, opened her laptop, and pulled up the reports on the Tawandian war refugees. Kicking off her shoes, she put her feet on the ottoman, sipping her drink while she read.

Done with input, Sybil's eyes closed as the information swirled around her brain. She knew key components would separate from the maelstrom and reveal the answers she sought. The sound of Lidia's voice jolted her into the present.

"What are you doing home so early?"

"I came home to work on a new project. I needed a change for inspiration."

Lidia walked over to her, leaned over, and gave her a hug and a kiss. She took a sip of Sybil's drink and said, "What are you working on?"

"Peter called me from Tawanda and asked me to address its human rights abuses. I don't think that's a big enough situation to get world-wide attention. Therefore, I'm trying to figure out how to harness eyewitness and documented reports on global atrocities reports to maximize their combined impact. I want to make sure the world and it's leadership can't ignore the problem and must address it."

"Go big or go home," Lidia said. "I like that about you."

"It's more about best use of time."

Lidia had heard Sybil's philosophy on this subject many times and yawned.

Sybil saw the disinterest but couldn't help herself. "You caught me in the middle of mulling over cause and effect, identification, and action response."

"Uh huh." Lidia disengaged.

Sybil changed the subject. "What's happening with the gallery?"

"Gavin asked for my opinion on his set-up. In return, he's going to give me some feedback on my paintings. I'm so stuck it's making me crazy."

"Are you sure he'll be objective?"

"Why not?"

Sybil sipped her drink. "He's putting up a show in your gallery and depending on your business contacts and advertising for his show. Do you think he'd jeopardize your working relationship?"

"You think he'd lie to me, so I don't smash every one of his pieces?"

Sybil checked her cuticles. "It's a possibility."

Lidia laughed. "I love you and your dark side." She took another sip of Sybil's drink. "He's doing it tomorrow night. Come if you like." Lidia walked toward the kitchen, changed her mind, and returned to face Sybil. "One thing, though. Please don't argue with him. If you disagree, we can talk later when we're alone."

Chapter 42►Gramercy Avenue, NYC

Tuesday, 18 March
She saw the gun aimed at her head. Heard the gunshot and cartilage snap. She tossed and turned, trying to get to Donovan. If she got there fast enough, maybe this time….

Rachel couldn't move. Pressure on her chest. Wetness on her face. She used her hands for protection and woke with a start.

Zeus lay beside her, his front paws on her chest, lapping at her face, tail slapping the duvet. She threw her arms around him and smiled as her breathing returned to normal. "Good boy, Zeus. Good boy." He laid his head on her chest, his nose almost touching hers, and she scratched behind his ears.

Chris turned over and said, "Lucky dog."

She turned to him, "I'm sorry, Chris. I didn't want to wake you. I wanted our first night together since the dreams started to be… perfect."

"It is. I can't tell you how happy I am that you're back."

They kissed.

Zeus whined and squirmed over Rachel, putting his nose in Chris's face.

Chris laughed. "The dog, though, is an unanticipated bonus."

"I don't know what I'd do without him. He's made a huge difference."

"Huge is right."

Zeus lay on his back in the coveted space between them. Rachel petted his exposed belly and Zeus's tail went into overdrive.

Chris said, "I think I'm jealous."

"I know a cure for that," Rachel said. "Off, Zeus." The dog squirmed to his feet, jumped to the floor, and lay down next to the bed. Rachel rolled toward Chris and caressed his midriff. "Still jealous?"

Chris took her into his arms. "I love you."

Her arms circled his neck, fingers slid into his hair, and her body arched against his. "I love you too," she said, lips close to his, so he could feel as well as hear her words. He kissed her, lightly, pulling her body close with one arm and her head with the other. He kissed her again. This time their lips locked, and their passion exploded. She felt him with every part of her being, outside and in.

<~<~|~>~>

Afterwards, Rachel said, "Does all this affection come with coffee?"

He said, "You're very demanding."

Before she could answer, Zeus bounded onto the bed, stepped all over them before plopping down in the center and separating the lovers. His tail thumped with joy.

She said, "I guess it's time to get up."

Chris's phone rang. He checked the ID. "Security client. Have to take this. You shower first, and I'll start breakfast." He got out of bed and put his robe on while he talked.

Before getting up, Rachel stretched in bed. Zeus whined and crawled up to her shoulder. "Want a little attention?" Her hands fondled his ears; her fingers massaged his head and body. Zeus yawned and turned over, belly-up. She scratched his belly, and his body went limp. After a couple of "we're done" pats, she got out of bed and went to shower.

Chris walked into the bathroom before she finished. "Don't turn the water off. I'm coming in."

Rachel giggled. "Why, Mr. Gregory, that must have been some phone call."

"Very funny. I've got your towel ready, and Nikolai's walking Zeus. I swear those two have a psychic connection."

They kissed as they changed places. Rachel said, "Don't dawdle if you want both halves of your bagel." She didn't have to wait for his reply. She knew he'd be quick because he hated it when she touched his food.

<~<~|~>~>

By mid-morning, Rachel sat engulfed in a paper sea. She reviewed all references to the Tanner girl's first two husbands, Zych and Pickens. Mansonati may have caused insurmountable problems for both men. He had the connections. He might even have spent his work weeks in New York City and gone west for weekends. Proving it, however, seemed useless since all parties were dead except possibly Mrs. Stella Zych Pickens and her son.

She searched for Stella Pickens in the New York State death records and found nothing. There might be a chance she'd still be alive.

The late Mrs. Mansonati said something about a financial consultant. Rachel searched online for the

1941 Pickens bankruptcy filing. If she could find the lawyer, she might find the consultant.

It didn't take long to find an online resource. She registered with PACER: Public Access to Court Electronic Records, did her search and found the case. The trial proceedings did not reveal a financial consultant, so she researched the attorney. She found his firm, which, after several mergers, occupied the upper floors of the Empire State Building.

She called Chris. "Hi. Want to come on a road trip?"

"Can't. I've an important client call this morning. He needs his computer security upgraded ASAP. My team can do the upgrade, but I'm the one who has to do the critical new code. Call Jack."

<~<~|~>~>

Rachel and Jack arrived at the legal firm's offices at noon. Rachel explained her purpose to the receptionist, who took down their information and sent them to the waiting area.

Before they got comfortable, a woman of stature and confidence, dressed in a dark tailored suit and sensible heels, appeared and said, "May I help you? I'm the executive secretary to the managing partner."

Rachel said, "I hope so. I am looking for the law firm's financial consultant for the 1942 Thaddeus Pickens bankruptcy case. Here's the information I printed from PACER."

She handed the woman a piece of paper. "I traced the lawyer's papers to this firm."

"May I ask why you're so interested?"

"I am looking for Mr. Pickens's wife. I have come into possession of some things that I'd like to return to her. I understand she became friendly with the financial consultant, and I'm hoping the file can give me his name."

"I see. Interesting. Wait here. I'll talk to our librarian. If we have the information, she'll find it."

An hour later the woman returned. "Normally, we don't let outsiders check our files. In this case, all primary lawyers and witnesses are deceased, so we will allow you a half hour to peruse it yourselves as long as one of our librarians may be present."

Rachel said, "Agreed."

The woman led Rachel and Jack into a small conference room. The ancient information sat on the polished wood table. They sat down and leafed through the material, ignoring the transcript, and searching through notes.

Jack wrote down every name they found and why it appeared.

At one point Rachel laughed. "Here's where it all went downhill. Pickens went to a loan shark, who in exchange for the money forced Pickens to hire his corrupt cronies on a job site." She read a little further. "And look. It's the very site where the building collapsed."

Jack said, "Pickens should have known better."

"I think a mobster named Mansonati engineered the problem and brokered the deal."

"Why?"

"He was the biological father of Pickens's wife's son."

"Jesus."

In the appendices, they found the financial statements and the verifying paperwork.

Rachel said, "If we're going to find his name, it'll be here." She went through these pages at a slower pace to be sure she didn't miss anything. "Jack, have you noticed the initials B.S.V.? They're at the bottom of each page, maybe to approve the figures."

"Might be the consultant," Jack said. "The accountant's name is on the returns, and those are not his initials. He must be our guy."

The file yielded nothing more. No name. No reference. No leads.

Rachel said, "I'm very disappointed. I really expected to find something."

He said, "We have names. Something will turn up."

On the way out, Rachel stopped to talk to the receptionist. "Please thank the firm for letting us use the library."

"I will," she said. She picked up an envelope from the desktop and handed it to Rachel. "One of our senior partners, who prefers to remain anonymous, wanted you to have this." Before Rachel could respond, the phones started ringing. So she waved the envelope and mouthed the words, "Thank you," and they left.

She gripped the information in her hand.

Jack said, "Aren't you going to open it?"

"In the car. It's sealed, so I want to protect the giver."

Jack laughed. "It's about a case from the nineteen forties. Who cares?"

"It's my mystery, so I care. And besides, if it's no big deal, how come whoever gave us this didn't talk to us?"

"Point made," Jack said.

He put the car in gear and drove out of the garage. After merging into traffic, he said, "How about now?"

Rachel lifted the flap and pulled out a yellow sticky.

Jack said, "Well, tell me."

Rachel said, "Bastiaan Vanderhagen." The name hung in the air until her phone rang. She checked the ID and said, "Hi, Sybil."

"I'm calling to find out when we can meet. I've come up with a plan for PRAISE."

"I can stop in now. I'm near PRAISE offices."

"No, not here."

"Okay," Rachel said, her tone skeptical. "Meet me at my building. We can talk and take Zeus for a walk. Very private."

"I'm on my way."

Rachel hung up and stared at the name in her hand. It felt familiar but she couldn't place it. Odd.

Jack said, "Do you want any help tracking this Vanderhagen person?"

"No, not at the moment. It's a little curiosity project of mine. No big deal."

He pulled into the drop-off space in front of 215. "Home sweet home." He jumped out and opened the door for Rachel. "Call me if you need me."

Rachel smiled. "I always do."

Zeus's tail wagged his body into spasms at the sight of Rachel. She entered the building, and he gave her a hero's welcome complete with verbalizations, body pressing, nuzzling, and licking of hands.

Nikolai said, "He did not miss you for a moment. He told me I had become his favorite. I am disappointed at the obvious lie."

Rachel laughed. "When you're not with the one you love, you love the one you're with."

"You are a poet also?"

"No. Credit goes to Stephen Stills."

"I am not consoled."

Rachel walked up to Nikolai, pulling a chair behind her. She sat down and placed her elbows, arms folded, on the table. "I've been having dreams. Last night I heard a pistol shot and felt warm blood oozing from my head, covering my body."

Nikolai nodded. "I too have had dreams. However, they diminish over time."

"How much time?"

"I cannot say. I have been through war. Many bullets have struck their mark. I see each and see all. I have made my peace. I did what I had to do to save my people. I live to tell about it by God's grace. I am not proud. I have forgiven myself and those who fought me. I would not be here otherwise. The burden is too heavy to carry."

"And here I am, a wreck over one incident, one gunshot, one death. I must seem ridiculous to you."

"Not at all. The responsibility is the same."

"I'm grateful for your understanding. Thank you, Nikolai."

Zeus barked. Nikolai checked the door and released the latch. Sybil Powell walked in.

Rachel stood and said, "You got here in record time."

Sybil said, "I'm becoming as reckless as a cab driver. It's like playing a video game."

Rachel put on Zeus's leash and said, "Nikolai, we're going for a walk. Be back soon."

The women, accompanied by Zeus, went outside into the bright sunlight.

Rachel said, "I'm intrigued by your secrecy."

"I admit to a degree of paranoia," Sybil said. "Our discussion and resulting plan may ruffle a few feathers in the world of no-holds-barred megalomaniacs."

"Feather ruffling isn't always bad. I've been accused of the same thing in my time."

"I'd like to have a firm action plan up before we put it out there. So, for now, I'm just taking precautions."

Rachel said, "You've really piqued my curiosity. What have you got?"

Sybil outlined her strategy. "…And PRAISE takes it directly to the media. We don't go to the various governments—individually or as a group…. So, what do you think?"

"You've crafted a powerful initiative," Rachel said. "After approval from the PRAISE board, I think it has to go to President Sandford for review before it's released. We are a U.S. based organization and don't want to cross purposes with the White House."

"But this is a world-wide crisis, even in our own country, and we are a global organization."

"Sybil, I agree. Still, to protect ourselves, I insist." Rachel waited for Sybil's response. When it didn't come, she said, "I've got some exiting news. Remember the diary mystery I was working on?"

"I do. Did you find the owner?"

"Not yet. However, earlier this afternoon, I found out she married a man named Bastiaan Vanderhagen."

Sybil stopped in her tracks. "Who?"

Rachel turned to face Sybil. "Bastiaan Vanderhagen, a financial consultant on her ex-husband's bankruptcy."

"Rachel, that's my grandfather. I'm named after my grandmother, Stella Zych Pickens Vanderhagen."

"Oh my God."

Rachel took Sybil's arm and walked her over to an outdoor café. They sat down and Sybil said, "Please, tell me everything you know."

After ordering sandwiches and wine, Rachel recited the *Reader's Digest* version of her research.

The wine came out first and Sybil finished the first glass while she listened.

She ordered another and said, "Let me get this straight. A mobster, who was also a pedophile, raped and impregnated my fourteen-year-old grandmother, and when she ran away, he tried to ruin her life so he could take the child."

Rachel said, "I'd say that covers it."

Sybil said, "Would you like to hear what my grandmother told me?"

Chapter 43▶New York City, NY

Tuesday, 18 March
At the café, while they sipped their second glass of wine, Sybil told her grandmother's story.

"Grandmother Stella loved to sit in the garden," Sybil said. "As a little girl, I would follow her so she'd tell me a story. My favorite was the one about my grandfather. I must have heard it a thousand times.

"She'd sit in the gazebo, look at me and pat her lap. I'd climb in. She'd put her arms around me, kiss my forehead, play with my hair, and, in a soft voice, she'd say, 'Once upon a time and long, long ago, I lived in a small town in rural New York.'"

Rachel said, "Apalachin?"

Sybil nodded. "Yes. In a small brick and wood house on a street just outside of town. Her parents didn't have much money, and the Great Depression took most of what was left. As soon as she was old enough, she helped out by taking menial jobs like cleaning, babysitting, and running errands for other families."

Rachel said, "The depression hit in 1929, so she'd have started working sometime between ages nine and twelve."

Sybil nodded. "At eleven, she worked for a woman who played the violin and offered to give her lessons. After the first swipe of her bow across the strings, Grandmother said she fell in love with music. In fact, she encouraged me to play piano. I wasn't very good and gave it up after three torturous years."

"At least you tried. I never played an instrument. No. Wrong. I did try to teach myself how to play the guitar and failed miserably." Rachel smiled at Sybil. "Thank goodness we have other talents."

Sybil paused for a bite of her sandwich and a sip of wine. "Grandmother told me about falling in love at fourteen when the soldiers suddenly appeared—the first wave of young men conscripted by the new 1934 draft.

"The soldiers lived in tents by the woods, were much older than she, looked very handsome in their uniforms, and had all the young girls batting their eyelashes. Grandmother said she was too shy to flirt, but she noticed and dreamt about them."

Rachel said, "I can imagine."

"She only watched from afar until one day when a soldier rescued her." Sybil said, "I know from here on this will sound like a B-movie, yet the story enthralled and inspired me."

"I understand. Tell me anyway."

"Grandmother had gone to the general store for some items her mother needed, the last one being a bag of flour. When she lifted it off the shelf, it slipped through her fingers and splattered all over the floor. She didn't have enough money for two bags, so she fell to her hands and knees and tried to scoop the powdery stuff from the floor and put it back in the ripped bag.

"As much as she tried, the flour seemed to migrate into ever widening circles. That's when she heard those fateful words, 'Don't worry, Miss. I'll help you,' from the handsomest soldier she'd ever seen. She described him as the movie star John Wayne's twin."

"I bet her heart went into double time."

"It did. She wasn't even sure she'd be able to walk. Somehow, she followed him as he grabbed a new bag with one hand and her hand with the other and went to the sales counter up front. He explained to the storekeeper what had happened, showed him the defective bag, and put its replacement on the counter. The storekeeper looked back and forth between the soldier and the girl several times and then made his decision—she'd have to pay only for the new one."

"Did our hero have a last name?"

"She never mentioned Johnny's last name, just that he walked her home. After that, they began seeing each other on the sly. They'd meet in the woods and picnic by the lake. She loved him and loved being with him. Every time she said that, I knew I wanted to be in love just like that."

Rachel said, "We all do, and sometimes it happens." They clinked wine glasses in agreement. "She said they sat on the bank of the river, and he would tell her all about being a soldier and shared his excitement about having a chance to help stop Hitler. She found his bravery intoxicating. And just before he had to leave town, Johnny convinced Grandmother to let him make love to her—so he'd have something to remember during the tough times."

Rachel coughed. "Very smooth."

"Grandmother seemed to think so. Her eyes would tear up every time she spoke of her Johnny leaving. Do you think it's possible she believed in her fairytale?"

"Why not? Better to remember true love than being dumped by an old man who raped you."

"I guess that's true," Sybil said. "My father arrived nine months later, on the same day she found out Johnny had died in the war—a hero who fought evil to make the world a better place."

Sybil drank some wine. "You know, all through my first marriage, I believed her story, wishing I could have felt one-tenth of the joy she did with her true love. The contrast made my situation even worse."

"And now that you know," Rachel said, "how do you feel?"

"Betrayed. I can see why she'd never tell me the truth. Now I have the kind of love she described with Lidia. And you know what? I don't think I'd have recognized it if she hadn't told me the story."

"Strange how it all works out."

"Very. In addition, if you can believe it, I patterned my whole life to be like Johnny, a figment of her imagination."

"Maybe that's why she told you her story over and over. She saw you as a hero, brave and caring, just like her Johnny," Rachel said. "Is your grandmother still alive?"

"She passed three years ago, and Bastiaan died seven years before that."

"You might be interested to learn your biological grandfather is Johnny Mansonati, and your grandmother has two brothers who are still alive. One lives in a New York City nursing home and the other in the Tanner family home in Apalachin."

"Amazing."

"Since the mystery's solved," Rachel said, "and you're her heir, would you like the diary?"

"Yes. I'd like to read it and find out the real story in her own words." Sybil picked up her glass and swirled the wine around. "What about my biological grandfather?"

Rachel told her what she'd found out.

"Wait a minute," Sybil said. "Gabriella Mansonati? The woman just murdered?"

"The very same."

"And the FBI thinks the killer might be her son? Which would make him what? My cousin?"

"Half-cousin."

Sybil's mirthless chuckle ended with a smirk. "The Bastiaan Vanderhagen family has always been considered the pinnacle of Philadelphia society. Always so proper and perfect. My father subscribed to all that high and mighty bullshit. And now, the truth surfaces. He's the son of a mobster, brother to a hitman, and uncle to a maniac who may have killed Ilse?"

"Well, we don't know for sure."

"Yeah, maybe not. But it does explain my father's ruthless disregard for...for anything besides wealth management."

"Are you sure? She must have told him the same story she told you. Your father might be honoring Johnny's memory by trying to change the world on a larger stage."

"Don't defend him, Rachel. Believe me, he's a son-of-a-bitch."

"You do realize that as of this minute, everything I've told you is based on my research. There's no DNA proof."

Sybil asked the waiter for a paper cup and a plastic bag large enough to hold the cup. She licked the rim, spit into the cup, stuck the cup in the plastic bag, sealed it, and handed it to Rachel. "You do now. Start with mine."

Chapter 44▶Soho, NYC

Tuesday, 18 March

In the bedroom, Lidia wore a clean smock and fiddled with her hair and make-up. "I can't believe how nervous I am about Gavin's critique."

Sybil changed from her work clothes to her jeans. She'd decided not to share her lineage information with Lidia until after the DNA testing. "It's always hard to hear comments about personal and creative endeavors."

Lidia turned to Sybil. "Remember, you promised."

"I did. I won't challenge any of Gavin's opinions. I'll be as quiet as a mouse."

"Good," Lidia said. "And don't defend me or my work. This isn't about you. It's about me. Okay?"

Sybil pursed her lips and mimed locking them together. "My lips are sealed. I'll sit off to the side and observe. However, my darling, if you give me a questioning look, may I answer?"

"I'll do better. I'll say, 'What do you think, Sybil?'"

"It's a deal." Sybil stuck her feet in her shoes and said, "Lead on. I'm behind you all the way with one stop at the bar."

Sybil carried her glass of bourbon and followed Lidia into the studio. Gavin stood behind the worktable, on which he had prepared two glasses of wine, a plate of grapes, cheese, and a French baguette, torn into pieces. "I'm sorry. I didn't expect we'd be three."

Sybil forced a smile. "No problem, I brought my own drink." She held it up for him to see.

Lidia gave her a stern look and then looped her hand through Gavin's arm and laughed. "You're so sweet. I bet you figured if I happened to get a little tipsy, I'd take the criticism better."

Gavin said, "Let's agree on relaxed."

Sybil pulled a stool to the table and sat within arm's reach of the food. She took a sip of her drink. "Let's agree to get started. I'm beyond interested in the critique."

Lidia shot her a look and returned to face Gavin. Her voice turned to honey. "Mr. Critic, I'd like a glass of wine."

Sybil picked at the bread and cheese as she tracked every move the others made.

Gavin took a step back and gave Lidia room to move between him and the table. He handed her one glass and held the other. He said, "To your increasing skills as an artist. May they know no bounds." They clinked glasses.

Sybil raised her glass. "I'll drink to that." Glasses tapped all around. "Now can we start?"

Lidia moved to her canvases. The finished three were turned away from the viewers. One by one, she revealed her work.

Sybil's mouth dropped. She shoved a couple of grapes in to cover. Gavin froze in place, his face in rictus.

Lidia was unfazed by their reaction. She said, "Well? What do you think?"

Gavin came back to life, took a gulp of wine, and said, "I'm stunned. It's so different from your last show."

"This new direction is thanks to Sybil. She opened my mind and heart to the plight of others. These images give them a voice."

Sybil sipped her drink, avoiding eye contact when possible, and otherwise presenting a non-committal visage offset by a slight smile.

Lidia said, "Sybil? Are you going to say something?"

Sybil covered. "So far, I agree with Gavin."

The man cleared his throat, sipped his wine, and put the glass down. He moved to the first painting and said, "Lidia, in general, you have a spectacular knack for composition, form and color—my eye travels the canvas and takes in each component as well as the whole."

Lidia listened like Moses hearing the Ten Commandments for the first time.

"They are truly unique, and I can't say whether it's good or bad at the moment, because I'm trying to understand why you've chosen a lollipop-cotton-candy palette to correct or cover the pain."

Lidia cocked her head. "I'm not sure what you mean by good or bad?"

Gavin pointed to the first painting. "Here, your adult-self has drawn a striking, well-done triplet of emaciated children in black and white. Your childlike self has obliterated the image's starkness with a pastel palette overpaint. Are you suggesting we live in self-imposed obliteration of the truth?"

"Ummm."

"Perhaps your statement says that the pain is so disturbing it must be altered into a palatable candy-like state to be truly appreciated?"

"I'd say both are true."

He pointed to the second painting. "You've repeated the themes in the crisscrossing hands pierced by over-sized barbed-wire and," he walked over to the third painting, "the opposing arching bodies where you've split the female in two by the male's sword, literally, emanating from his penis root." He turned to Lidia. "I find it shocking, disturbing, and mesmerizing—all at the same time. Far different from anything I've seen."

"I've merged the psychedelics of child-like denial with the harshness of war's collateral damage," Lidia said. "I want to ruffle feathers and get people to pay attention."

Gavin took another gulp of wine, replenished his glass, and turned to Lidia. "I think you've done exactly what you set out to do."

"Wonderful," Lidia said. "Still, Gavin, I want to know. Should I continue or retrench?"

Gavin stroked his chin as he regarded each of the paintings. "They are done so well, I can't say."

"But that's why we're doing this, "Lidia said. "Tell me what to do."

Gavin said, "If you pressed me, I'd suggest less obliteration of the underlying image and maybe a stronger palette more in keeping with the images."

"If I did that, it would change everything."

Sybil said, "I don't think you have to *do* anything except reflect on Gavin's critique."

Lidia said, "It's going to be tough to decide which approach fits my vision better."

Sybil said, "Maybe both. Why not experiment and compare the two? I'm guessing you'll have a definite preference, and that's the one you should stick with. Or you might consider expanding your vision to include both interpretations."

Gavin sidled up to Lidia and put his arm around her shoulder. "Lidia, be bold. You've got good instincts."

Lidia leaned into him. "You always know just what to say." She patted his hand and slipped away. She walked over to Sybil and gave her a hug. "Give me some time to think and maybe experiment."

Sybil said, "Good. It's getting late. Are we done here?"

Lidia said, "We are. You two are the best, and this has been a breakthrough moment for me." She picked up her glass downed the remaining wine. "Thank you, Gavin, for the small repast. The perfect complement to the evening."

Sybil said, "You seem to have thought of everything."

Gavin collected the glasses, wine, and plate. "I'll see you tomorrow." With that, he disappeared.

Lidia turned to Sybil. "You were just perfect and didn't ruin my evening."

Sybil said, "It's not over yet."

Lidia laughed. "Come on. Time for bed."

<~<~|~>~>

In the bedroom darkness, after making love, Lidia sighed. "Lovely."

Sybil said, "You're lovely."

"What did you mean before?"

"About what?"

"When I said thank you for not ruining my evening, you said it's not over yet."

Sybil lay silent.

"Well, it's over for me and it was the best." Lidia snuggled next to Sybil.

Sybil embraced her, remaining silent.

Lidia pushed away. "Wow. It must really be bad." When Sybil still didn't respond, she said, "You tell me right now or I will…"

Sybil pulled her close, tucking Lidia's head under her chin and stroking her hair. "Sweetie, I want to… buy the gallery from you."

Lidia sat up and put the light on. "You what?"

Sybil turned to look at her. "I want to buy the gallery so my father can't hurt you. He has put you in a dangerous position to manipulate us."

"Sybil, why are you so paranoid? Your father's been nothing but kind to us."

"Exactly. He is not a kind man. It's all bullshit."

"I don't believe it."

"I know," Sybil said. "I believe he's laundering money through the offshore non-profit set up in your name."

"Isn't that illegal?"

"You bet."

"Are you sure *my* non-profit is involved?"

Sybil said, "I'm sure enough to be afraid you'll go to prison if the wrong people, like the federal government, found out."

"If you took it over, wouldn't you go to prison?"

"Maybe, however, you'd be safe."

"Sybil, you're scaring me. What's happened?"

"It's very complicated, but the short version is that I'm planning a no-holds-barred assault on the inhuman treatment of war refugees—the very people represented in your paintings. It will affect, according to my conversation with Peter, my father's mining interests."

"Don't do it if you think it will destroy us."

"That's not an option."

"It has to be," Lidia said, her arms tightening around Sybil. "I don't want to lose you."

"I love you too, Lidia, and I'm not afraid for myself. I'm convinced my father has systematically removed everyone I've ever cared about or loved. I'm sure he'd never hurt Peter, so the only person left standing is you."

"He's going to destroy me through the gallery?"

"Probably. And through Gavin."

Lidia jumped out of bed and paced the room, ranting. "I hate being used. Why can't people be straight with me? State the facts and the desired outcome and let me make my own decision." She took a deep breath and sat on the edge of the bed. "Vanderhagen told me he and his contacts would make my gallery a major player in the current art scene. Put me at the heart of 'What's Happening,' and secure my place as a noted international contemporary artist."

Sybil said, "For what it's worth, I think he meant it. He didn't lie. He just didn't tell you the whole truth or clarify your risk. He never does, and that's one of the things that makes him so poisonous."

Lidia stared at Sybil and said, "Okay. I'll sell you my shares for a dollar. Do the paperwork."

"Thank...."

"I'm not finished. There are some conditions. First, no one knows. I'm not walking away or letting anyone hurt us. This is strictly to protect us should the Feds get involved."

"Lidia...."

"Say no more. I get it. Your concern is for me."
Lidia jumped to her feet. "Let them come and do
their worst. We'll be ready for them. I bet they felt
they could use me because they see me as an air-
head." She didn't wait for confirmation. "Those bastards. They have no idea they're dealing with a lethal
little honey-pot." She stopped and turned to face
Sybil. "You can count on me because I love you…
forever."

"Come here, Baby," Sybil said.

Lidia fell into her lover's outstretched arms.

Sybil embraced her wife's lustrous spirit, feeling
grateful and blessed.

Chapter 45▶Washington, D.C.

Wednesday, 19 March
President Sandford's secretary knocked on the door and entered the Oval Office. "Sir, this came hand-delivered." She handed him a manila envelope. "It's from Sybil Powell of The PRAISE Foundation."

After reading the contents, Sandford summoned Wendell Waters and Uriah Henderson. The men arrived and they sat on the facing couches.

Sandford said, "Don't get too comfortable." He held up the envelope. "This arrived today. It is pertinent to an issue Uriah and I discussed yesterday and will put us all on the same page." He handed each of them a copy and read aloud.

"All lives matter. Classifying any human being as 'them,' collateral damage, those people, not-our-problem, or any term which removes concern and recognition for an individual's humanity is neither acceptable nor tolerable.

"Let it be known any and all incidents of geno-cide; internment without representation and due pro-cess, denial of basic needs including, but not limited to, clean water, proper waste disposal, food, and housing will invoke an immediate export boycott and suspension of trade with any government supporting the above behavior, excluding non-profit monies and services that directly support individuals in need.

"PRAISE demands that governments direct attention and monies into programs that feed, house, clothe, educate, and care for their poor, indigent and refugee populations. In the absence of effective positive action, a large group of dedicated humanists will electronically cripple communications, financial and otherwise, of offending governments.

"PRAISE is dedicated to supporting and encouraging those more fortunate to end starvation, dehydration, hygienic diseases, false imprisonment, kidnapping, disappearances, and human trafficking. Our programs, as stated above, start the first of June." Sandford paused and said, "Well?"

Waters said, "It's illegal. Tantamount to a terrorist threat. Give this to homeland security and let them deal with it."

Sandford said, "Before we do any such thing, let's take a close look at what PRAISE is proposing. The threat is outrageous, but I do believe they are looking for a way to enforce compliance."

Henderson said, "It contains some of the language we are putting together but we have nothing as strong as this, mainly because we can't enforce action on foreign soil."

Sandford said, "How do we contain PRAISE when they are doing exactly what we should be doing? What the United Nations should be doing? Er…uh…legally, of course."

Waters said, "And whatever *we* do, it better be before the statement's release."

Henderson said, "We can ask PRAISE to cease and desist, citing interference with the country's impending human rights initiative."

Waters said, "We can ask. However, to get any kind of compliance, we'd have to offer a date so it doesn't appear the idea has been or will be sitting in development forever."

Sandford said, "I'd like to see the positive and negative results of a scenario where the countries of the free world back PRAISE's statement. I'd also like to see a revision the U.S. could either back or announce tomorrow on its own."

Waters said, "You're not really going to consider this, are you? We cannot get into a situation where we can't hold our position. Mr. President, you have one of the highest ratings of any president because you've been making good on all your campaign promises. Please don't change our strategy. The next election is around the corner."

Sandford stood and retrieved a bottle of water. He removed the cap, tossed it into the wastebasket, and downed half the liquid. "I am certainly aware of the hold of financial interests on campaigns in this country, and, in particular, the presidency. I walk a fine line between the interests of our diverse population and those of our largest donors who foot the bill. In this case, do I try to maximize my one chance in my one term or compromise to insure a second term so I can finish the job without the threat of re-election hanging over my head?"

Waters said, "That's an executive decision if I ever heard one."

Sandford said, "It plagues me every day." He took another sip of water and returned to his desk. "Uriah, get me the scenarios I asked for. We don't have a lot of time."

Henderson got up to leave.

Sandford said, "Don't you find it interesting this document arrived virtually on the heels of Powell's report and concerns in Tawanda?"

Henderson stopped and said, "Now that you mention it. He's using his mother as an end run against our neutral response."

"Jesus." Sandford said, lowering his eyes and running his fingers through his hair. "The reports, please, Uriah—ASAP. I have a sinking feeling we may be in a no-win situation. Let's be sure we go down standing on the moral high ground."

"Yes, sir. Right away."

"Wendell, I'd like you to get in touch with Rachel Allen. She is on the PRAISE board and may have some influence with Sybil Powell. She may be able to help us contain the declaration until it serves our purpose as well."

"I'll take care of that," Waters said and left Oval Office.

Sandford turned toward the window and scanned the Washington landscape. After a while, he shook his head, and went to the bar. This time, he went for a Scotch chaser. He lifted his glass to the Oval Office. "Here's to hoping for the best, knowing the worst is yet to come."

His private phone buzzed. He glanced at the ID and answered. "Philip."

"Franklin, I've been concerned about the Human Rights Initiative currently on the table. It is in our mutual interest that you deal with it decisively before it becomes public."

"How on earth...." Sandford couldn't hide his surprise.

Vanderhagen ignored him and continued. "You have the power to control the leaks, end speculation, establish a committee. Better yet, have the UN look into it. They haven't done anything noteworthy to date."

Sandford regained his composure. "You're way out of line and well aware I do not have absolute power."

"Really?" Vanderhagen paused. "I am of the opinion you have much more control than you know." He cleared his throat and hissed. "Inaction might result in the release of information labeling you as a sex offender."

Sandford gulped down his rage. "That's a lie. You wouldn't dare."

"Don't test me. You're fucking around with a gazillion dollar enterprise in charge of the world's economy. We're friends but, in truth, we've got someone lined up to take your place. So, you have to ask yourself, do you want a second term or not."

"Don't threaten me."

"Franklin, all I'm suggesting is that we cooperate on a course of action to support the global initiative to shore up financial reserves, encourage trade, and boost employment."

"At the cost of thousands of lives."

"Collateral damage."

"How can you…."

"I need to go, Franklin. Do the right thing."

The connection ended.

Franklin made a beeline for the bar, took two gulps of Scotch straight from the bottle, and called Waters.

"Get me deep background on Philip Vanderhagen."

"Sir?"

"I want to know everything down to what brand of toothpick he uses. Understand?"

"Yes, Sir. When, Sir?"

"Yesterday."

Chapter 46►Gramercy Avenue, NYC

Thursday, 20 March

Rachel walked into the lobby at 215 with Zeus strutting beside her, head and tail held high.

"I see Zeus is wearing a new vest," Nikolai said. "He must have passed his final exam."

"With flying colors," Rachel said. "He's now a bona fide service dog. I have his certificate and everything."

"Zeus is a very smart dog."

Zeus's tail ramped up to overdrive at the mention of his name.

"My trainer had no doubts, so she registered him in advance."

"My congratulations to you both."

"We're going upstairs to show Chris."

"You will find Chris in his apartment. You have a guest."

"Who?"

"No name. Jack's on his way."

<~<~|~>~>

Rachel and Zeus entered the apartment. Chris rose from his seat and walked over to her. "We have a guest."

Rachel peered around Chris to get a glimpse of who it could be. "So I've heard."

"He's here to see you… alone."

Rachel stepped to the side and faced the visitor head on. She considered the well-dressed man in his mid-eighties, and knew she'd never met him before.

"He said he'd explain everything to you and only to you," Chris said. "Do you want me to take Zeus?"

"No, Zeus's staying with me."

Chris said, "I'll be downstairs." He closed the door behind him. Before it latched, Jack stepped in.

The guest said, "Alone please."

She said, "Thanks, Jack. I'll be okay with Zeus."

Rachel and her dog walked toward the gentleman sitting in the high-backed chair. She took a seat opposite him. Zeus lay down, positioning himself between Rachel and the man, staring at him with intense distrust.

Rachel waited a few heartbeats and said, "Who are you?"

"My name's not important, although the group of world leaders I represent are. Please forgive this unplanned visit, but time is of the essence."

"I'm unaware I'm involved in any time-sensitive actions."

"You have influenced Sybil Powell. She has submitted a proposed document to the President of the United States that would undermine other initiatives currently underway. I urge you to get Mrs. Powell to withdraw the document and all plans for implementation."

"Are you talking about the human rights statement from PRAISE?"

"I am."

"How did you get a copy?"

"My methodology isn't up for discussion. All I want is for you to see to it that the statement is withdrawn from presidential, private, public, or non-profit consideration."

"Why would I do that?"

"Miss Allen, I'm not here for explanations, nor am I making a request. The PRAISE document will upset the world order as we know it and cannot be considered, in any form, at this time." The man stood. "I hope I've made myself clear."

Rachel stood, as did Zeus, his body tense. She said, "Are you threatening me?"

"I don't make threats. Every action one takes or ignores has consequences. Please withdraw the statement." He took a step forward, and Zeus let out a warning growl. Rachel stepped aside and called Zeus to her. The dog backed up to Rachel, never taking his eyes off the man.

The visitor reached the door and opened it. "Thank you for your time. I'll see myself out."

Seconds later Chris and Jack raced into the room. "We've got him."

Jack said, "I traced the car. It's a rental. I'm tracking it down."

Chris said, "I took his image from surveillance and ran it through facial recognition software borrowed from a client, with permission, of course, and I have a name."

Rachel said, "Okay, spill."

"Philip Vanderhagen."

She gasped and sat down. "Oh my God. I can't believe it."

Jack said, "Same last name as the financial consultant."

Chris said, "Let me see."

Rachel retrieved the slip of paper with Vanderhagen's name from her purse and gave it to him.

"The spelling is definitely the same," Chris said. "Vanderhagen is also listed as a financial consultant. Plus, he's listed as a major donor to Sandford's presidential campaign."

"And," Rachel said, "he could be Sybil Powell's father."

"Not necessarily," said Jack. "There could be hundreds of U.S. citizens with that name."

Rachel said, "Sybil said her family home is in Philadelphia."

Chris went to his computer and searched.

Rachel and Jack watched the screen over his shoulder. "There it is," Chris said. "A B.S. Vanderhagen lived in Philadelphia. Died almost ten years ago."

"Wait," Jack said. He pointed to the screen. "I think that's his obituary."

Chris clicked on the link. The photograph didn't resemble the man who left minutes ago. "Bastiaan S. Vanderhagen went to Yale, member of Skull and Bones, a Freemason, President of the Organization of Financial Consultants, and served several presidents, and… he leaves behind several children from his first marriage, and a son, Philip, from his second marriage to Stella Pickens." Chris turned to Rachel. "You were researching this man because of the diary?"

"Patricia Tanner's diary. After being raped and impregnated, she changed her name to avoid a mobster named…."

"Mansonati. The same name as the woman you visited who's just been murdered."

"Yes."

Jack whistled. "I think you may have stepped into it this time."

"Me?" Rachel went on the defense. "I was just trying to do the right thing."

Chris said, "Well, I think now's the time to stop before you get hurt."

"Stop doing what? I haven't done anything."

"You must have done something catastrophic. Why else would this Vanderhagen character appear out of the blue?"

"Sybil and I worked on a statement to address the broad, ruthless, and horrendous abuses of human rights ignored by the free world. Before going public, she submitted our statement first to the PRAISE board and, with its approval, to President Sandford as a courtesy, and asked for feedback."

"And?"

"And nothing. I haven't heard from Sybil. She might have told her father, except I got the impression they don't talk."

"Do you think the president sent him?"

"How should I know?"

Jack said, "I've got to go. Call me if you need me."

As soon as he left, Chris said, "Rachel...."

"Don't say anything. I'm calling Beth and letting Sybil know what's going on."

Chris said, "And the President. Don't forget the President." His phone buzzed. He glanced at the text. "I've got to go." At the door, his hand on the handle, he stopped, turned, and walked back to her. He took her in his arms and held her tight. "I almost lost you once...." He kissed her. "And once is enough."

She smiled. "Agreed."

As he went out the door, over his shoulder he said, "Can you stay out of trouble for the afternoon?"

She gave him a thumbs up. "Sure. Just for you."

Chris shook his head and walked out the door, shutting it behind him.

Rachel called Beth and in return got a text. "*In a meeting.*" She called Sybil. The auto-answer said to leave a message. Rachel sent her a text, "*Call me!*"

Chapter 47▶Soho, NYC

Thursday, 20 March

Lidia luxuriated in the shower. She washed away the paint and frustration clinging to her after a long day wrestling with revisions to her ultimate vision. After her purification, wrapped in a plush bath towel, she glanced in the mirror and paused. She played with her hair. It needed something her hands couldn't fix. Addressing her reflection, she said, "Time for a makeover."

In the bedroom, Lidia threw on a comfortable kimono, covered it with an apron, and went to the kitchen. Tonight, her dinner menu centered on Sybil's favorite—homemade lasagna. She assembled the ingredients on the counter, retrieving noodles from the cabinet, vegetables from the refrigerator, pans from under the cutting board, and her favorite chef's knife.

She set the large pot in the sink and filled it with water. As she set it on the stove, her phone rang from where it sat—on the bedside table. She ran into the bedroom, executed a flying bellyflop across the mat-

tress, grabbed the phone, and answered without looking. "Hi! Be home soon?"

"Lidia?"

"Peter?"

<~<~|~>~>

Gavin was on his way out, hand on the doorknob,
when he heard Lidia's voice. He stopped and turned.
This morning he'd received a new contract, paid in
full. When he'd seen her name on the fax, he'd ripped
the paper to shreds in a fit of disbelief and rage, which
passed as quickly as it had come. After some tea and
a turn at the wheel calmed him, he was good to go.
Still, he had managed to avoid her all day until now.

He checked the deep pockets of his painter's overalls and touched the coiled cutting wire. Ready to ex-
ploit any opportunity, he went back up the stairs and
paused on the landing outside her apartment and listened.

Lidia's tone dropped, and the conversation became jumbled. Gavin tried the door. The knob
turned. He pushed. The door gave. Inside, he closed
the door, slipped out of his shoes, and tip-toed to the
corner of the central hallway, out of sight and within
hearing.

He had no interest in the conversation. However,
if it left Lidia vulnerable, it'd be easier to manipulate
her final moments. He waited to find out.

<~<~|~>~>

"It's me Lidia. I need to talk. Do you have time?"

"Peter, you know I'm always here for you." She
heard slurping sounds followed by inhaling and exhal-
ing. "What's going on? Where are you? Are you
drunk?"

"That's a lot of questions."

"Where are you?"

"Outside, on a hilltop overlooking Damir."

"What are you doing?"

"Talking to you on my SAT phone." Slurping and exaggerated breathing. "Drinking beer and smoking, ah, um, stuff."

"What's going on?"

Peter's tone turned evasive. "How do you know something's going on?"

"You called me, remember?"

Peter laughed. "Right." Another drag and his tone turned conspiratorial. He lowered his voice. "Lidia, I discovered the supervisors are cheating grandfather's company."

"Are you sure?"

"Sure I'm sure." Slurping. "They tried to kill me…."

"What? Did you go to the police?"

"They said I slipped." Peter coughed. "Did I say I have proof?"

"No. What kind of proof?"

"Slips of paper."

"Peter, what are you talking about?"

"Do you like diamonds?" Peter laughed. "Of course you do. 'Diamonds are a girl's best friend.' I'll get you some."

"Forget about the diamonds," Lidia said. "What about the slips of paper?"

"What paper?" Another sip and a drag.

"The proof."

"Oh yeah. The papers. I figured out their codes."

"What codes?"

Peter laughed. "Sure, you want to know? 'Cause if I tell you, I might have to kill you."

"Very funny. I'm hanging up."

"No. Wait. You still there? Lidia?"

"I'm here."

Peter lowered his voice to barely audible. "Each supervisor's daily record shows the worker's name and a stroke for each raw diamond his team finds. The supervisor receives the stone and adds a tick mark to the stroke to indicate its clarity and size. The higher the mark, the higher the value."

"What's wrong with that?"

"Lidia, the tick marks don't match the inventory. I think the supervisors carry a number of rough stones of their own and do an unofficial trade-up with the day's catch."

"Why?"

"They sell them as free traders back to the company or on the black market. It doubles their take. They get their normal commission in addition to what they make on the side."

"Seems harmless although clearly illegal."

"Exactly my problem. If I report the negligible discrepancy, who knows what the company will do. The Tawandanese workers at all levels are underpaid and can't afford to lose their jobs."

"So, reporting the issue hurts the workers far worse than the company?"

"Yes, yes. That's it. So, Lidia, what do I do?"

"That's a tough one." Lidia paused to consider the options.

"Lidia, are you still there?"

"Just thinking, Peter, that you should keep your findings under wraps, don't tell anyone else, and come home as soon as possible. Once you're safe, I know you'll do the right thing."

"I...."

Lidia heard an explosion over the phone. "Peter! Peter! Are you okay?"

"Uh, yes."

"What just happened?"

"My hotel blew up."

"Oh my God. The whole thing?"

"Yes. No. Wait. No, not the whole thing. Just the corner where my room used to be."

"Peter, get out of Africa—now!" She waited for a response. "Peter?" Lidia stared at her phone—no connection. She hit redial and got no answer. She waited, fingers drumming on the side table. She tried again. And again. Nothing. What was she going to tell Sybil?

<~<~|~>~>

Gavin backed away, slipped on his shoes, and went into the stairway, shutting the door behind him. He paused. Made a decision. Knocked on Lidia's door.

Powerless and agitated, Lidia walked to the front door.

Another knock. Lidia peeked through the peephole, recognized her visitor, and let Gavin in. "You okay?"

Gavin said, "Me? Fine. I was running out for supplies and heard you shriek. If something's wrong, I want to help."

"Talk to me. That would help. I need the distraction," Lidia said. "Pull up a stool while I get the lasagna ready."

She went into the kitchen, and he leaned on the pass-through counter. "How are you doing after last night's critique?"

"I'm fine. I like a good challenge if I'm unsure."

"I'm glad." Gavin watched her slice and dice a green squash with ever-narrowing eyes. Seconds later, his expression turned innocent—complete with a sheepish smile. "I, um, have a favor to ask."

"Ask away," Lidia said without looking up.

"I have several pottery pieces in the basement, including one I just finished. I could use your input about which two work best with the other pieces you've seen."

"When?"

"Now would be great."

Lidia turned to him. "I... I guess I can put dinner on hold for a few minutes." She put down the knife and took off her apron. "Let's go."

Gavin led the way. At the basement door, he flipped the light on and led her down the wooden stairs.

Standing on the cement floor, Lidia said, "Wow! You've done a great job cleaning the place. It looks twice as big as I remember."

"I divided it in two." Gavin stepped into the middle of the room and gestured as he spoke. "The pile of furniture, frames, and household items on the left was abandoned by the tenants before us."

She walked over to take a closer look. "I see some salvageable stuff in here. A good project for a rainy day."

"Over here," Gavin said, continuing the tour, "on the right, I've set up a table and stored my work in the boxes stacked behind it." He walked over, selected two packing crates, and placed them on the table. He removed the tape, opened the top, and scooped out the layer of paper wadding, letting it fall into an empty carton by the table. Stepping aside, he said, "You may discover the rest."

Lidia took his place and disposed of the remaining packing material with care, exposing the wrapped sculptured pieces. She unwrapped each and set them on the table. Gavin stepped up to the table and showed her how to assemble them.

The first one they finished resembled an iridescent aqua representation of seagrass. The second, stacked elongated cones glazed in green and brown metallic, reminded her of cattails. She said, "I love them both."

To get a better view, Lidia walked around the table, and stopped, her back toward the stairs. "From what I saw the other day, I'd go with the seagrass."

Garret stepped to Lidia's side, his shoulder behind hers. "I see what you mean."

"You don't sound convinced."

Gavin said, "No. I agree." He side-stepped, his shoulder now by her backbone. "You have a good eye."

She felt his breath on her neck and turned to face him as well as put some distance between them. She said, "I hope I've helped."

Gavin walked up to her. "I've two more…."

"Not now," she said. "I have to get dinner in the oven. Sybil will be home any minute."

He blocked her forward movement, so she backed up, bumping into the table and causing the delicate sculptures to break apart, crashing onto the table and tumbling to the floor.

Lidia's hands flew to her face. "Oh my God, I'm so sorry."

Gavin, rigid and tight fisted, roared like an injured lion. "Look what you've done."

Lidia ran around the table. Before Gavin could stop her, she knelt and scavenged the larger pieces from the dust and grit, placing each on the table. Her hand closed on a metallic object at the same moment Gavin bent down and grabbed her arm.

"Stop," he said and pulled her to her feet. "It's a waste of time. You've ruined both."

Lidia broke free and opened her fist. On her palm lay a pendant identical to Sybil's. With the recognition came the fear—her throat went dry, her body trembled, and her hand snapped shut.

Gavin said, "Too bad you've discovered my little secret."

Lidia, never letting Gavin out of her sight, moved backwards to be free of the overturned table and have a clear path to the stairs.

He said, "And I don't share." He cut off her escape.

Lidia said, "You killed Ilse. I know it's her pendant."

"If you say so."

"Why? What'd she ever do to you?"

"Nothing."

"Then, why?"

"I've no idea."

The blood drained from Lidia's face. "You're the Necktie Killer."

Gavin gave her a crooked smile. "An inherited family business."

"And me?"

"I'm sorry, Lidia. I really am." Gavin made his move.

Lidia ducked and ran for the stairs.

He caught her arm and pulled out the cutting wire.

She used her free arm to grab the stair railing so she could swing her body up the stairs. He yanked her back and released his grip to prepare the garrote. She leaped for freedom.

She was fast, but Gavin's hands were faster. He had the wire around her neck before her toe touched the first step. He squeezed and yanked her toward his body with such force, he staggered, falling under her dead weight. The blood from the deep cut in Lidia's neck splashed on the bib of his overalls, camouflaged by pre-existing splatters.

He pushed her body off his and stood. He scanned the floor for Ilse's pendant. It lay by a discarded picture frame. He retrieved it and, with a ceremonious kiss, put it in his pants' bib pocket. Next, he disentangled the wire cutter, wiping it clean with Lidia's blouse, and returned it to his back pocket.

He checked the time. If Sybil kept to her usual schedule, she'd be home in an hour. He'd have to work fast. Gavin pulled out a handkerchief, wiped his brow, and said, "Fuck." With dazzling yet efficient speed, he removed all evidence of his recent encounter—including Lidia's engagement ring, which now sat in the same pocket as Ilse's pendant.

Gavin whistled as he left the basement and walked up to his studio. He had a lot of work to do for his upcoming show. No more distractions. He shut off the fax and locked up his phones. Prepared a cup of tea and charted his course. The upcoming exhibit would be his best ever.

Humming, he prepared the clay and sat down at the wheel. He turned on the motor and wrapped his hands around the supple clay.

Chapter 48►Washington, D.C.

Thursday, 20 March

President Sandford summoned Nancy and demanded action. "Get somebody in here who knows what's going on!"

She scooted out the door, clutching the files to her breast, and mumbling, "I'd rather be out sick."

Sandford paced in front of the windows. He stopped and turned as Waters and Henderson burst through separate doors.

"Henderson, what went wrong in Tawanda?"

"Sir, I've been on the phone to Tawanda ever since the hotel explosion. Powell did not die in his room."

"Where is he?"

"We expected him on the first flight out, but have no verification he's on the plane, or any other plane for that matter."

"You're telling me Peter Powell is MIA?"

"At the moment, Sir."

"Find him and bring him home—now!"

"Sir, I'm doing…."

"Go do more."

Henderson flew out of the office.

Water said, "A little hard on him, Sir?"

"You tell me how hard I have to be when a U.S. agent and grandson of a major contributor goes missing? I'm not sure I want to be the brunt of an angry Philip Vanderhagen."

"I understand."

"Anything else?"

"Hearings on the Vice Presidency are going well. I understand she'll be confirmed sometime next week."

Sandford said, "Do we have the votes?"

"Our polling has us ahead by three and support is growing," Waters said. "And, Sir, one more thing."

"Go ahead."

"I've been in touch with Rachel Allen. She understands our position. She will convey our concerns to Sybil Powell."

"Good, because the PRAISE wording is strong, and, if Sybil doesn't back off, it will probably get her killed."

Chapter 49▶Damir, Tawanda

Thursday, 20 March

Peter ended the call with Lidia. Below him, a growing crowd of guests and curious onlookers gathered in front of the hotel. He walked down the hill and joined the gathering, his hat brim low, shading his face, in case people were looking for him. His time in Africa had darkened his skin and he blended in with the multi-shades around him. Only his features could give him away. It didn't take long before he stood among the hundreds of onlookers pushing and shoving to get a better look.

The police and soldiers barricaded the hotel, repeating the announcement, "No one allowed in or out without authorization."

Peter gazed up at the charred ragged gaping hole where room 229 used to be. All he had left, besides the clothes on his body, was his messenger bag, hanging by his side, closed and locked. He felt a tug on his shirt. Turning, he made eye contact with a boy about eleven, who shifted his gaze to the right.

Following the boy's line of sight, Peter saw Sam, who moved away as soon as their eyes met. After giving the boy some change, he worked his way to the edge of the crowd and followed Sam into a closed shop's shadowed doorway. Sam cocked his head. When he felt sure no one followed them, he nudged Peter and took off through the alley maze behind the shops. Peter stayed at his heels.

Sam stopped at a wreck of a car. "Official back-up vehicle. Get in and get down." Peter scrunched into the well of the passenger seat. The motor turned over on the first try, and the car sped away from the city center. Neither man spoke until Sam cut the motor and rolled into a space within the edges of the refugee camp.

Peter unfolded and sat on the passenger seat. "Now what?"

"Now you're a wanted man," Sam said. "When they didn't find your body, the Tawandanese government put out an all-points bulletin for your safe return."

"That's not good. It means I'm stuck in Tawanda?"

"Pretty much. Do you have any idea who wants to kill you?"

Peter said, "Not for sure. It could be the government or mining interests over living conditions or maybe it's Bakama. I'm pretty sure he knows I figured out how the managers are scamming the owners."

"So, it could be either this government or ours, the MiNe owners, or Bakama's people." Sam laughed. "Not bad for a posting less than three weeks old."

"Not funny," Peter said. "What are our options?"

"We can turn ourselves in to Ebu and hope diplomatic channels trump angry assassins. Or we can make a run to the border and hope we don't get caught."

Sam turned on the motor and edged out of the camp.

Peter said, "Did you make a decision?"

"Yeah. Let's get out of here before the whole place wakes up." He paused. "I think the border is our best option. There's a map in the glove box."

Peter pulled himself up and sat in the passenger seat. He retrieved a flashlight from his pocket, unfolded the map, and studied it. "South to Adumi Road and follow straight into Arua. Looks like less than two hours."

Sam said, "I've got this. We just have to make a stop. This baby's almost out of gas."

They drove in silence. Sam kept the car in a grouping with other cars, not wanting to stand out for any reason. As cars merged, he'd move his position up to the next pod, making the best time possible given the constraints. Peter kept watch for anyone following them.

"Over there," Sam said, nodding with his head.

Peter shifted his gaze. The gas station was part of a village, cobbled together from rundown shacks. More important, there seemed to be constant flow of cars.

Sam pulled in and up to a pump. "You do the honors. Keep your head down. I'll go pay and get us some breakfast."

Peter got out, arranged his hat so the brim touched his nose. After releasing the gas nozzle, he placed it into the tank and pulled the trigger. He leaned on the car as he waited for the "full" click. Trying to appear preoccupied, he checked out the cars, passing and pulling in. He recognized the small gray car idling off to the side, although not the driver or his passenger. It had been on their tail since they hit the open road, maintaining a two to three car distance.

He made a snap decision and opened the passenger door as Sam approached. "Get in, I'm driving."

Sam raised his eyebrows but didn't argue.

Peter slid into the driver's seat and said, "We're being followed."

Sam put the breakfast bag on the floor and sat up with a gun in his hand. "I'm ready when you are."

"A gun?"

"You saw the bomb blast. These people, whoever they are, aren't kidding around."

Peter started the engine and pulled onto the main road. "I think we'll be okay as long as the traffic holds." Sam put the gun in his lap and brought up the bag. "Let's eat while we can." He pulled out a coffee and a wrapped pound cake and held them out to Peter. "Here. This is for you, and I've got fruit for later."

After twenty minutes, the traffic thinned out, most cars taking the last turn before Adumi Road. Peter glanced in the rear-view mirror and said, "Here we go."

Sam threw the trash in the back seat, picked up the gun, released the safety and put a bullet in the chamber. "Ready."

The small gray car pulled out, passing the cars ahead of it until it pulled in directly behind Peter and Sam, and hit the wreck's back bumper over and over again.

Peter said, "How do you want me to handle this?"

Sam's response got lost in the smash of vehicles. It was so violent the wreck gave up its twisted appendage to the roadway, which caused the gray car to swerve. The pursuing driver regained control and kept coming.

The two cars raced, side by side, on the empty road.

Sam yelled, "Gun!"

Peter said, "Brace yourself." He slammed on the brakes and forced the other car to take the lead position, with Peter directly behind it.

"Hold on." Peter rammed the gray car on the left side of its back bumper, sending it into a tailspin.

Sam said, "Great driving. It should be clear sailing from here."

Less than three minutes later, the gray car appeared, gaining ground with every second.

Peter said, "I can't outrun it."

Sam turned, waiting for the car to get close. When he saw the passenger lean out of the window with an automatic rifle in hand, he aimed and fired his gun, three times. The passenger withdrew and the driver lost control. This time the grey car flipped several times, landing wheels up.

Before they could catch a breath, a green car zoomed into view. The driver managed to get alongside them, and his passenger exchanged bullets with Sam.

Peter said, "I think you got him."

Sam turned toward him, dropping the gun in Peter's lap, blood oozing from his left shoulder.

Peter gunned the engine. The car leapt forward. Then he braked hard and turned the wheel. The car spun out and stopped. "Sam, get down."

Peter grabbed the gun and jumped out of the car, using the open door for cover.

The green car followed, stopping fifty feet away. The driver, gun in hand, stepped out. "Mr. Powell, this will not end well for you. We have many searching and you are now only one. I suggest you…."

Peter's shot hit him square in the forehead. As he drew closer to the dead man, he could see the passenger, unmoving and glassy eyed. Sam's shot had hit its mark. He made sure both were dead before returning to Sam.

He opened the door, "It's okay."

Sam sat up. "See if the bullet went through."

Peter checked and nodded. "You're going to be okay."

Sam said, "In the back. First aid kit."

After tending Sam's wound, Peter said, "I need to get you to a hospital."

Sam shook his head and reached into the glove compartment, tossed the contents on the floor, and lifted the bottom. "Take the packet under there."

Peter retrieved it. Inside were a new set of travel papers for a David Duggins, Peter's twin with glasses.

Sam pulled a matching pair of glasses out of his shirt pocket and handed them to Peter. "Non-prescription." Next, he lowered the visor and grabbed the papers out of the holder. "The car's registration and insurance papers."

Peter feigned amazement. "You mean you actually registered this heap?"

"No. But I did get a set a papers made for it to make it possible to cross borders," Sam said. "Now help me out. I'll take the green car back to Damir."

Peter helped Sam to the car. He put Sam in the driver's seat and the two bodies in the trunk. He returned Sam's gun to him and gave him the dead men's cell phones. "I put the machine gun in the trunk."

Sam smiled, nodded, turned on the engine, and said, "Good luck."

Peter watched the green car disappear over the horizon and walked back to the wreck. He put his wallet and passport in an x-ray proof compartment in his bag. Sitting behind the wheel, he put the glasses on, the new IDs in his pocket, and his foot on the gas.

<~<~|~>~>

At the Ugandan border, the guards checked the car, his license, and papers. They asked him if he had seen anyone on the road or two men traveling together in a Land Rover.

Peter shook his head. In Tawandanese, he said, "No, Sir. I'm so sorry. I have business and have thought of nothing else today."

"What is your business in Uganda?"

"It's personal. A family emergency."

The guard nodded and waved him through.

Peter took a deep breath of freedom and raced to the Arua Airport.

Chapter 50►Washington D.C.

Thursday, 20 March
Waters hurried into the Oval Office with Henderson on his heels. "Sir, Peter Powell is still missing."

President Sandford said, "And you know this how?"

"The Tawandanese Police have confirmed his hotel room was bombed. No bodies were found in the blast zone and Powell is not answering his phone."

Henderson rushed in. "Sir, I've heard from our operative. Sam sustained a bullet wound in his shoulder during a shootout. He's fine and recovering at Damir Hospital under police watch. He arrived with two dead bodies. I've sent one of our people to talk to him. I'm sure he knows what happened to Peter, and we'll get the full story."

Sandford said, "Peter must know he's a hunted man. Where would he go?"

Waters said, "To the airport."

Henderson said, "No record of a Peter Powell buying a ticket in Damir or surrounding countries. No record of his crossing any border either."

Sandford said, "Stay on it. Let me know as soon as we have his location. Also, let Kwanh Ebu know we expect full cooperation from the Tawandanese government. He's met with Peter, so maybe it'd be more personal than if we went directly to President Okoro."

"Done." Henderson exited the office.

Sandford said to Waters, "Does Vanderhagen know?"

"To my knowledge, no one stateside knows, although we both know that doesn't mean anything."

"I'll handle Vanderhagen. Who can we send to Mrs. Powell?"

"Special Agent Elizabeth Neilson. She worked with us on the Donovan debacle, and I can trust her to have our interests covered."

"Good. Keep her informed and be sure she knows we're doing everything we can to bring Peter home safe."

Waters left.

Sandford stared at his phone for several heartbeats before calling Vanderhagen.

After the president shared his information, Vanderhagen said, "What do you mean my grandson is missing?"

"Someone bombed his room. I have no idea why at this moment. His mission for the United States did not warrant any such action. Have you heard from him?"

"No."

"Do you have any idea where he might be?"

"No."

"At this point, we have no record of him leaving the country. He has not crossed any border nor gone to any airport. We are waiting for our agent to wake up from surgery to interrogate him and find out what happened."

"I'm beyond outraged. You'd better find him and fast."

"Philip, we are doing everything we can. I'll call you when I have more definitive information."

"I won't rest until I hear from you."

"You'll be my first call."

Chapter 51▶Arua, Uganda

Thursday, 20 March
Peter parked the wreck at the Arua Airport and entered the terminal. At the ticket counter he used his David Duggins IDs for the first flight out: LASER Airlines, bound for Valencia, Spain. The plane boarded in thirty minutes. Just enough time.

He went to the men's room, relieved himself, and washed his face and hands. It felt good to get the dust off his skin. He reached for some paper towels and checked the mirror to make sure he appeared presentable. When he saw an unexpected second reflected image, his body tensed. Wembe stood behind him.

"What are you doing here?" Peter remained leaning over the sink, his hands grasping the sides, his arms supporting his upper body.

"Many men and many families depend on our way of life. We cannot let one man ruin what we have built."

"We?" Peter turned around to face Wembe. "Did you plant the bomb in my hotel room? Try to kill me on the road?"

"My people have found a way to survive and not you or anyone else is going to change that."

"They live in shit and get paid even less. I want to change that and make life better."

"You can only make things worse. Our tick system keeps order."

"I never intended to tell anyone."

"I cannot take the chance. I must make sure no one gets hurt."

Peter stared at Wembe. "Except me."

Wembe pulled a knife and sprang like a cat, his blade finding flesh. Peter groaned as he twisted and caught Wembe's hand before he struck again. They wrestled with fierce determination—Wembe's wiry body against Peter's training. The knife clattered to the floor, sliding into a stall. The African kicked him and crawled for the weapon. Peter recovered and jumped on him, one hand grabbing Wembe's wrist and the other around the man's neck. In a massive effort, he pulled back, getting his legs around the struggling man, torquing his body. Once the knife was out of his reach, Peter released Wembe's wrist and cupped his chin. With a quick jerk, Peter snapped Wembe's head—twisting his neck and severing his spine.

Despite the searing pain in his arm, Peter dropped the knife in the toilet and propped Wembe's body on the toilet seat. He locked the door, took off the man's shirt, and slid under the divider into the next stall. Here, he removed his own blood-stained shirt, ripped it into strips, and bound his arm. It probably needed stitches, but that would have to wait.

Peter washed up and put on Wembe's shirt. With his wound hidden, Peter dashed for security and made it through without a hitch as his flight's final boarding announcement blared through the loud-speakers.

Peter dashed onto the tarmac and saw the plane waiting, stairs down, a steward with a clip board waiting to check him on board. He raced to the plane, skidding to a stop when he reached the stairs.

As if by magic, the police appeared, confirmed he was indeed David Duggins, and took him into custody.

In the back seat of the police jeep, Peter cursed his luck as his flight took off without him.

Chapter 52▶Soho, NYC

Thursday, 20 March
Sybil felt good. She had approved five projects and prepared them for the upcoming PRAISE board meeting. In addition, the human rights initiative's computer support team confirmed their readiness to act, pleased for another opportunity to undermine the general idiocy masquerading as governments.

Besides her briefcase, she carried two bottles of Lidia's favorite wine and a bag of groceries. Lidia's short list would put the finishing touches on her famous lasagna dinner. Humming, she climbed the stairs to their apartment. Tonight's combination of good food, drink, and conversation portended great sex.

She shifted the bag to free her hand to unlock the door. When she tried to insert the key, the door swung open. Her smile faded. She couldn't remember how many times she'd told Lidia to lock the door and engage the deadbolt. Sybil caught her anger and pushed it away. Nothing was going to spoil this evening.

"Lidia?" Sybil called several times. No answer.

She set her things on the dining room table and hung her jacket on the coat rack. "Lidia, where are you?" She heard nothing from the kitchen, although the lights were on, and preparations sat on the counter. She walked to the bedroom and checked the bathroom. "Lidia?"

Sybil checked her phone. Five o'clock and no messages. Unusual. She opened the door to the gallery and called out, "Lidia? Where are you?" Her words echoed in the emptiness. She went downstairs and into the office, the studio, storage area, and shipping bay. No Lidia. Her heartbeat quickened as panic crept in.

She ran back to the apartment, pulled out her phone, and called Lidia's. The familiar Beach Boys song came from the bedroom. Sybil grabbed Lidia's phone and checked her messages. Nothing enlightening. She checked her phone calls. The last came from an unknown number. She hit redial. No answer. Now what? She opened Lidia's calendar. No scheduled appointments.

Sybil sat down on the bed to gather her thoughts and consider various scenarios. Lidia could have run out for ingredients. Her eyes shifted to the dresser where Lidia parked her purse. It sat there, silent, waiting. She went over to see if Lidia had just taken her wallet. No. She found it inside her purse with her keys.

The panic started. She ran to the bar and poured a drink. After one gulp, she started pacing. Lidia would never go out without a purse, money, or her cell phone—two out of three maybe, but not all. She took another sip. Where else could she be?

Sybil put her drink down and searched the apartment and first floor again. She even opened the basement door, descended half-way down the steps, and called out, "Lidia?" Nothing.

Her heart pounded in her chest as she returned to her apartment and took another gulp of bourbon. The only place left to look was the third floor, with Gavin. Sybil needed to calm herself down before going up to his studio. She didn't want to barge in there like a hysterical shrew if Lidia happened to be having an innocent conversation with the man. A final sip and Sybil felt the panic subside as she chided herself for letting her imagination run wild. Of course Lidia was fine, upstairs, with Gavin.

She stood up and made herself presentable—ran her hands through her hair and smoothed her clothes. As she opened the door the outside buzzer demanded attention. She stopped and pressed the intercom. "It's Rachel. May I come in?"

Sybil released the door and greeted Rachel and Zeus on the landing. "Come with me. I think Lidia's upstairs with Gavin. It'll be fun. You'll get a chance to see his studio." She led the way.

At the top of the stairs, they found the studio door propped open. Sybil knocked for courtesy, and they went in, passing the drying shelves and the glazing table. They found Gavin, eyes closed, sitting at his potter's wheel, wet hands engulfing a large clump of clay.

Sybil said, "Hello, Gavin."

He ignored her.

She peered into every corner of the room before she said, "Where's Lidia?"

Gavin gave no indication he heard her.

She repeated her question and shook his shoulder.

Zeus had his nose in the air, sniffing and whining, while pulling at his leash. Rachel had never seen him so agitated. She got the dog's attention and said,

"Sit." Zeus obeyed with great difficulty—his butt would not stay still.

Sybil's lack of restraint superseded Zeus's. Her frustration erupted. She stood in front of Gavin. Stamped her foot. Shouted. "Gavin. Lidia."

He didn't even jump. If anything, he leaned in more, hands caressing the clay, and said, "The moment of perfect alignment. Experience it. Don't rush."

Rachel's hand flew to her mouth to help stifle a scream of recognition. She scrambled for her phone and texted Jack, waiting in the car. "*911 call beth asap 3rd floor.*" She slid the phone into her pocket, shortened Zeus's leash, took a few steps forward, and touched her friend's elbow. "Sybil, let's go."

When Sybil didn't move, Rachel reached for her arm, but she jerked away and hooked her hand around Gavin's forearm. "Lidia. Where is she?"

This time, when he said, "The moment….," she jolted his arm and the clay moved to the outer edge of the wheel, escaping his grasp. Gavin jumped to his feet, hands balled into fists. "You bitch."

Zeus started barking, straining forward.

Gavin and Sybil were nose to nose when Jack catapulted into the room. He flew by Rachel and put his hands between the confronting two. "Let's calm down. Everyone, take a step back and see if we can work this out."

Nobody moved—waiting.

Gavin looked at Jack, raised his hands, and stepped away.

Sybil tried to take a step toward Gavin. Jack stopped her. He said, "There, that's better."

Zeus dropped to the floor. Rachel said, "Good boy." Believing him to be relaxed, she released the tension on the leash. Seconds later, she heard the low growl before the dog charged Gavin. At the last moment, Zeus leaped at the man's chest.

Gavin shoved the dog away with one swipe of his massive hand. Zeus landed with a crash.

Rachel let out a screech and ran to the dog's side.

While Jack's attention went to Rachel, Sybil stepped forward and slapped Gavin across the face. "Answer me. Where's Lidia?"

Before Gavin could retaliate, Jack was back. He stepped in to restrain him. At the same time, Rachel jumped up and yanked Sybil out of Gavin's reach. "Sybil. Come with me."

Sybil jerked free. "I'm not going anywhere until I find Lidia. Where is she?"

Gavin shot back. "How would I know?"

Jack, now between them, his arms outstretched to separate them, said, "Easy everyone. Easy."

The stairwell echoed with footfalls. Seconds later, two policemen rushed in.

Gavin pointed to the police and said, "Thank God you're here. These people are trespassing and," he pointed at Sybil, "she attacked me. I want to press charges."

The taller of the two policemen walked toward Sybil, and the other pulled out his notebook and pen.

Zeus wobbled to his feet and shook his body.

"Wait," Rachel said, standing up, leash in hand. "Leave her alone. It's him," she pointed at Gavin. "He's the man you want."

Gavin said, "These women are harassing me."

Rachel said, "Like hell. Officers, that man's name is Anthony Mansonati, and he's wanted for questioning in the death of Gabriella Mansonati and her nurse."

Gavin shot back. "She doesn't know what she's talking about. Get these people out of here."

She refused to be silenced. "He's also wanted for questioning in the Necktie Killer murders."

Gavin strained against Jack's palm planted in the center of his chest. "I repeat, get these people out of my studio."

More footfalls in the stairwell. Beth and Eric dashed in, badges out. Beth said, "FBI Special Agents Neilson and Jarrod. Jack, what's going on?"

Pointing to Gavin, Rachel said, "Beth, he's Anthony Mansonati."

Jack stepped aside as Eric approached Gavin and said, "Is that true? Are you Anthony Mansonati?"

Gavin stuck to his guns. "These people are trespassing, and Sybil attacked me. I want to press charges."

Beth addressed Rachel. "How do you know? What proof do you have?"

Rachel said, "I knew as soon as I heard him quote his grandfather, using the exact same words as Patricia Tanner used in her diary. No one else would know."

Gavin's jaw dropped. "Are you fucking kidding me?"

Beth said, "Rachel, what did he say?"

"He said, 'The moment of perfect alignment. Experience it. Don't rush.' It's all in the diary. They're the same words Patricia wrote."

Gavin said, "You have no proof."

Sybil said, "They will have. I've given them a sample of my DNA."

Beth said, "It's been processed. We'll compare it to yours."

Gavin said, "What'll that prove?"

Sybil said, "If they match, you're my half-cousin because our fathers were half-brothers."

Gavin shook his head. "You and me? No way. You've got the wrong man."

Eric cuffed Gavin and read him his rights. "Let's go and figure this all out," he said as he steered the man out of the room. As they passed Zeus, he jumped on Gavin, pawing at the man's chest and whining.

Rachel pulled him off. "He must smell something on Gavin. Zeus's been agitated since we got here."

Sybil ran forward and pleaded with Eric. "Wait. He's got to tell me where Lidia is."

Eric said, "I'll find out what's going on. Don't worry." He turned to Jack and said, "You, come with me. I'll need your statement."

The policemen turned to leave. Beth stopped them. "Wait, let's listen to Sybil."

Sybil recounted her search for Lidia—the phone, bag, wallet, and building search. "She'd never have gone anywhere without her phone or money, and definitely not without both."

Beth said to the police, "Search the place, top to bottom. I'll take everyone else to the apartment downstairs." Beth put her arm around the Sybil's waist for support. "Come on. Stay strong. We'll find Lidia."

Sybil, Rachel, and Beth entered the apartment and came face to face with Philip and James Vanderhagen. Sybil stiffened.

Vanderhagen raised a hand. "Don't say anything. I'm merely here to tell you, in person, Peter's gone missing."

Chapter 53►Arua, Uganda

Thursday, 20 March

"So, tell me, Mr. David Duggins, how is it you've arisen from the grave?"

Peter raised his hand in his defense. "Chief Inspector, I admit I'm not Duggins. My real name is Peter Powell. My documents are in the messenger bag on your desk."

"Ah, yes." The Chief Inspector held up the two passports. "Were you aware it is illegal for one person to possess two different passports, with two separate identities?"

"I had to use the false Duggins passport to get out of Tawanda."

"I have checked. The Tawandian Police are not looking for you in connection with a crime, merely to determine your whereabouts."

"Someone tried to kill me by blowing up my hotel room. They chased me to the border and tried to kill me. I have no idea who. Or even why."

"You thought it might be the police?"

"I didn't care. I just wanted to get home alive."

"And the illegal passport?"

"A deception so I couldn't be traced."

"Why?"

"I can't say. It would get a lot of people in trouble."

The Chief Inspector chuckled. "Very good, sir. I am impressed with your ability to counter-punch with the guile of a child." The man leaned forward, elbows on his desk. "I have been at this job far longer than you have been in Africa. I have talked with smugglers, killers, pickpockets, and thieves, all of whom sat in the very same seat as you. So, while I can tell you are a master at avoiding my questions, you should know I am a master of getting to the truth."

"I am telling you the truth."

"You are telling me half-truths." He waved his hand and the two officers in the room grabbed Peter's upper arms. "We will talk again later."

"No. I need to get…."

"Need?" The Chief Inspector half smiled. "The only thing you need to do is tell me the truth. Take your time because I have all the time in the world. I am in my own country. I will go home to my family, play with my grandchildren, eat a hearty meal, have sex with my wife, and sleep soundly until morning. You will not."

The officers hauled Peter to his feet and kicked the chair out of the way. The Chief Inspector placed a pile of folders on his desk and opened the first, ignoring the commotion.

Peter struggled against the officers. "Chief Inspector, I'll tell you what I know in private, for your ears only. I can't take the chance idle gossip may ruin thousands of lives."

The Chief Inspector looked up and nodded. The two police officers left, closing the door behind them. Peter sat down and told his story.

The Chief Inspector said, "Do you have proof of fraud with you?"

"No. But I can look at any original daily count and decipher it. You see, the only way into the mining area, much less review the process, is as an authorized agent of the company. My grandfather, Philip Vanderhagen, gave me the permissions and instructions. I am Peter Powell."

An officer knocked and came in with a fist full of papers, placed them on the desk, and stood by the door. The Chief Inspector reviewed the information. "I see there is a new police inquiry. Mr. Bakama claims Peter Powell stole from him and put his job at risk." He looked at Peter. "This supports your account."

The Chief Inspector pushed the papers aside and picked up another set. "These documents are from the United States State Department confirming the documents hidden in your pouch and stating your fingerprints match those on file." He placed the papers on top of the others.

Peter said, "So I can go?"

"You have not asked about Sam."

"Is he okay?"

"He is. The police picked him up for erratic driving. His story matched yours. He's been released and received treatment for his shoulder."

Peter let out a sigh of relief.

"One last question." The man's gaze fell to Peter's bandaged arm. "Do you want to tell me about your injury?"

Peter's hand covered the spot of blood oozing through his makeshift bandage on to his shirt's fabric. "It's nothing."

"That's what I thought you'd say." The Chief Inspector shuffled papers on his desk and then looked at Peter. "The American Embassy has sent a car for you and will arrange for your immediate return to the U.S. I leave it up to your superiors to clean up whatever mess you have left in Tawanda. This officer will accompany you out. You may retrieve your pouch at the front desk. Now leave before I change my mind."

From his window, the Chief Inspector had an unobstructed view of the police station's front entrance. As the U.S. Embassy car pulled away, his phone rang.

"Sir, a man's dead body has been reported at Arua Airport. A cleaner discovered him sitting on a toilet in a locked washroom stall."

Chapter 54▶Soho, NYC

Thursday, 20 March

Somewhere deep in Sybil's soul the cry began and erupted from her throat in a blood-curdling wail. She fled to her bedroom and dropped onto the bed, hugging herself and sobbing. Her body shook with despair until calmed by exhaustion.

When she returned to the living room, Sybil confronted her father.

"You did this." She slapped him across the face. "You've stolen him from me and probably gotten him killed." She went to slap him again. This time he caught her wrist.

"Be careful," Vanderhagen said, "before you say or do something you'll regret."

Sybil laughed. "I don't think that's even possible." She went to the bar, poured herself a drink, and took a sip. She put the glass down and faced her father. "Look at you all smug and confident. You finally have me where you want me, stripped of every meaningful relationship, devastated, with only you to turn to."

He said, "I have no idea what you're talking about."

"Liar." She went nose to nose with him. "Where's Lidia?"

The police stood in the doorway talking to Beth. She listened and spoke to Sybil. "Lidia isn't in Gavin's place or in the attic crawl space. Are you sure she's not here, in the apartment?"

"Absolutely."

Beth spoke to the policemen. "Please go through the first floor and the basement."

"Oh my God," Sybil said. "The basement's where Gavin stores his stuff." She flew out of the room, down the inner staircase to the gallery, through the workroom to the basement door. She flung it open and flipped on the light. "Lidia. Lidia. Where are you?" She descended the stairs and stopped on the last one. "Lidia?"

Beth, Rachel, Zeus, and the police were behind her.

Beth said, "Sybil, wait here. Let us look for her."

Sybil nodded and flattened against the wall so people could pass her. Rachel and Zeus stayed by her side, letting the professionals handle the search.

The two policemen were rummaging through the tenant debris on the left while Beth examined the table and floor by Gavin's boxes. She said, "This floor's been swept recently."

They said, "Not seeing any disturbance or hiding places."

Zeus stood and began whining, shifting his weight, and straining against his leash. When Rachel tried to calm him, his sensitive nose pointed in one direction. She patted her dog and said, "Beth. I think Zeus knows where to look," and held out the leash to Beth.

Zeus led Beth to a large box, positioned behind all the others, next to the far wall.

Zeus sat and barked.

Beth leaned over the box, straightened, and put on a pair of vinyl gloves. Once again, she examined the box, this time opening the top flaps. With fingertips and flashlight, she got her answer. Pulling out her cell phone, she called Eric. "We found something… In the basement… Send a team. The officers with me will secure the site."

Beth put the phone away and walked Zeus back to Rachel, gave her the leash, and turned to Sybil. "I'm so sorry."

Sybil's face contorted with horror as she collapsed, chanting, "Oh no. Oh no. Oh no."

Beth looked up at Rachel and then up the stairs.

Rachel understood. "Come on, Zeus, let's go."

Beth knelt down next to Sybil. "Come with me, Sybil. Let me help you get upstairs."

Sybil shook her head and pushed Beth's hand away. "No. Have… to be… here for… Lidia."

Beth persisted and brought Sybil back to the apartment where Rachel and Zeus waited with Philip and James Vanderhagen.

Sybil sank into the couch. Rachel brought her the rest of her drink, which she finished in one gulp and held up the glass. "Another." Rachel did as she asked and sat down next to her.

Vanderhagen said, "What's going on?"

Beth said, "We're investigating the contents of a box. I'm waiting for our forensic team."

Sybil finished the second drink, her body now limp and her expression dazed. Without warning, she clutched Rachel's arm and stared at Beth. "Tell me."

Rachel and Beth exchanged glances. Beth cleared her throat and said, "We found… Lidia. We believe

Gavin killed her. At headquarters, Eric frisked him and found the garrote as well as two pieces of jewelry." She tapped her phone. "Can you identify these?" She showed Sybil the items.

Sybil groaned, tears flowed down her cheeks. "Fucking bastard. That's Ilse's pendant and Lidia's engagement ring."

Beth called Eric with the information and returned to Sybil with a box of tissues. "Eric's going to keep me updated. If there's anything else, I'll let you know immediately."

Sybil lapsed into noiseless anguish—broken only by the occasional sound of tissues, snatched from the box, two or three at a time.

The Vanderhagen men stood between the bar and the window—out of the way and with a full view of the room. Philip looked at his watch and nudged James, who answered with a shrug.

Rachel looked up and realized no one had spoken since Sybil broke down. She figured enough time had passed in silence. She patted Sybil's shoulder and stood. "Is anyone hungry? I'm going to check the fridge and then order in. Sybil's got to have something to eat." She looked around and got no response, so she made her way to the kitchen.

Vanderhagen stepped forward and said to Sybil, "My condolences."

Sybil sprang to her feet and responded through clenched teeth. "This is all your fault."

Vanderhagen raised his chin and adjusted his jacket. "You're upset."

Sybil, her fists balled, nails biting into her palms, approached him. Her strained voice clipped her words as she said, "You hated her. Used her."

"I did no such thing," Vanderhagen said, smooth as ever. "I hardly knew the woman."

Sybil poked him in the chest. "Admit it. Tell the truth for once in your life, mister bigshot-master-player-global-manipulator."

"Sybil," Vanderhagen said, brushing her hand aside. "I know it's the liquor talking. To preserve both our dignities, I'm going to ignore your outrageous accusation. Perhaps you should consider resting."

She glared at him and turned away. "Ilse, Lidia, and, oh God, maybe even Peter." She faced him again, tears trickling down her cheeks. "You killed them all."

"My dear, your assertions are baseless."

"How about Peter? Huh? I'll bet you're behind his posting to Africa."

"How...."

"Tell him," Sybil said turning to Rachel, who stood behind the counter dividing the kitchen from the main room. "Tell him how he used his own nephew as a contract killer."

Vanderhagen said, "Nephew? What are you talking about?"

James said, "Yes, what nephew?"

On the edge of hysteria, Sybil started laughing. "You two think you're so sophisticated and beyond reproach when you're nothing but mobster seed, grown in better soil, but rotten anyway." She walked over to the counter and picked up a cracker. "My biological grandfather, your father, was the infamous Johnny Mansonati—mobster, hitman, rapist, and pedophile. Gavin's real name is Anthony Mansonati." She gave her father a crooked smile. "Your half-nephew."

She shifted her gaze to James. "Your first half-cousin." She put the food down and took a step toward Philip. "When people find out, you'll be laughed off your precious pedestal."

Vanderhagen maintained his poker face throughout Sybil's tirade. With a voice tightened by rage, he said, "You know this how?"

"I told her," Rachel said. "Agent Beth Neilson," she nodded toward Beth, "found, and I researched, the diary of fourteen-year-old Patricia Tanner. Raped by Mansonati, she kept his baby—you, Mr. Vanderhagen. Under the name of Stella Zych Pickens, she married your stepfather, the man who adopted you."

Vanderhagen said, "Absurd."

James said, "Impossible."

Beth said, "All true."

"I don't believe a word of it, "Vanderhagen said. "Neither will anyone else."

Beth's phone buzzed. She read the text and looked at Vanderhagen. "Eric confirms Sybil's and Anthony's DNA are a match."

Sybil said, "That proves it. Thanks to you and Anthony, I've got no one left. Ilse's gone. My beautiful, talented Lidia's gone. And my precious Peter is MIA, possibly dead." Sybil grabbed the back of a chair to keep from collapsing and slid onto the seat, sobbing.

Rachel came out of the kitchen and handed Sybil a glass of water. She took it and flung it across the room. James looked up just in time to deflect the glass, batting it into the mirror, which shattered.

Vanderhagen said, "James deserved that. He's played a major role in all my, our, decisions."

James's mouth dropped open.

Sybil blew her nose. "Since when?"

"Since he came of age."

"When?"

"At twenty-one."

Sybil got to her feet, staggered, and used the back of a chair to regain her balance. Eyes on James, she said, "You. You knew, you cretin, that Father pimped me out?"

James, now ashen faced, hands up in denial, said, "I had no idea."

Vanderhagen said, "Don't be modest, James. You suggested it."

"No, no," James said. "I only verbalized a fleeting thought as I pondered my rook's move to d4."

Instant comprehension and revulsion tightened every muscle in her body. Enraged, she shrieked, "You were playing with chess pieces and my life?"

"No. It wasn't like that," James said. "We'd play and conjure up scenarios and do hypothetical risk analysis. It was just a game. I never expected Father to actually consider my babbling."

Vanderhagen said to James, "How else were you to learn the repercussions of powerful ideas?"

Sybil's face turned red, and her body began to shake. Rachel went to her side and put an arm around her waist and the other on her arm to support her.

"Not your fault?" Sybil said. "Mother disagreed with you, and you had her thrown from the roof." Sybil laughed. "Not your fault. Yeah, that's going to sound great in court."

James said, "Nobody's going to court."

Sybil said, "Someone has to pay for murdering Lidia." She pointed her fingers at her brother and father. "And that's going to be you two."

"Sybil," James said. "You're distressed. Get a good night's sleep. When you're thinking clearly, we'll discuss a course of action."

"Wait a minute," Beth said, entering the fray. She faced Vanderhagen and said, "You followed the ideas of an adolescent male's partially formed brain to teach him responsibility after the fact?"

Vanderhagen gave her a wry smile. "I see you have a problem with that."

Beth said, "You're the one with the problem. You've just made James culpable for actions made with or without his knowledge."

James, recovered from his father's accusation, said, "We have done nothing wrong."

Rachel said, "Oh, I don't know. Mr. Vanderhagen threatened me."

Vanderhagen said, "Ridiculous. I simply let you know your Human Rights Initiative, if pursued, would severely impact global initiatives already in place, and there would be consequences. I never said there would be personal repercussions of any kind."

Rachel said, "And I told Sybil about our meeting. That's when we decided to remove my name and submit the proposal under PRAISE, with Sybil as the signatory."

Vanderhagen lifted an eyebrow but said nothing.

Sybil said, "Don't you dare look surprised. You knew, you bastard. You found out your own daughter planned to sabotage your perpetuation of the status quo." She paused. "And you couldn't kill me, so you went after Lidia."

"Preposterous."

"You killed Lidia, whether you pulled the trigger or not. And you did it just like that." Sybil snapped her fingers.

Vanderhagen said, "She...."

"Lidia. Her name was Lidia Lundon. She was my wife."

Vanderhagen cleared his throat. "Miss Lundon...."

"Mrs. Lundon-Powell."

"Mrs. Lundon-Powell played a key role in the cartel re-establishing funding for our world-wide oversight activities. Her first show, a more than passable tribute to the hippie years, attracted an audience. Her new work did not appear promising."

"How…." Sybil shook her head. "So, you're saying you had her killed… over bad art?"

"Again, I did not kill her, although she did violate our contract."

"You killed her."

"Sybil," James said. "You know in a well-run campaign there is no room for slackers, dissenters, or trouble-makers. Everyone has to play their part, as designed, as required."

"Shut up, James." She looked past him to address Vanderhagen. "And Peter? What did he do?"

"Perhaps he interfered with the status quo."

"At your request."

Vanderhagen's phone buzzed. He checked the text and smiled. "Peter's okay. He'll be home on the next flight." He pocketed his phone. "There. Crisis averted." He paused. "You know what? I'm hungry." He looked over at the counter. "Cheese and crackers are not going to do it." He turned to James. "Make reservations."

Beth said, "You're not going anywhere." She released her gun's safety strap.

James said, "You've got nothing to hold us. Even if you think you do, our lawyers will have us out in minutes and forestall any action for decades."

"Nevertheless, you are under arrest."

James put his hand into his jacket and Beth raised her gun. He said, "I'm getting my phone."

Vanderhagen said to Beth, "That's not necessary. We are unarmed."

Sybil said, "Is it true their case may never come to trial, and they'll be free to continue their work?"

Beth nodded. "Maybe. We'll find out."

Sybil staggered to the bar and fussed with a glass and bottle of liquor as if making another drink. Instead, she removed something from the array of the bar equipment. She turned, eyes red-rimmed, lips tight, nostrils flared, and knuckles white. She took a deep breath and flung herself into Vanderhagen's arms. "Oh, Daddy, I'm sorry."

"It's okay, my dear. Everything will be fine."

Sybil whispered in his ear, "Fuck you," and plunged the ice pick deep into his chest, using the full weight of her body to pierce muscle, tissue, and puncture his heart."

Vanderhagen grunted and fell into James's arms.

Rachel and Beth pulled Sybil away. She never broke eye contact with her father.

Vanderhagen stared back, mute, unaware blood oozed from the corner of his mouth.

Rachel screamed. "Sybil, what did you do?"

Zeus raced to Rachel's side and started barking. Rachel gave him a "down" signal and he dropped to the floor, quiet.

Beth ran to James. "Lower him to the floor. I'll check his pulse." She put two fingers on the man's neck and shook her head.

James stepped away from the body and backed up until he stood against a wall.

Beth turned to make a call and saw the police in the doorway. "We need another bus." She texted Eric. "*Vanderhagen dead,*" and walked over to Sybil. "You are under arrest for the murder of Philip Vanderhagen."

Sybil, head held high, didn't respond.

Rachel said, "Don't say anything, Sybil. Call your lawyer."

"Don't worry," Sybil said. "Lidia told me what I had to do, and I did it. I'll be fine."

No one moved until the ambulance arrived. Within moments, the EMS team pronounced Philip Vanderhagen dead at the scene.

Sybil, without emotion or comment, watched her father's body bagged and removed. Next, she observed a team of FBI agents arrive, place James under arrest, and escort him out in handcuffs. She said, "Good riddance to bad garbage."

Beth cuffed her. "You're coming, too."

Chapter 55▶Washington, D.C.

Thursday, 20 March

Uriah Henderson stood in front of President Sandford. "We have him, Sir. He'll be here in approximately nine hours."

"Good work. Does Wendell know?"

After knocking on the Oval Office door, Wendell Waters entered. "Peter Powell's in the air."

Sandford said, "Excellent."

Henderson said, "He'll come to D.C. for a debriefing before heading home."

"I'd like a word with him before he goes home."

Waters said, "I've got more good news. Sarah Mitchell has been approved by the Senate. The House votes this afternoon."

Sandford said, "Let me know as soon as the vote goes through. I'd like to congratulate her personally." He turned to Henderson. "What's the status on the human rights statement?"

Henderson said, "I suggest we table it until we hear what Powell has to say. His verbal report will tell us whether it needs our comment, and, if so, how strong it needs to be."

"Good." Sandford stood. "Thank you, gentlemen. I'll see you later."

After the men left, Sandford used his private phone to call Vanderhagen. After a few rings, a voice said, "Philip Vanderhagen's phone. This is FBI Special Agent Elizabeth Neilson. May I ask who's calling?"

"President Sandford."

"Sir."

"What's going on, Agent Neilson? Where's Mr. Vanderhagen?"

"Sir, he's dead by his daughter's hand. She and his son, James, have been taken in for questioning."

"Thank you, Agent."

Sandford hung up and stared at the phone. He called the Director of the FBI with specific directions to keep the investigation under wraps as much as possible. After that conversation, the president leaned back, sighed, and called Wendell with the news. He ended with, "We're going to keep this between us for the time being. When it leaks, it won't be from here, and we can comment appropriately."

"I understand, Sir. His passing, and I say this with respect, means a significant decline in donor contributions for your second term."

"No doubt. Let's try to equalize the gap by encouraging voter support, reducing the chance we'll have to deal with any one donor as influential as Vanderhagen."

"I'll look into it," Waters said. "I believe your attention to campaign promises will bring in many new supporters who have doubted you in the past. You and the party will be okay."

Sandford said, "I will enjoy not having my every move second-guessed. Vanderhagen's generosity had strings—power and control—which proved difficult to manage and more than challenged my integrity."

"You're your own man again."

"Hardly. I understand the politics and don't mind being shoved this way and that. However, I now answer directly to the people of the United States, as a president should."

"It must be a very gratifying feeling."

"Wendell, it's the best."

Chapter 56►New York City, NY

Wednesday, 26 March

The Obituary Page, *New York Times*

Philip Vanderhagen, eighty-four, died surrounded by family. A renowned international financial advisor and philanthropist, he used his far-reaching influence to the betterment of humankind. Vanderhagen employed over a million people in business enterprises spanning the globe, notably helping new nations kick-start their economies.

Vanderhagen overcame a difficult and disadvantaged childhood to find a higher purpose. Shielded by his mother, the late Stella Zych Pickens Vanderhagen, he never knew his birth father. His stepfather, the late Bastiaan Vanderhagen, of Philadelphia, PA, adopted and mentored young Philip.

Vanderhagen was predeceased by his wife, Thea Parsons, heiress to Parsons Industries, and is survived by his son James, his daughter Sybil, and his grandchildren, Peter Powell and Sarah Mitchell.

The family will hold a private service. In honor of Vanderhagen's human rights work, they ask any donations be made in his name to The PRAISE Foundation.

<~<~|~>~>

At the Bellevue Hospital Center, Sybil read the obituary and shook her head. "The man always comes up smelling like roses when he's actually the goddamn thorn."

Rachel said, "I know."

"Did James write it?"

Rachel nodded.

Sybil said, "Left Lidia out of it all together. Bastard."

"We'll write Lidia's obituary when you're feeling better."

"Let's do it either later today or tomorrow. I'll jot down some ideas, and we can go over them."

"Sybil, have you talked to James?"

"No. He's on my shit list and my no-visit list."

"You can't believe everything your father said in his blatant attempt to evade blame."

"He came close enough to the truth for me."

"If you let him split up your family, he wins for the last time."

Sybil said, with a strong hint of sarcasm, "Well, we can't have that, can we?"

"Do you want to hear the update?"

"Sure. Entertain me."

"James hired lawyers to represent the family. Even though he's a person of interest, no charges have been brought against him."

"The old pimp was right."

"His lawyers got you out of the psychiatric division's prison ward and free on bail, based on your state of mind at the time—intense grief and shock over Lidia's murder and Peter's disappearance. Beth thinks that'll stick, and you won't do any jail time."

"Finally, some good news," Sybil said. "What about Gavin, er, Mansonati?"

"Not so lucky. They have him for the murders of Lidia, Ilse, Gabriella Mansonati, and who knows how many others. Beth's sure he's the Necktie Killer."

"And you? How are you doing?"

"I'm okay—coming to terms with my Lake George experience, back on track with my book, and getting ready to deal with my wedding-planner mom. When you're out of here, I'm planning to work with you and President Sandford on the Human Rights Initiative."

"And the diary?"

"I've packed it all up for you. It's your grandmother's story. You should have it."

Sybil sighed. "It's going to be tough once I'm released. I don't know if I can go back to the apartment."

Rachel said, "Chris and I have talked. If you're interested, I've got a vacant beautiful two-bedroom penthouse apartment on the East Side, overlooking the Brooklyn Bridge. It's much closer to the PRAISE offices and… no awful memories."

Sybil's face lit up. "I'll take it. Draw up the papers."

A knock on the door and Peter walked in. "Hi, Mom."

Sybil's outstretched arms welcomed her son.

Rachel left to give mother and son much needed time together and stepped into the hall. Chris and Zeus greeted her. She said, "Sybil's doing much better, and she'll take the apartment."

"Good, one thing less to worry about," Chris said. "Are you ready?"

"Sure. For what?"

"I think it's hot fudge sundae time."

Zeus's tail went into overdrive.

"Okay, okay," Chris said, patting the dog's head. "Everyone gets one, even you."

Chapter 57▶New York City, NY

Wednesday, 26 March
In Sybil's hospital room, she released her son and pushed him away with a big smile. "Peter, let me look at you." She gave him a mother's once over. "None the worse for wear. I'm so glad you're back home. I went out of my mind when I thought you were dead."

Peter said, "Mom, you had me worried. After Uncle James called to tell me what happened, I still had to go through an intense debriefing. I could hardly concentrate thinking about you and what you had to be going through." He took her hand. "I'm so, so sorry about Lidia. I liked her from the moment I met her. You guys were a great team, and she always made time for me."

Sybil teared up, rivulets running down her cheeks. "I know. I still can't believe she's gone."

"Me either. But I don't want you to worry. I'm back and I'll take care of you. We'll go forward together."

Sybil reached out and stroked Peter's arm. "I love you."

He said, "I hope so because I've quit the State Department to be with you and PRAISE."

"What do you mean?"

"If you'll have me, I want to spearhead the drive to end the exploitation of workers and war refugees. I'll be your 'on-the-ground' observer and activist. How does that sound?"

"It sounds wonderful. Best present ever."

"Good. I've sent in my resume and application. Rachel said she'd present it to the board next week. By the time you get out of here, everything will be in place."

Sybil held out her hands as Peter leaned in for the hug.

"Speaking about places, I just agreed to take a penthouse apartment. You're welcome to live there with me until you get settled."

"That'd be great. Get me the info, and I'll make sure all your things are moved and ready for you when you get out of here."

"This is one of the… wait," Sybil said. "What about James?"

Peter said, "What about him?"

"Weren't you working with your grandfather in Tawanda?"

"Yes, and I've spoken with James. He's agreed to rethink the cartel's position and broker a workable deal to ease the workers' living conditions."

"Be careful. James has had plenty of experience working with Vanderhagen and can't be trusted."

"I knew you'd say that. Still, I'm trying to use family leverage, so we don't enter into an all-out war with him and the cartel."

"I don't want to argue with you. Maybe it will be different. Let's work on strategy when I'm out of here and at full strength."

"Good. James'll be glad to hear that."

"Don't lower your guard. James may well have been instrumental in ordering the attacks on your life."

"You can't really think that?"

"I think you were about to threaten your grandfather's tight secretive little world and had to be stopped."

Peter leaned back in his chair, his fingertips touching in an open tent formation with opposing forefingers resting on his chin. He stared at his mother for a few seconds, dropped his hands and leaned forward. "I believe you. We'll do whatever we have to."

Sybil said, "I love you, Peter." *Keep your enemies close.*

<~<~|~>~>

Peter stood and gave her a kiss on her forehead. "I'll be back, Mom. Sweet dreams." Outside the hospital he walked into the small park by the entrance. He pulled out his phone.

James answered before the first ring ended. "How'd it go?"

"Good. She's amenable to considering an arrangement."

"Thank you, Peter."

"She's no push over, Uncle James. Don't underestimate her."

"Sybil? Never."

Chapter 58►Harrison, NY

Wednesday, 26 March
Lucy pulled out her throwaway phone and texted, *"Deliver."*

The signal bounced around the world to another throwaway phone which texted back, *"Accepted."*

Minutes later, she got another text, *"Confirmed."*

<~<~|~>~>

TV stations all over the world cut into their regularly scheduled programs.

The on-site news broadcaster said, "Adebowale Okoro, President of Tawanda, has been assassinated. Friends and family, who were gathered in his private garden for his granddaughter's birthday celebration, looked on in horror, helpless, as his body exploded.

"We are standing here, outside the palace, waiting to hear the police report. We can tell you the private guarded Presidential Gardens were breached. The word we've just received indicates a new hi-tech silent drone with stealth technology, delivered the fatal shot. Authorities have confirmed the floor plans for the palace and government offices are closely held. Therefore, they believe the architect of the attack may be an insider.

"Behind us, the citizens of Tawanda are gathering to pay tribute to the late President Okoro, Father of Tawanda, hero and leader of the independence revolution. His vision and guidance will be missed."

The broadcaster put his hand to his ear, listened, nodded, and faced the camera. "We've just heard his appointed successor is Counsel to the President Kwanh Ebu, his cousin and most trusted advisor.

"Ladies and gentlemen, Tawanda's new president is Kwanh Ebu.

"Further updates as they happen. Again, President Adebowale Okoro has been assassinated."

Chapter 59▶Washington, D.C.

Wednesday, 26 March

President Sandford read Vanderhagen's obit, reached for the phone, and called Waters. "Wendell, is Vanderhagen's granddaughter the same Sarah Mitchell just ratified as Vice President?"

"I believe so."

"In all the time we talked that never came up."

" Wasn't that one of the reasons you approved her?"

"I had no inkling. Vanderhagen's request for Peter Powell's appointment must have thrown me. I missed it in her documentation."

"I don't believe it was present in her *curriculum vitae,* anywhere in her voting record, or in the vetting process. Give me a few minutes to confirm. I'll call you back."

Five minutes later, Waters informed the president of his findings. "My people have scoured her documentation. The Vanderhagen family name is definitely absent."

Sandford said, "Interesting, in an odd sort of way. Yet, I'm surprised she never mentioned it in conversation."

"Why would she? She'd have no idea about your relationship with her grandfather."

"Hmmm." Sandford's gut told him otherwise. Vanderhagen had someone in the West Wing on payroll.

"Sir, I wouldn't worry. Mrs. Mitchell has a strong voting record in your favor, and she is smart, savvy, and tactful. She will be a great asset to you and your administration."

Sandford hung up the phone and stared at the obituary. *Sarah Mitchell's appointment was not a coincidence.*

He looked up when he heard the knock on his door. Waters and Henderson ran in. Waters found the remote and turned the TV monitor on.

The three men watched the report of Okoro's assassination and Kwanh Ebu's appointment.

Sandford said, "Did we do that?"

Waters said, "Absolutely not. I checked with the CIA. There are no covert operations in Tawanda."

Henderson said, "Nothing from any of my sources either."

Sandford said, "Then who?"

Henderson said, "We're on it, but we haven't heard any chatter at all about Tawanda, much less an attack on the president."

Sandford said, "Get the press secretary to prepare a statement ASAP. I want to issue my condolences as soon as possible."

The men left.

Sandford opened the Oval Office door and went outside. The balmy weather and shifting winds filled the air with the fresh smell of spring. Secret Service followed him as he walked the White House Garden, hands clasped behind him, his pace slower than usual.

He stopped at a bench, sat down, and pulled out his phone. After scrolling through his email and texts, Sandford sighed and put the phone away.

Leaning back, arms draped over the back of the bench, he lifted his face to the sun.

His phone rang. His private phone. He answered.

"Franklin, this is James Vanderhagen."

The End.

A Note from the Author

I hope you enjoyed reading PERCEPTION as much as I enjoyed writing it.

If you did, please consider leaving an unbiased review on Amazon or the site where you are a verified purchaser.

PREVIEW—ISOLATION

Love, Loss, Leverage, Murder
A Novel by C.L. BLUESTEIN
Seduction series-Book #3

Chapter 01 ▶ Damir, Tawanda

Monday, 30 March
Under the morning African sun, a small boy jumped
to his feet and ran, zigzagging around home-made
tents, leaping over troughs of human waste, and
avoiding refugees, old and young, in his path. He slid
to a stop in front of the sector mayor. Arm outstretched, he pointed and said, sucking air between
each word, "Four. Buses. Coming."

The mayor left the shade of his makeshift office in
a corner of his elaborate six-foot square home, four
wooden posts supporting a corrugated steel roof, and
walls of faded fabrics. He stepped out into the morning light as the buses braked at bottom of his section.

The vehicles had been whitewashed for continuity, but it didn't hide the multiple paint jobs applied over the years. Wind and sand stripped away layers in patches, burnishing exposed metal and the edges of color. Shadows under the thin overcoat gave the appearance of camouflage. But nothing hid the fact that these buses had been around a long, long time.

Doors on the first bus squeaked open and the driver stepped out, cleared his throat and pulled a paper out of his coat pocket. He whipped it open and read the announcement.

"Refugees, your new home is Hope City. It will have food, shelter, schools, work, and medicine.

"Mayors must keep extended families within their sector together.

"You may bring what you can carry. The first groups leave in three hours."

The mayor approached the man. In a quiet voice, he said, "May I ask if there is a choice? For many, it's home or here. Relocation is not an option."

The man said, "We will take the willing first. If necessary, the army will encourage the resistors."

The mayor nodded and returned to his home, trailed by the elders. They gathered around a small table, and he said, "This is a chance to better our lives."

"Just like that," an elder said, snapping his fingers. "The government cares about us." He shook his head. "I don't believe a word of it."

Another said, "Maybe we go look first."

Noises outside rose to a crescendo. The men emerged and saw the lead bus draped with a poster showing Hope City's crisp white tents against the African landscape.

"Pick us." Refugees crowded the elders. "Pick us."

Someone found a wooden box, and the mayor stood on it. "Please quiet down and form a line. We will need your family members' names and their original village." He pointed to a man, "One." Then another. "Two." And another. "Three. That's it for now. I will come around to get everyone's information."

By ten that morning, families filled the buses and began their journey to Hope City. Their excitement vented in singing and conversation. No one heard or saw the drone flying high above the caravan.

<~<~|~>~>

Lucy Kilmer watched the first evacuation from the drone's feed. The buses, crowded with people. Children leaned out the windows to catch the breeze. Possessions, strapped to the roof, were tied down with ropes and fraying bungee cords.

She felt a shiver of excitement. This ambitious and intricate operation, her biggest yet, would save thousands from the agony of starvation and disease.

The Hope City initiative also saved Lucy from excruciating boredom. She'd been under FBI scrutiny, capture, and questioning, ever since they found a photograph of a woman who looked like her on a missing person's phone.

The late Theodore Donovan, mastermind vigilante and her mentor, had taught her well. Together they had arranged disappearances for a number of deranged psychopaths. After he died, the FBI tried to pin the disappearances on her. The photo did not prove she had anything to do with anything. Still, they persisted and requested more time to complete their investigation.

Lucy looked down at her ankle-bracelet. She was out of one prison and in another, her home in Harrison, New York. She smiled. Fortunately, the precautions she had taken to hide a complete computer center now served her well. While the FBI kept tabs on the main set-up in her office, she worked under an invisible cloak of electronic wizardry hidden behind her bedroom closet.

Her keen mathematical mind and her penchant for details put her at the top of a small but competitive industry—first choice for those who could afford her.

Her new contract came from Tawanda's President, Kwanh Ebu, via James Vanderhagen. Ebu needed to clean-up the refugee problem if his country intended to comply with human rights initiatives put forth by the United Nations, and an even stronger declaration expected from the United States.

Lucy checked her watch. The buses' ETA to Hope City's receiving tent gave her two hours of free time. She checked in with her ground crew, worked out, and showered. She returned to her monitor in time to observe the first group of refugees.

Cameras, positioned outside and inside the main tent, started sending a live feed to the site manager and Lucy from the moment the first bus entered the unpaved road.

Pristine white tents lined the drive leading up to the large receiving tent. In the distance, heavy equipment prepped the ground behind a sign— "Hope City Mines." A large white truck, positioned next to the tent, housed command central and sported a large banner, "WELCOME."

Refugees spilled from the buses in a matter of seconds. They formed lines to check in and enter the air-conditioned tent with a canvas floor mat. Once inside, the travelers found food, and drink, and outside, portable restrooms. After the receiving agents checked in the last family, the site manager welcomed everyone. He explained their tents would be ready and assigned in a few hours. They were to relax and get some rest until his return.

After everyone ate and used the rest rooms, the journey's tension evaporated, and the refugees dozed. The cameras stopped recording. Command central released nitrous oxide into the filtration system, sending all into a deep sleep, followed by the potent anesthetic, sevoflurane. The <u>coup de' grace</u>, in the form of carbon monoxide, killed them in less than thirty minutes. No pain. No sound.

Lucy watched as her team removed the tent top and, by means of ropes, gathered the corners of the canvas floor and offered them to the crane claws. The bundle of bodies and belongings rose in the air, swung over and placed in an over-sized dump truck.

She switched her view to the drone the semi-crew had launched. Lucy saw the vehicle travel to a prepared burial site, empty its load into the deep hole, and leave. The earth mover filled the pit and tamped the dirt. The operators swept the area and removed any tell-tale signs of a major disturbance—save the top of a small pipe inserted into the pit to release the gases.

Lucy smiled, stood and stretched. She looked at the time. She had four hours before the final preparations for the next group arrived. She decided to have lunch on the porch, play a few expert Sudoku games, and, if her head cleared, take a short nap.

This is turning out to be a great day.

The End of Chapter 1

Continue reading
<u>ISOLATION - Love. Loss. Leverage. Murder.</u>

ABOUT THE AUTHOR

C.L. Bluestein lives in Slingerlands, New York. Her ideas for projects are fueled by absurdity and puzzles—i.e. how, why, and how come things work—whether it is functional or mental, psychological or physical, political, or just plain interesting. She is a member of the International Women's Writing Guild (IWWG)(2008-),
https://iwwg.com/ and a writer for The Good Men Project 2016-), https://goodmenproject.com/
Other writings available at http://carolbluestein.com/

Check out the rest of the political thriller Seduction Series featuring Rachel, Chris, Beth, & Eric.
- SEDUCTION – Book 1
- PERCEPTION -- Book 2
- ISOLATION – Book 3
- DECEPTION – Book 4

You Want Me To Do What? Walk in the sandals of our ancestors through this engaging interactive contemporary scripted Story of the Exodus/Passover for Jewish and Interfaith Families. Targeted but not limited to tweens.
REVIEW: "You Want Me To Do What" is the most innovative addition to the Passover literature I've seen. This is not just another pretty Haggadah....these interactive mini-dramas will make ANY Seder using any Haggadah come alive for all ages." Cantor Charles Bergman, Los Angeles, CA **Free download** at
http://carolbluestein.com/

Twitter: @clbauthor
FB: Carol Bluestein
Web: http://carolbluestein.com/

www.ingramcontent.com/pod-product-compliance
Lightning Source LLC
Chambersburg PA
CBHW060934120726
47910CB00002B/318